It Happened at the SUNSET GRILLE

It Happened at the SUNSET GRILLE

WILL CUNNINGHAM

THOMAS NELSON PUBLISHERS

Nashville

Published in Nashville, Tennessee, by Oliver-Nelson Books, a division of Thomas Nelson, Inc., Publishers, and distributed in Canada by Lawson Falle, Ltd., Cambridge, Ontario.

Published in association with the literary agency of Alive Communications, P.O. Box 49068, Colorado Springs, Colorado 80949.

Scripture quotations are from The King James Version of the Holy Bible; the New American Standard Bible, © 1960, 1962, 1963, 1968, 1971, 1972, 1973, 1975, 1977 by The Lockman Foundation, used by permission; and the HOLY BIBLE: NEW INTERNATIONAL VERSION, copyright © 1973, 1978, 1984 by the International Bible Society, used by permission of Zondervan Bible Publishers.

Printed in the United States of America.

Library of Congress Cataloging-in-Publication Data

Cunningham, Will, 1959–
    It happened at the Sunset Grille / Will Cunningham.
        p.   cm.
    ISBN 0-8407-9199-2 (pbk.)
    I. Title.
PS3553.U54I87   1993
813'.54—dc20   92-43370
                                                                  CIP

1 2 3 4 5 6 — 98 97 96 95 94 93

As in my previous writing,
I acknowledge my wife,
Cindy.

In the great, wide world,
she is my best chance
of feeling God's hand
in mine.

My companions asked me to cite and recite this story, though admitting they were already familiar with much of the tale.

And so might it be with you. Perhaps this is your story, too.

THE MEMORY

WITH *a crack of lightning, the hole tore open below us. Cries went up from the field. Fists once raised in rebellion now clawed desperately for an anchor. Some hung above the universe by clumps of grass, kicking at the colorless chasm below. Others fell on their swords before plummeting through the divide. To my surprise, none of them bled.*

The split came right up to where I was hiding and stopped, as if it knew which ones to claim and which ones to spare. Those who fell changed immediately. They were monsters before they had fallen two feet into the nothingness. Or perhaps, now that their rebellion was known, they became outwardly what they already were on the inside.

When I had summoned the courage, I ran along the edge looking for him. He had to be here. We were together just moments before it started—when he began shouting things. I tried to stop him, but he ran onto the field. Honestly, I think he believed it was a game. He had never even held a sword.

"Lukas!" I shouted over and over, my voice wavering, lost between confusion and panic.

Then I saw him clinging to a rock. Our eyes widened as

they met: his, due to the sheer terror of falling out of Heaven; and mine, at the sight of his lower extremities. Black, leathery legs, with talons for toes, kicked frantically at the air. The rest of him held a tenuous, ebbing grip on holy ground. Above the waist he was still my brother. For a few seconds, this familiar freak, this impossible hybrid of good and evil, balanced on the precipice. Then he started to slip.

"Lukas!"

"Skandalon!"

His shoulders sprouted powerful, dark flappers. His fingers slid. His neck swelled and bulged. At last his face dipped below the edge and withered into a hideous mask. I dove for his hand and grabbed it. He swung his free arm up and latched onto my wrist. Already the flesh of that arm was grotesque. His clawed fingers dug deep into my forearm, bathing his hand with my life-essence. I looked through the hole in Creation, and a demon's face stared back at me from where, moments ago, my brother's face had been.

"Help me!" he whispered. I heard my own sobbing.

"Holy, holy, holy is the Lord God Almighty," he sputtered, "who was ... and is ... and ..." He broke into a string of vile curses. Our grip weakened.

"Don't let go! Don't drop me!" he wailed.

It was no use. He no longer had a purchase on Heaven. Diminishing, he slid into the void as a piece of ice slides down a hot strip of steel. His nails tore down through my palm. I suppose at that moment he reverted to his earliest memories, just as aged, dying humans at the moment of death often cry out for mothers who passed on a half-century previous.

"Lukas!" I screamed, as he slipped into the yawning darkness below.

He tore my bracelet from my wrist as he fell ...

I.

THE MIRACLE

A CERTAIN man was assigned to me one late fall and early winter. He was my first assignment, for I was one of the less seasoned members of the legion. I am, in fact, the youngest of my kind in Heaven, though I come from good blood—not "blood" as you know it, however. To us, ancestry is a matter of wisdom and guidance rather than parentage. Like you, we have but one ultimate Father. Unlike you, we don't have biology to confuse the fact.

My name is Skandalon, and I am a Trial. You may call me an angel, but that's only part of the truth. There are many types of angels, you see . . .

MY TRIP through the pipe would have seemed uneventful to a more experienced Trial—but this was my debut on earth. I felt my eyes widen with apprehension and more than a little nervousness as I slid down the long chute. Then, abruptly, I came out earthside, landing with a bump in a small, closed room. To you it would have been dark, but our vision isn't affected much by physical light or its absence. I stood, dusted myself off, and looked around me.

The room had obviously been kept in good condition. Fifty-pound cloth sacks of flour were stacked neatly along one wall, and a large electric mixer stood in another corner. There was no smell of dust or cobwebs—in fact, everything smelled of pine cleaner, and recent attention. I surmised I must be in the location to which the dossier referred as my "probable entry point," the attic storeroom of the Paradise Donut Shop.

I looked up at the hole in the ceiling through which I had dropped. The opening was just wide enough for one of your house cats to pass through. There was a large discoloration to the left of the opening—the only evidence of anything unkempt in this tiny, closed room.

Perhaps I should explain: Volume, mass, and density are relatively intangible terms to my kind. It's not that we're immaterial—far from it—it's just that our matter and yours are not subject to the same limitations. I would be as comfortable in a breadbox as I would be in a bank vault. When I use terms like "pipe," "slid," and "opening," I'm trying to convey our method of travel in words comprehensible to you. You may wish me to mention something more traditional—say, wings and harps and such. Well, all I can tell you is: There are many surprises to encounter for those who come Home. It's a wonderful place, a perfect place in fact. But it's not always what you expect.

The Supreme One, in the beginning of the ages, laid the vast network of pipes—I might better describe them as causeways of light, or rays of time—across the universe for future travel. Each pipe sits unused until the appointed time. Then, the hatches at each end are unlocked and whoever is assigned to the particular task is sent on his way. The agent is expected to follow orders without deviation, and upon completion of the assignment must be punctual in arriving back at the pipe before it is sealed and destroyed. As the pipes are used one by one, the Supreme One severs the network until, someday, there will be only one pipe left, and only One who may use it. And after that final, glorious, overwhelming approach, there will be no further need of communications with the earth—at least with the earth as you know it. But I digress.

As to punctuality—there are no excuses for being late returning to the pipe. Those who are late must wait in your world until that final way is opened. In time, they will get back in. And, as always, the Supreme One is prudent with His resources. He has been known to grant bodies and, sometimes, significant missions to those tardy ones. You yourself may have entertained one of them without knowing it. Such has happened.

On the broad lip of the pipe, stenciled in yellow paint, were the figures "E–2," and in smaller print beneath, "1103–1210." Hanging from a peg on the side of the pipe was a leather pouch marked "T." I took this off and hung it by its thong around my neck—I'd need it when the time came for my return. The other pouch, labeled with the letter "W," was hanging on a peg beside mine. When he arrived, my partner on this assignment would take this pouch. And speaking of my partner—where was he?

I had been told that on most assignments our kind worked in pairs—sometimes in threes. This was because of the different gifts given to us by the Supreme One. Trials had one set of abilities, and Ways another. My partner was a Way. And he was late. I stifled the resentful thought that this type of behavior was typical of Ways—it wouldn't do to start my first assignment with friction between my partner and me. I wondered how his strengths would complement mine. Then I wondered what he'd look like—when and if he ever arrived. *Doesn't*

5

he know how to read a dossier and a map? I fumed, before realizing I was getting resentful again.

To occupy my mind more productively, I opened the dossier I had been given in Heaven and started reading again the abstract for the mission.

THE TOWN in which this donut shop stood was called Ellenbach. It was a smallish community in a mostly rural area. The few square miles of the municipality were surrounded on all sides by grain fields and rangeland which were the economic mainstays of this region. Ellenbach clustered at the crossing of two highways which, in earlier times, had been well-used wagon routes for settlers in this part of the land. It was a simple place, peopled with residents who led simple lives. The folks here were still close to the earth, and the earth had been mostly good to them.

A few years ago, however, hard times came to Ellenbach, as they did to many small towns and cities. Grain prices went down. It seemed the only time they recovered any at all was coincident with the bottom falling out of the cattle markets. Farmers and ranchers who weren't making any money certainly had nothing to spend in town, so the merchants of Ellenbach saw their trade dry up to a mere trickle.

Then, five years ago in early June, something strange happened. Some of the city fathers eventually called it a miracle.

One morning the residents of Ellenbach woke to find that Menconi's Feed & Seed was closed. This in itself was not unusual: Ellenbach had grown drearily accustomed to signs in the store windows which were permanently turned to "Sorry—We're Closed." Most of the businesses downtown had the dusty-paned, boarded-up look of vanished profits and abandoned hopes.

6

But Menconi's was not just closed—it was cleaned out. Looking through the store windows, all one could see was the empty planking of the floors. Also, Frank Menconi's house down the street was locked and vacant, its owner nowhere to be found. It was as if Frank Menconi had vanished into thin air, taking with him any trace that he had ever lived or worked in Ellenbach. All that was left was the faded sign over the abandoned store.

Even that didn't last long. Before noon that very day, Ellenbach was astonished to see a gleaming red, unmarked eighteen-wheeler pull into town, its air brakes squawking it to a halt in the street in front of Menconi's Feed & Seed. A huge work crew got out of three like-colored vans which parked behind the semi-trailer-truck, the men swarming over the vacant store like vengeful ants.

They began the swift, efficient demolition of Menconi's Feed & Seed. By sunset, the brawling, swearing workers, as if devouring some victim, had stripped the building to its gaunt skeleton of a superstructure.

Within two more days the wide-eyed Ellenbachians began to witness another inexplicable thing: The crew was erecting a new structure on the former site of Menconi's Feed & Seed. A high fence only partially obscured the diesel fumes of the digging machines as the crew delved deep into the earth. Apparently, whatever would take the place of Menconi's would have a very deep cellar.

This whole process was entirely new to the locals. Never in memory had a new business arisen to take the place of a closed one. A cautious optimism budded shyly in the hearts of some of the Ellenbach city council members. If one business thought Ellenbach worthy of such urgent, immediate endeavor, might not others follow?

Some folks, however, were not so sanguine about this eruption of activity in the town. "Look at the fellas on them crews," someone would say. "Not an Ellenbach boy in the bunch—nor anyone else a body might recognize."

"Yep," another might concur. "And have you heard the language they use? Why, it'd make a sailor blush. And I've seen 'em drink enough beer up on the roof beams in the middle of the day to float a small boat. . . ."

And it was true. The behavior of the hard-bodied men with the unseasonable tans was a far cry from the demeanor favored by most Ellenbachians. The crew whistled at the local girls and women who passed the contruction site—and sometimes made more pointed suggestions. They cursed loudly, and swung their hammers far into the night, daring the sky to rain on them.

Indeed there wasn't a drop of rain while the crew toiled—odd in itself. Then there was the heat—unseasonably warm for Ellenbach. Even the nights had a sticky, stifling quality about them, as if the whole area was holding its breath, afraid to inhale while the loud, brash men were building. Soon, many local people began to avoid the construction site. Mothers wouldn't let their daughters go downtown unattended; schoolchildren banded together in groups when forced to traverse the area.

By degrees, it became known what the men were building: It was to be a steakhouse—or something similar. A name began circulating among the gossips in town: The Sunset Grille. Afterward, no one could recall exactly who had first mentioned the specific name for the establishment, but the anonymous namer was proved correct. One day toward the end of July a sign appeared over the broad, beckoning doorway of the almost completed building. In bright new neon it read:

THE SUNSET GRILLE
Fine Steaks and Spirits

Beneath, almost as an afterthought, were these words:

Live Entertainment

No meeting of the Ellenbach city council had ever been half as well-attended as the one which took place after the sign went over the door. It was easy to infer that the heretofore unknown owner or owners of the Grille intended to serve liquor, beer, and wine at the restaurant. As to the ramifications of "Live Entertainment," what was left unsaid was far more ominous than what was spoken. Ellenbach was a dry town in a dry county, and there were plenty of citizens in attendance to voice their objections to the representative of the Grille's owners— who, as advertised, was to be present at the meeting to respond to questions and concerns.

Seated with the city fathers on the stage of the high school auditorium (the expected attendance tonight required the move from the small council room in the city hall, which was normally more than adequate), the Grille representative sat quietly, apparently oblivious to the murmuring, beetle-browed hostility of the townspeople. He was a narrow-shouldered, clerical type, complete with steel-rimmed glasses whose lenses brightly reflected the lights overhead. The glittering reflections gave him an anonymous, goggled appearance which matched perfectly with his neat, buttoned-down shirt, his tie, and his suit of respectable, if unremarkable, color and cut. The meeting was called to order, and the representative rose to speak. An uneasy hush settled over the gathering.

"I represent a large consortium of investors," he began in a bland voice, "who are engaged in building a chain of restaurants like the one being completed in, ah—" he consulted his notes, the lights glittering on his spectacles as his face angled down, then back up—"Ellenbach. My employers believe that Ellenbach is the perfect location to showcase their business strategies."

A farmer, seated in the front row, stood abruptly. He held his cap, which bore the logo of an agricultural chemical company, wadded in a thick fist. His tan ended just above his eyebrows. He wore new blue bib overalls, and his blue chambray shirt was unbuttoned at the collar. The representative paused, his eyeglasses flashing toward this unexpected interruption. On the stage, the council members stirred uneasily.

"I didn't catch your name, mister," the farmer began in a loud, flat drawl, "but I got somethin' to say." He paused, half-turning toward the rest of the audience. "I reckon most folks here are worried over the same thing I am, and that's this: We don't much like the idea of some sorta honky-tonk comin' into this town. Have you got anything in your notes there that might make us feel any different?" The farmer's chin jutted as he finished his statement, and he sat down to spontaneous applause from the rest of the crowd.

The spokesman waited for the clapping to subside, sifting back and forth among the sheets of paper before him on the podium. If he was nervous or apprehensive, he gave no sign. Emotion seemed to be something that never occurred to him.

He cleared his throat. "Certainly my employers realize that in order to be successful in the long-term, the enterprise must be of benefit to the community, as well as to themselves." His voice was unchanged from the bland-ness with which he had started. "The Sunset Grille will benefit Ellenbach in a number of ways. First, of course, in terms of employment. The Sunset Grille will provide some, ah—" his glasses winked down, then up—"fifty jobs. We'll need cooks, waiters, waitresses, and, ah, et cetera. . . ."

A thoughtful quiet settled on the auditorium. Fifty jobs were significant in a community this size. That would almost re-employ all the helpers, cashiers, sales-people, and assistant managers laid off in the closure of downtown businesses. Some of the council members began gazing in calculation at the ceiling.

"Second, and perhaps more important," the spokesman continued, "are the benefits which would accrue to the main industry of the area—that is, ah, agriculture."

If the hall had been quiet before, it was positively silent now. Every farmer and rancher in the auditorium sat forward to hear what the representative was saying.

"My employers have a policy of utilizing local suppliers whenever possible," he said. "In fact, this is a significant part of their marketing strategy. The Sunset Grille will serve only beef which has been grown and processed in this immediate area. We believe this gives us an advertising niche not enjoyed by our, ah, competitors."

Now the ranchers were peering at the same spot on the ceiling studied earlier by the council members.

"Further," the speaker added, "my employers have major holdings with several large brewers and distillers. Here again, an effort will be made to purchase the necessary grains from this immediate area. We believe this will enhance market acceptance of our products."

The farmers joined the cattlemen in the upward squint.

"I understand," said the speaker, "that the economy of this area has been through a rather severe downturn. I believe you can see that this, ah, proposal has the potential for a major impact on such an unfortunate situation. As a matter of fact," he concluded, "if the Sunset Grille performs at all in accordance with our market research, I believe I can assure you of an imminent turn in the fortunes of this community."

Cautious smiles were stealing across many of the faces in the auditorium. Fifty new jobs! A private market for local beef and grain! Maybe, some speculated, if things went well enough, the old slaughterhouse on the outskirts of town could be reopened. And who could surmise what else might happen if the pockets of the still-unknown investors behind the Grille were as deep as they appeared . . .

By the time the representative sat down, much of the animosity with which the meeting had begun had been drowned in a rising tide of euphoria. This might be just what this town needed! Maybe things were going to turn around. . . .

The surge of optimism was almost strong enough to choke out the still, small voice of doubt and mistrust that most Ellenbachians felt, but were embarrassed to admit to each other. The necessary resolutions and ordinance changes were largely formalities. The Sunset Grille opened exactly on schedule, and the doubters among the population maintained an uncomfortable silence.

I SIGHED, closing the dossier. The story was an old one: Even good, honest people like the citizens of Ellenbach could be swayed by a smooth presentation and an appeal to self-interest. The possibility that they hadn't gotten the entire story hadn't occurred to them in the glad rush of hope which swept the whole community after the council meeting. And by the time they figured that out, it would be very late in the game. . . .

THE CALLING

A WHITE station wagon slowly rounded the corner of Washington and Terrence, rolling quietly past the parking lot of the Ellenbach Community Church. It turned into the gravel driveway of the parsonage, a modest whitewashed frame structure across the street from the church building. Dr. Larry Ravelle shut off the engine and opened the door of the car only wide enough to poke out his umbrella and unfold it against the drizzle which fell from the early morning sky above Ellenbach. *Looks like another sloppy day,* he thought, stepping over a puddle as he got out of the car and closed the door.

The house had a faintly Victorian look, with its meticulously painted green trim and its starch-white paint. The driveway was lined on one side with a row of Russian olives. In front of the bay window which stared across the street, Dr. Ravelle's rose garden slept away the winter.

Larry Ravelle was an Ellenbach native. He and his twin brother, John, had grown up on a farm near here. Both boys had left Ellenbach for a number of years; both had returned by circuitous routes which left scars far less obvious than painful.

Their father had farmed a mid-sized parcel southwest of town, juggling the tasks of provider and sole parent to the boys, whose mother died when the twins were nine. Wallace Ravelle was far from being a garrulous man even before the death of his wife; her passing left him more taciturn and withdrawn than before. He loved his boys, after his fashion and to the best of his ability—but there was a darkness hovering just at the edge of their young lives which the twins, though having no vocabulary to express it, knew and dreaded with an anxiety beyond words.

Even in their childhood a pronounced inner difference in the two Ravelle boys was apparent to the folks of Ellenbach. While Larry inherited the sunny outlook and disposition of his deceased mother, John retained the brooding, aloof manner of his father. The difference was all the more strange because the boys physically were like two peas in a pod: blond hair, blue eyes, and a lithe, athletic build which made them the object of many an admiring female glance. John's physique was marred, however, by a childhood bout with polio which, though mild, left him with one leg slightly shorter than the other. Ellenbachians came to habitually distinguish the Ravelle twins by John's limp and Larry's easy smile.

There were other differences, however. For all of John's moodiness, he was possessed of a brilliant, agile mind. Schoolwork always came easier for him than for Larry. And so, the boys adopted a kind of symbiosis: John helped Larry along with academics, and Larry used his winning personality to repair the damage John's dourness inevitably caused among their friends and the wider community.

For John was not an easy child to like, and adolescence

didn't improve his disposition. He was sometimes cruel to farm animals, more so to strays. His temper was notorious, his bloody noses frequent. And many a teasing child learned to fear the patient, thorough revenge of John Ravelle.

After high school graduation, John felt the call of the wide world and resolved to go "back East" to further his education and begin a career. His father encouraged the endeavor, perhaps subconsciously realizing that the more John distanced himself from the memories and expectations of Ellenbach, the better for him. John went away, and was gone for many years. Larry wished his brother well, and the town breathed a sign of relief.

Larry stayed on, taking whatever work he could find during the slack times when his father didn't need him on the farm. He worked at the slaughterhouse for a time, then at the grain elevators. All the while he basked in the glow of Ellenbach's approbation and blessing. He was the town's darling, as much as his brother had been its derelict.

The Bible had always been important to Larry, and he showed an aptitude for teaching. Perhaps his frequent interventions on John's behalf had made him more sensitive to the minds and hearts of others. At any rate, he became a valued member of the Ellenbach Community Church, where on any given Sunday he might be found instructing a children's class, or hanging lilies in the sanctuary, or even substituting for an absent minister by delivering a brief sermon with a technique that made up in earnestness what it lacked in polish.

After several years of being told that "the call of God" was upon him, Larry went to Bible college and seminary. With time and much hard work, he earned a doctorate in theology. He met and married Rose, his wife, and returned to his birthplace, after various ministries in cities and towns more or less distant from Ellenbach. The town received him back with the enthusiasm usually reserved for a returning war hero.

But there was a difference in Larry Ravelle after his homecoming. Some lurking shadow, some obscure echo from his upbringing haunted the corners of his eyes, stalked his dreams by night and day with an implacable, patient tread. Unlike his brother John, Larry Ravelle's limp was concealed from the admiring glances of Ellenbach, from his parishioners, and even from his loving wife. He wished, daily and fervently, that he could conceal it from himself.

On this gray morning, the pastor paused in his walk toward the house to look at his winter-browned lawn; he shook his head. He might have been saying again to himself, as he had at least weekly since autumn's first freeze, "Got to get that mower fixed before spring." Even in dormancy, the Ravelle lawn was not tidy. In contrast to his carefully tended rose bed, great straggling clumps of dried dandelions and crabgrass lurched across the lawnscape, their shape and shade evoking a sense of shabby discord when compared with the uniform textures of the trimmed yards on either side of the parsonage. His wife tolerated the lawn's condition, and his children were too young to be embarrassed by it. But he suspected Mrs. Pickard and the Spradlings, whose neat lawns bordered his, were less accommodating in their opinions about weeds in the preacher's yard.

Yes, ordinarily he might well have been reminding himself once more to fix the mower, but today, standing on the walk next to his lawn, his mind was elsewhere. He was praying, and something in his pained, prayerful longing compelled him to stop and close his eyes before entering his home.

All was still for a moment on that gray morning. Then

he opened his eyes, shook his head again, and turned toward the house.

Climbing the three steps to the front porch, he wiped his feet carefully on the doormat as he propped the furled umbrella against the wall beside the front door. He unlocked the door and went inside, after tossing the plastic-wrapped newspaper in ahead of him. Under his arm, he carried a long, thin box from the corner florist. It contained a single red rose.

In one of the counseling classes he had taken at seminary, the professor told the students to do something "special" for their spouses every single day. In response, Larry had adopted the practice of daily giving his wife a bloom from her namesake flower. Hence, the carefully tended rose bushes in the front yard. Out of season he had to rely on the corner florist, who knew of the pastor's chivalrous custom and always had roses available. Larry only recently had mentioned to the florist with pride that his marriage was well over four thousand roses old.

He removed his overcoat and hung it in the entry closet, then paused beside the grandfather's clock to wind it with the key that lay atop the cabinet. He went into the kitchen and opened the refrigerator, placed the rose inside, and retrieved two grapefruit, which he began methodically slicing and sectioning.

These morning rituals comforted him, allowed him to drift, unconnected to the concerns of the future or the present. But he could never quite escape the past.

As he did every morning, he looked up at the framed snapshot on the windowsill above the kitchen sink. The face staring back at him was stern, with a smile forced grudgingly, as if from a high-pressure hose, onto its features. It was a picture of John, his twin brother. The photo was five years old. It showed John sitting in a floral-print easy chair, with the detritus of Christmas morning scattered about him on the floor. He was holding up, like a trophy won at great difficulty, the shirt and tie received from Larry—the offering for the year from one estranged brother to another.

There was another figure in the photograph, bur Larry rarely attended to her. She was forgotten, for her abrupt departure had been the final nail in the coffin, the onslaught which had driven his brother away from ever achieving friendly, pleasant, respectable living. In the photograph, Karen Ravelle was crouched on the floor beside John's chair, peering with a guilty smile into the camera, her pose that of a captive who would spring toward freedom as soon as the guard looks away. The guard had apparently dozed. Karen had made good her escape not long after the photo was taken. Some five years ago, John had skulked back to Ellenbach, his countenance darker than ever, trailing behind him a tattered train woven of betrayal, guilt, and hidden fears. Without any ceremony he had moved in with his aging father, and resumed farming the parcel of land southwest of town which he had left so long before. He rarely came into town, never to church. He and Larry had spoken perhaps a dozen times in the five years since his return. Two of those occasions had been in the time surrounding their father's funeral, when the need for making arrangements had forced them together.

"Lord God," Larry prayed silently, without much hope for the prayer's success, "help my brother. Help him get past his pain. . . ."

What about my pain? What about the guilt that never goes away, that mocks me after every phrase of every sermon?

Larry closed his mind quickly on the voice inside his head. He glanced at his wristwatch. Seven-thirty. Time to wake Rose and the kids.

He pulled the rose out of the refrigerator, then removed it from its box. From the windowsill he took the simple white bud vase that he had used every morning for the past twelve years, filled it with tap water, and inserted the rose. He walked from the kitchen down a hallway lit dimly by a nightlight in the socket by the bathroom door. Arriving at the first of the bedrooms, he pushed open the door quietly, gazing in at the piles of T-shirts, inside-out blue jeans, and half-untied Nikes, dimly lit by the light filtering through the closed, football-patterned curtains. The room smelled of boy.

Larry heard the soft thumping of a tail under the bed, and smiled to himself.

"Come here, Lord Byron," he called softly. "Here, boy!"

The long-haired mongrel scurried from under the bed and wiggled toward him, wagging his tail and licking his chops in greeting.

"Hello there, fella," Larry whispered, scratching the dog behind the ears. "You better get to your bed, before Peter's mother catches you in here. Go on!" he admonished. "Bed!" The dog whimpered and slinked off toward the utility room beyond the kitchen, his officially sanctioned winter's night residence.

Larry walked over to his son's bedside. He excavated among the tumbled, twisted sheets and blankets until he discovered Peter's tousled, ten-year-old head.

"Time to get up, son," he said, shaking Peter's shoulder gently but firmly. "Rise and shine!"

"Urffff," replied the covers.

"Let's go, partner," Larry persisted, "we don't want to be late."

"Do we have to go to church today?" mumbled Peter, rousing slightly.

"No, we *get* to go to church today," corrected Larry, giving the boy's hair an affectionate ruffle. "Now crawl out of the sack, and come into the kitchen. I'll get your breakfast, as soon as I call Mom and Annie."

"Okay," Peter muttered grudgingly, sticking his feet over the edge of the bed.

"Atta boy," said Larry, going back into the hallway.

The next door across the hallway led to the room of Annie, age six. Larry opened the door to find his daughter wide awake, standing on her bed with her arms outstretched. "Morning, Daddy!" she called.

Larry made a courtly bow. "Good morning, my princess," he intoned, face toward the floor. "And what is my lady's pleasure this fair morning?"

"Take me to Mommy's room," the princess ordered.

"Very well," Larry responded, bending low next to the bed as his daughter clambered aboard for a piggy-back ride. "To the land of Mommy we shall go—posthaste!" He bounced and jiggled out of the bedroom door, to the loud delight of his passenger, then down the hall toward the remaining bedroom.

The steed and his giggling rider burst through the door. Rose Ravelle was, to no one's surprise, awake and sitting up in bed, her white lace nightgown low on one shoulder. She smiled and shook her head at the two of them, cavorting in the doorway.

Larry thrust the rose toward his wife and, just as he had every morning for the last dozen or so years, announced, "Rise, Rose! The sun has risen!"

Rose Ravelle was a beautiful woman—not in the cool, svelte manner of many women who are beautiful for a living, but in the fresh, wholesome, durable way of a woman who was, all in all, pleased with her life.

She had long russet hair which cascaded in a shining tangle past her milk-white shoulders. Her face was round, with elegant cheekbones and smiling lips which she now offered to her daughter for a good-morning kiss.

Annie slid off Larry's back and padded toward the kitchen, sensing that her ride was over.

"Good morning, my love," she murmured as Larry brushed her lips with his. She was not entirely satisfied with the offhand nature of her husband's greeting, but decided to say nothing. She took a whiff of the proffered rose and placed the vase on her bedside table. She looked at her husband, who had turned away.

"When did you come to bed last night, dear?" she asked, pulling the bedclothes aside and padding to her closet for a robe.

"Pretty late," replied Larry in a low voice. "Today's sermon didn't fall together quite like I'd hoped." He glanced at her, then away. "I'm sorry, Rose. I've been agonizing a lot over this thing I'm getting myself into, and—"

"You're not in it by yourself," Rose stated, quietly but firmly. "You know I'm with you." He looked at her from under his eyebrows, and nodded slightly as she went on. "And even more important, the Lord is with you, Larry." She studied him thoughtfully, then asked, "You *do* still feel a sense of calling about this, don't you?"

He looked up at her again. He closed his eyes, then opened them. "Yes," he whispered hoarsely.

"Then that's all there is to it," said Rose matter-of-factly. "If God is calling you to this burden, He'll give you the strength to bear it. He enables whom He anoints." She came to him, looped an arm behind his neck, and drew his face to hers. "And I'll do all I can, too. Okay?" She kissed him lightly on the lips.

He smiled grudgingly, backing away from her. "All right, honey. I'll remember that." He felt her eyes on him—questioning, perhaps? Evaluating? He couldn't meet her gaze this time. "I'd better go get breakfast started," he said, half-turning from her.

There was more to be said, but Larry was bound to silence by the familiarity of her expectations, the comfort of an unrocked boat. *No need to worry her. I just need to sort some things out....*

Rose nodded, more to herself than to her husband, and went into the bathroom. Larry went to the kitchen, closing the bedroom door softly behind him.

THE BATTLE CRY

W HEN from inside the attic of the Paradise Donut Shop I heard the church bells chiming, I knew I could wait no longer on my overdue partner. I tucked the dossier into my satchel, dusted the flour off my clothes—strictly a habit, since you can't see us—and stepped through the ceiling and roof into the Sunday morning air above Ellenbach.

Even in gray November, morning painted Ellenbach with flattering features. The scene was a peaceful tapestry, a model portrait of a small town which could almost let you forget that anything could spoil such an idyllic setting.

Almost, but not quite. For our vision is not of your world, and many things hidden to you are woefully visible to my kind. Despite the town's peaceful Sunday morning facade, there was evil lurking just below the surface in Ellenbach. After all . . . that's why I was sent.

I alighted in the belfry of the Ellenbach Community Church. The church, constructed of the tan-colored native stone of the area, stood on a slight rise above the town, and from the steeple, one commanded a view of quite a large surrounding area. I watched the sedans, station wagons, and pickup trucks filing into the parking lot. Farm families, town families, dad-mom-and-the-kids families, single-parent families, single adults, young, old, suit-and-tie professionals, boots-and-big-buckle ranchers—all were represented in the congregation pastored by Larry Ravelle. They met, greeted, shook hands, and conversed good-naturedly in the parking lot and on the front steps.

As my gaze randomly roved the ingathering of the parishioners, my heart was struck by the poignancy of the scenes which greeted my eyes.

Here, for example, was a farmer—painfully shy, judging by his demeanor—whose assignment this day was to give a written order of worship and a verbal greeting to everyone who came in the front door of the church. A tie, several earth-seasons out of style, was knotted inexpertly beneath his chin. Though his cheeks had the scrubbed-raw look of one who had taken extra pains before the bathroom mirror that morning, I could still see traces of engine oil beneath his workman's fingernails. He hewed manfully to his task, bobbing his head at each person who came in the door, handing them the liturgy and giving them an eyes-averted, duty-laden smile and single-word greeting. It is likely that very few of the recipients knew what that simple courtesy cost the timid farmer at the front door, yet he persevered. It was, that morning, his gift to the Creator.

Here came a young mother, trudging wearily toward the front steps with two rambunctious toddler-aged boys dangling from the ends of her arms and twining themselves about her ankles. Her eyes bore the haunted, desperate look of a person who is staring at an unavoidable, unpleasant fate. Then an older woman approached from the flank, bent down in front of those two rowdy young-sters and enfolded them in a warm, cushiony hug. "Oh, just look at these sweeties!" she exclaimed. The young mother smiled weakly and nodded, as if unconvinced.

"Wanna go sit wif Miss Laura!" the boys chanted. "Wanna go sit wif Miss Laura!" I saw the look of sheer relief on the younger woman's face as the older woman asked, in all seriousness, "Would you mind if the boys sat with me today, Claire?" Claire shook her head, weak with joy.

I was in prison, and you visited me, I thought.

My spirit sang with sadness and joy as I watched them come in: these wandering, bewildered, lame and weary sheep of Adam's lineage. In their weakness they longed for strength. In their confusion they sought clarity. In their best moments they found in each other that spark first kindled by the Supreme One at the founding of your world. They craved a message from Home, and came here to discover it, at whatever level they were equipped for the search.

It was almost time for the worship assembly to get under way. I made my way inside, just above the left shoulder of a young, broad-shouldered lad with closely cropped hair and swarthy skin. I perched above the choir loft, just behind an arching beam, and watched as Larry climbed the stairs to the pulpit and seated himself in one of the big, velvet-cushioned chairs at the front of the sanctuary.

A deacon with a raspy voice read the call to worship, as chosen by Larry and printed in the photocopied liturgy: "O God, do not keep silent; be not quiet, O God—be not still. See how your enemies are astir, how your foes rear their heads ... Let them know that you, whose name is the Lord—that you alone are the Most High over all the earth."

The organist mashed a dense hedge of chords, catapulting the choir into the opening anthem as the congregation rustled to its feet.

> *Rise up, O men of God!*
> *Have done with lesser things;*
> *Give heart and mind and soul and strength*
> *To serve the King of kings.*

I swooped unseen among them, conducting my own call to worship. "Sing!" I shouted into the strained ears of their souls. "Sing a new song! Clap and shout and whirl about with praise!"

I buzzed the balcony, where sat a few with willing spirits and labored flesh. "Wheeee!" I called as I slalomed among them. "Don't bask in His love! Burn with it! Set yourself ablaze in the fire of His holiness!" And it worked! Praise the Supreme One, it worked! A few of them sat a little straighter, had a slightly more thoughtful gleam in their eyes as the words to the hymns became, if only for a moment, something more than obstacles inked on a page.

I dove headlong into the dark, dreary reaches of the pews directly in front of the altar, down among the tight-lipped, dry-eyed note-takers and dutiful, downcast readers of Scripture. I sang to them a new song—one meant for hearts too shackled by obedience to recognize freedom when it is offered.

"Sing! Laugh and shout for joy to the Lamb—for He alone is worthy! If He makes you free, you are free indeed!"

With the next hymn I glided along the front rows:

> *Hear Him, ye deaf; His praise, ye dumb,*
> *Your loosened tongues employ;*
> *Ye blind, behold your Savior come;*
> *And leap, ye lame, for joy.*

The color rose in a cheek here, a smile struggled for birth there. Joy bubbled from me in a glistening shower of laughter, a praise-ode to the Source of all delight.

Then I wheeled amidships to those seated in rows five through ten who by default numbered themselves among the aimless army of ambivalents: those whose convictions were neither hot enough to set their worship afire, nor cool enough to wash it down. I called fiercely to them, shouted a battle cry as the choir sang:

> *Thou and thou only, first in my heart,*
> *High King of heaven, my treasure thou art.*

Finally, I drifted toward the elders and deacons, seated in the pews flanking the altar. Coursing among them, I tasted one or two spirits who reclined in the smug assurance of their authority. For them, proximity to the pulpit represented a grip on their place in the hierarchy, a satisfying endorsement of their self-worth. For such as these I might weep and beseech, but I had no song.

But others fairly seethed in their affection for this flock. I felt their anxious concern for their own inadequacies, sensed their tenderhearted solicitousness for the welfare of the church, as the Supreme One gave them the grace to see it. And I offered them words of comfort and of hope.

> *Do not fear, little flock,*
> *for it is your Father's good*
> *pleasure to give you the*
> *kingdom.*

I returned to my vantage point above the choir as Larry rose from his seat and paced slowly to the pulpit. He took a white-knuckled grip on the sides of the heavy, age-darkened oak lectern, as if he intended to pick it up and heave it into the first row of pews. All eyes were on him as he bowed his head for a moment, then peered at his open Bible.

"Lord God," he had prayed, "let my tongue proclaim what You would have said this morning." At least that was what I heard. We aren't allowed to eavesdrop on everything you humans think—just things that pertain to our specific missions. And this morning's sermon did, believe me.

As Larry continued his silent contemplation of his open text, I saw a few of the parishioners begin to look at each other from the corners of their eyes. *What's on Brother Ravelle's mind this morning? Why is it taking him so long to get started?* Their silent queries were easy to imagine.

Larry looked up, catching the eye of his wife, seated in the right-hand pews, aisle end, second row. She winked at him. He sighed deeply, lifted his well-worn Bible in his hands, and stepped down from the pulpit. Before the widening eyes of his congregation he slowly and carefully descended the steps toward the front of the altar. It was so quiet in the sanctuary that each creak of the carpeted wood risers could be heard. When he had reached the center aisle and stood between the altar and the pews, he opened his mouth to speak.

"Brothers and sisters," he began, "I stand among you today, because I am one of you. This morning I will not preach from up there," he said, pointing back toward the abandoned pulpit, "because I don't think I have the right to look down at you while I say what God has placed on my heart. I'm not above any one of you, spiritually. And today I don't want to be above you physically either. God in Heaven knows I don't deserve to be. . . ."

In the long pause that followed, I don't think I was the

only one who noticed that Larry's hands were trembling. "Be strong, Larry—be strong," I urged, wishing again for my partner's presence.

Larry looked up, swallowed, and said in a loud, clear voice, "Give attention now to the reading of God's word." I breathed a little easier.

"From the seventh chapter of the Proverbs," he announced, glancing at the open Bible he held, then looking out over the congregation and quoting from memory:

> *At the window of my house*
> *I looked out through my lattice,*
> *And I saw among the naive,*
> *I discerned among the youths,*
> *A young man lacking sense,*
> *Passing through the street near her corner;*
> *And he takes the way to her house,*
> *In the twilight, in the evening,*
> *In the middle of the night and in the darkness.*
> *And behold, a woman comes to meet him,*
> *Dressed as a harlot and cunning of heart.*
> *She is boisterous and rebellious;*
> *Her feet do not remain at home;*
> *She is now in the streets, now in the squares,*
> *And lurks by every corner.*
> *So she seizes him and kisses him,*
> *And with a brazen face she says to him:*
> *"I have come out to meet you,*
> *To seek your presence earnestly, and I have*
> *   found you.*
> *Come, let us drink our fill of love until morning."*

Again Larry's voice faltered. I could hear the anguished workings of his mind: *Like an ox to the slaughter . . . like a bird darting into a snare . . . O God, help me!*

"Keep going, Larry!" I shouted. "You've got to tell them! Don't stop now!"

Once more he gathered himself:

> *Now, therefore, my sons, listen to me,*
> *And pay attention to the words of my mouth.*
> *Do not let your heart turn aside to her ways,*
> *Do not stray into her paths.*
> *For many are the victims she has cast down,*
> *And numerous are all her slain.*
> *Her house is the way to Sheol,*
> *Descending to the chambers of death.*

"Amen," Larry concluded. "May God bless the reading of His Word." His eyes roved the sanctuary, from the balcony down to the front pews. He took another deep breath, and launched himself into his prepared remarks.

"Brothers and sisters, the passage you've just heard describes a danger as old as mankind—or rather, as old as fallen mankind. The wise man is trying to warn his children—and us—about one of the most deadly temptations of the flesh..." He paused dramatically, and the congregation was practically leaning out of the pews when he said the next word. "...*lust.*"

The single syllable thumped onto the floor of the sanctuary like a brick through a windowpane. It seemed to echo, its ugly sound reverberating soundlessly within each heart and mind in the reach of Larry Ravelle's voice.

"Notice what the writer says about the end result of lust," Larry continued. "He says that lust has slain whole armies—'a mighty throng' is the phrase he uses—and that the house of a lustful woman is like a one-way road to the grave.

"Don't you think King Solomon cried just a little bit when he wrote some of these words?" challenged Larry,

30

after a pause. "After all, I'm sure he'd heard the stories about his daddy and mother. You remember her: lady by the name of Bathsheba.

"Do you think Solomon was proud of his mother and father? Do you think he ever felt guilty—that he ever imagined Uriah's death-moans mingling with the birthing cries of Solomon's very own brother?" He had them now; there were enwrapped in the rising and falling cadences of his voice, the richly hued portraits he was painting with his words. "No, friends, I don't think Solomon is exaggerating one iota when he says that lust can kill just as surely as a sword, or a gun, or—" he faltered for a half-moment—"a snare set for a bird." He allowed them to ponder this last thought for a few seconds, then continued.

"Now, folks," he said, his voice warming, mellowing, taking them all in his confidence with a kindly tone like a favorite uncle, "you might be asking yourselves, 'What in the world has Larry got stuck in his craw?' After all, we don't see many painted ladies inviting our young men into their houses here in Ellenbach, do we? We don't have a real problem with prostitution. Matter of fact, it hasn't been too many years back when the high school kids had their first prom—before that, dances were considered a little too risqué for Ellenbach." A few veiled snickers were heard as some of the teenagers rolled their eyes.

"And most of you remember when alcoholic beverages weren't available anywhere in Johnson County," Larry said, his voice dropping ever so slightly, "not to mention other things...."

A few of the farmers ducked their heads and suddenly became very interested in their fingernails. They could sense what was coming next.

"But things have changed in Ellenbach, friends," Larry

31

went on, raking the audience with his eyes, locking gazes sternly with anyone who would meet his stare. "And some of the changes haven't been for the better.

"You all know what I'm talking about!" he said, boring into them like a prizefighter going on the attack. "There's a bad smell in Ellenbach! For a while we could cover it up with perfume, pretend it wasn't there. But every day it gets a little stronger, a little riper—like a corpse in the parlor.

"And God help us, brothers and sisters," he said, his voice modulating into a desperate, beseeching tone, "if we get comfortable with the stink! If we ever get so we can't tell a cesspool from a drinking-spring, then it's all over. The battle is lost, and the enemy has won it all.

"The enemy I'm talking about," he warned, his voice dropping to a low rumble which carried to the farthest corner of the balcony, "is that temple of perdition we allowed to be built in the very center of our town—you know it as the Sunset Grille."

As his challenge rang out in the sanctuary, I could sense the polarities forming in the pews. I could hear the justifications being summoned to the silent defense of those who felt they needed them. I could feel the self-righteous agreement of those who believed themselves above the rebuke implicit in Larry's words. And from the rest—the majority—I discerned a vague, undefined malaise, as if they were suddenly jarred from a comfortable doze by a disturbing noise that could no longer be ignored.

"Now people, notice I said *we—we* allowed it to be built!" Larry cried. "I was here! I remember! And I share the blame—there is plenty to go around." By now he was pacing the center aisle, pouring his heart out in a voice that vibrated with intensity.

"'It was hard times, Larry!' you say. That's right! The times were bad, and a little bit of hope was hard to turn down. I understand! I was raised on a farm just southwest of town. I know what it means to tighten your belt one more notch—and realize you've just run out of notches.

"'It was good for the town, Larry!' you say. And I'll grant you, Ellenbach sure wasn't in any position to turn down jobs at that time. I don't like to see our young people leave any more than any of you.

"But brothers and sisters," he said, his voice heavy with concern, "how can anything which is bad for the souls of Ellenbach's people be good for the town?" An uncomfortable silence ensued as the congregation wrestled with the difficult implications of this question.

"Now don't get me wrong," he said, his voice brightening a bit. "I've got nothing against a good steak." A spattering of relieved laughter greeted this remark. "And while I don't approve of strong drink, I'm not really talking about that, either."

Almost as if he were talking to himself, Larry mused quietly, "How many of us can look in the mirror and say we don't know—or at least suspect to the point of certainty—what goes on in the basement of the Sunset Grille? What perversions, what filth is carried on there, under the heading of 'Live Entertainment'? Oh, sure . . . they keep everything quiet. Adds to the mystery, the allure. But word gets out. . . ." He looked up at them, a strange, indefinable expression on his face. "Doesn't it?"

I smelled guilt rising like a cloud from some of the worshipers.

"Friends, how long can we go on worshiping the Holy God on Sunday and laying sacrifices on the altar of lust Monday through Saturday? What will it take to make us realize, like King Solomon, that the doorway to places like the basement of the Sunset Grille is like the entrance to a tomb?

"We're talking about death, brothers and sisters," he insisted, rounding the final curve and heading full steam into the home stretch of his appeal, his challenge to the people of Ellenbach. "We're talking about a spiritual cancer eating away, whether we realize it or not, at the bowels of our community. And I appeal to each of you—to each of us: Let's look deep within ourselves. Some of us have sinned by actively participating in the nasty enticements offered by the Grille. Some of us have sinned by providing trade and support for its less distasteful attractions. And some of us," he said, patting himself on the chest, "have sinned by keeping quiet.

"But I say to you, brothers and sisters," he finished, his voice rising like a gladiator gathering himself for a charge, "that I won't be silent any longer." His eyes glittered with purpose. "Here and now, I lay down the gauntlet. It is time, I believe, for all of us—all of us who will—to meet prayerfully together and plan to *do* something. I'll be speaking with you again about a specific time when we can meet and share our hearts about this, after you've had the opportunity to ponder your own commitment.

"In the meantime, in the name of Almighty God, I affirm this: I shall no longer bow to the Sunset Grille! And I ask you: Who will stand with me? Who will join me in this holy struggle?"

On cue, the organ pealed forth, and the congregation stood to sing the closing anthem.

> *Onward, Christian soldiers, Marching as to war,*
> *With the cross of Jesus Going on before!*

I couldn't tell how many of them were singing, and how many were trying to see who might still be seated.

Well, I thought, *the first sword has been unsheathed. It shouldn't be long before the adversary takes the field. . . .*

THE ASSIGNMENT

IN ANOTHER assembly, the forced praises of thousands ricocheted from rock walls and bounded upward. There were no windows in this place, no slanting, multicolored rays angling in through stained-glass scenes of Moses and the Lamb. No, the only light here was that grudging, fevered glimmer emitted by lumps of smoldering brimstone. It was midnight in Hell, and the Low Service of Satan had begun.

From the back of the hall crashed a raucous, frenzied burst of organ music. The tangled chords rose to the unseen ceiling above, spinning for a moment in the soot and ash before raining down upon the backs of the prostrate worshipers. The backs of the congregation, splayed in helpless terror on the floor of the place, were masses of welt and burns. None dared turn his head so much as an inch to the right or left, for fear of attracting the brutal ministrations of the gaff-wielding, demonic acolytes.

None of the congregation breathed any more than absolutely necessary, for to inhale the sulfurous oven-breath of Hell was to add another misery to the constant torments already inflicted. Some even tried to suffocate themselves, but of course that was no use. The gate of death had been passed by these wretched ones; for them it opened but once, to a single destination.

Even the demons despised the heat—though they could tolerate it slightly better than the condemned mortals—for nothing in all of Creation had ever been intended for this horrid place. Despite their swagger and cruel bravado, the demons knew they were here only because of the War. They talked of strategies and campaigns, of the eventual overthrow of the oppressive Other. They loudly endorsed the shrieking threats which the Head made against the Enemy, and swore their eternal vengeance on the One who had forced them into this inconvenient, temporary bivouac.

But they knew. Not even in the dark reaches of Hell could they convince themselves in their deepest hearts that the battlements of the Other would be stormed by such as they. They knew that one day, even such influence as they had over the despised humans would be removed, and then... Most of them didn't allow themselves to wander too far down that path. Instead they swore and shouted, and continued practicing the deceit first taught them by the Father of Lies. It was almost enough to make them forget... but not quite.

At a place not too far distant from the hall—though such terms as "distance" and "place" are somewhat irrelevant in Hell—was a lake of oily, gaseous water. In the middle of this ill-smelling tarn was an island, and on the island was the abiding place of the Head.

At one time the Head had been a whole individual, with limbs and torso. But he had been only a head for so long now that many wondered—when they paused to think of anything other than their own advantage—if his body was still actually present in the soil beneath him.

The propaganda the Head gave out was that he had himself buried here, the better to meditate and scheme the overthrow of the Enemy. But others snickered, when they were reasonably sure of not being betrayed to Intelligence, that the Head had been ensconced there forcibly—buried like a carrot up to his neck. He might give orders and commands and directives, but his actions were severely constrained by his near-complete burial.

Not that the Head was powerless. Even in his greatly limited capacities, the evil force of his personality pervaded this part of Hell like a foul vapor, twisting and bending to his will those who shared in his enmity to the Other. By fear, intimidation, and bullying he maintained himself—for the present, at least—supreme regent of this region.

From time to time, some denizen of Hell was conscripted to row out to the island to feed the Head. This was supposed to be a great honor, and could not be readily refused by the chosen one. But feeding the Head had certain liabilities attached. One never knew precisely what mood the Head would be in. Those who fed him and tended the jagged gash on his forehead—which never quite healed—tended to cut their visits short because of the Head's unpredictability. His caretakers had been known to lose fingers—even entire limbs. And while these wounds could not be fatal, neither could anything in Hell regenerate. The casualties of the Head's capriciousness were thus permanently maimed. It was fearful duty to row out to the island of the Head.

At this particular time, a lone demon pulled against the oars, heading across the lake. At his feet sat a pail containing the Head's ration: a bowl of fine flour—some whispered it was only common dust—and bitter capers to season it. *No wonder the Head is always in such a foul mood,* thought the demon, coming cautiously ashore. *Who'd want to eat this swill?*

Nearing the island, he came about, sculling quietly toward the shore. As he peered intently at the oversized, battle-scarred visage of his master, it appeared that the Head was asleep. Just as the demon stepped from the boat, the pipe organ in the church sounded a particularly loud blast. The Head's eyelids fluttered, and he opened his eyes.

Or at least they had once been eyes. Now they were shrunken, atrophied slits of red sclera, with glowing pupils, not the visual apparatus one would expect of a creature who lived in perpetual twilight. But then, even the Head had been created for a more well-lit environment. Thus the demon with the food-pail, standing ankle-deep in the muck at the shoreline, appeared to the Head as a barely moving blur against the larger, indistinct darkness. But the Head could feel him with his mind.

"Well, don't stand there staring, you moron," the Head snapped, "come here!"

The demon pulled his feet from the mud with an unpleasant sucking sound, and inched toward the commanding presence.

"I suppose you're the volunteer," snarled the Head sarcastically.

"Yes, your Excellency," replied the demon, warily eyeing the slightly bared fangs of his liege, "but I would like to think of myself as . . . well, more than a volunteer. . . . Actually, I—well, that is . . ."

"What? What?" interrupted the Head testily. "Quit your stuttering, fool, and say what's on your mind!"

"Yes, sir," responded the demon meekly, edging a halfstep closer to the Head. "Well, sir, I . . . I'd like to think of myself . . . as an admirer, sir. . . ."

An ironic chuckle rumbled from the head. "An admirer, eh? Well, well, well . . ." His slitted eyes peered from the pail to the abashed demon, then back. "Do you know what I'd say to that?" he queried, bending his full attention toward his nervous attendant. "Do you?"

"I . . . No, sir," the demon stammered, carefully studying his clawed toes.

"I'd say you ought to get on with my feeding, you idiot!" screamed the Head in a voice like a million buzzards.

"Oh . . . yes sir!" snapped the demon, his eyes wide with fright. He stared about him in panicked confusion, half-retracing his steps to the boat, then back—as if he had lost something.

"Well? What is it now?" snarled the Head. "What are you looking for?"

"I'm sorry, your Excellency, but . . . the scullery staff have apparently forgotten—that is, they didn't issue me any, ummm . . ."

"Any what?" sneered the Head, knowing what was coming.

"They gave me your food," said the demon, peering about in disarray, "but they didn't put in any—"

"Utensils?" grinned the Head. "Is that what you're looking for? A nice spoon—with a very long handle, perhaps?" An evil smile had spread across the Head's features.

"Uh—yes, sir. As a matter of fact, I had assumed there would be—"

"*There aren't any!*" snapped the Head, smacking his lips.

"Oh . . . well, then," said the demon brightly, "I'll just row back, quick as a wink, and get some—"

"You're not going anywhere!" the Head growled.

The demon halted his retreat toward the boat, slowly turning to face the Head, although he was afraid to look directly at the teeth which now gleamed threateningly in the half-dark. "Then, sir," he stammered, "what am I—how shall I—?"

A broad, tooth-baring smile was smeared across the Head's visage. "You'll just have to use...your fingers." These little interchanges, and the terror they inevitably produced in his subjects, were one of the few really enjoyble pastimes left to him.

The demon could have left the island and the Head any time he chose. He could have walked around behind the Head and kicked him, had he thought of it. But he didn't think of it—so complete was the Head's terrifying domination. He could only move to obey. He scooped a handful of the powdery flour into his palm, and reached, trembling, toward that gaping, eager mouth. He averted his eyes, for he knew that if he once looked into those red, glowing slits he would not be able to pull himself away.

He dropped the portion onto the Head's tongue, and pulled his hand away a little quicker than he probably should have. The Head grimaced at the tastelessness of the food, then smiled sardonically at his attendant.

"There—you see? Nothing at all to be afraid of, right?"

"Yes, sir," answered the demon dutifully, still averting his eyes.

"You aren't the first to feed me, and you won't be the last. By the way, how are you called?"

"I am called Pitch, sir," the demon replied.

"Very well, then, Pitch," the Head smirked, "give me a handful of those capers." The Head's tongue flicked the corners of his mouth, licking away a few stray flecks of flour. Pitch cautiously fed him the morsels, his eyes shifting anxiously from his hand to the Head's teeth.

"Now, then," continued the Head, noisily crunching the capers, "about this business of your admiration of me..."

Pitch fidgeted, dreading the Head's next swallow, for then it would be time for another serving.

"If you truly wish to gain my favor, there is an excellent opportunity to do so. Are you interested?"

Pitch calculated desperately. One could usually expect a down side to these "opportunities." There had been, for example, the unpleasantness with that Luther human—a good friend of Pitch's had gotten splattered with ink for his troubles. Then, even worse, there was the misbegotten spectacle remembered in Hell—though not in the Head's hearing—as the "Persecution Debacle." Horrified whispers rumored the gruesome punishments meted out to the author of that ill-fated, utterly ineffective campaign to obliterate the Enemy's followers. And of course, the Head's own burial here on the island was said to have resulted from his unsuccessful attempts to oppose the Other's fleshly assault upon the world of humans. One never knew. Venturing onto the field of battle with the Enemy was a chancy affair. But of course, to refuse the Head's request was also distasteful....

"What's the matter with you, Pitch?" the Head shouted, shocking Pitch back to the present. "I'm ready for my next bite, fool!"

"Sorry, sir," Pitch mumbled, delving a handful of powder from the pail. "I was thinking about your suggestion . . . about the opportunity you mentioned."

"I don't make suggestions, Pitch," the Head growled, when he had swallowed the gritty mixture. "I give orders."

"Yes, sir."

"Now, then," the Head continued. "It so happens I have a little . . . assignment . . . up on the battlefield. I need someone with just the right touch. Someone who isn't afraid to mix it up a little bit." The Head cut his near-blind orbs toward Pitch's face. "What do you say, Pitch? Think you're up to it?"

"I . . . well . . . your Excellency, I've never, uh, exactly been on an assignment to the earth. . . ." Furiously, Pitch tried to calculate the odds. A successfully completed assignment earthside usually entitled the agent to perks—such as exemption from feeding duty. And success was not unheard of, under the right conditions. "Oh, your Excellency," Pitch asked, "can you tell me a little about the . . . the intended subject?"

"Well, for starters, he's a professional agent."

A professional! If it were possible, Pitch felt himself sweating more heavily than normal. "Do . . . do you mean, sir," Pitch stammered, ". . . do you mean to say that he's an . . . an enemy clergyman?"

"What's the matter, Pitch?" demanded the Head petulantly. "Don't tell me you've got superstitious notions about the Enemy's so-called 'ministers'! The professional designation doesn't mean a blasted thing, in and of itself. We've got a pretty passel of the breed right here in Hell, don't forget!"

"True, sir. And yet," Pitch squeaked, "on my first assignment?" A thought occurred to him. "I don't suppose . . . Surely he's not an actively praying type, is he?" Pitch waited in dread for the answer.

"Unfortunately . . . yes," drawled the Head. Pitch felt himself sinking into a pit of despair. "But," said the Head importantly, "he's got one very important weakness, one that fits very nicely into this particular situation. Almost poetic, you might say. If you've got any talent at all, you should be able to find a way to insert your influence between this pretender and his prayers."

"Yes? What weakness is that?" Pitch asked, a desperate note of hope in his voice.

The Head called him uncomfortably closer, and whispered in his ear. Pitch felt slightly less dejected than before. "Hmmm," he murmured, scratching his cheek. "This mission sounds . . . interesting," he said. He paused long, feigning thoughtfulness. "All right, sir," he said, nodding decisively. "I'll do it."

"Wise choice," remarked the Head sarcastically.

"When do I leave?"

"As soon as you've finished feeding me," the Head replied. "You'll report to Central Files and read this human's dossier. Ravelle is his name, Dr. Lawrence P. Ravelle. Then you can leave immediately. You'll have one earth-month. That should be enough time."

"What exactly am I supposed to do to this Ravelle?" Pitch asked.

"Stupid! Do to him what you're trained to do! How long have you been here, anyway?"

"Since the . . . the beginning, sir," answered the cowed demon.

"Then act like someone who knows something!" spat the Head. "And give me more food!"

Pitch dipped his hand into the pail and proffered the meal toward the Head's maw, feeling the flesh crawl along his arm from the breath of his hideous, ill-tempered master. *I'll complete this mission, all right,* he swore to himself. *And I'll never set foot on this stinking little island again.*

THE BASEMENT

"O NWARD, Christian soldiers" was still ringing within me after the service, as I went back to the attic of the Paradise Donut Shop to see again if my partner had come through the pipe. But still nothing. The pouch marked "W" still hung from its peg, unclaimed. Shaking my head in irritated wonder at such tardiness, I pondered the best course of action to take. I decided it was time to make a closer inspection of the enemy's chief beachhead here in Ellenbach. Normally, I would have had my partner with me to guard my flank, and I his. But he still hadn't arrived, and was it really wise to wait?

Alone and with no little misgiving, I made my way across the street that separated the Paradise Donut Shop from the Sunset Grille.

Washington Avenue was the main east-west thoroughfare that ran through the town, linking it with other towns scattered across the miles of farms and ranchland beyond. A few blocks west was the major intersection where the other highway, a north-south route, came through Ellenbach. The Grille wasn't sited exactly at the center of town, but it was close enough.

In the five years since its construction, the Sunset Grille had become, for better or worse, a tradition. Like a bad habit, an unpleasant family secret, the Grille was scorned publicly by most Ellenbachians, when it was mentioned at all. One didn't brag about going to the Grille, and one certainly didn't admit to entering its multileveled basement. The Grille was mainly overlooked by the respectable. *It means business for Ellenbach,* they thought, and that was about as far as it went—until Larry issued his challenge.

The building was a friendly looking red-brick affair, with stylish, forest-green false shutters and neatly painted green trim. Approaching the place from along Washington Avenue, one had the impression of a solid, respectable, comfortable place—like a bank, or a country club for the well-heeled. Stones, piled to form a wall, lined the sidewalk outside the Grille, along with artfully placed driftwood and other bits of colorful flotsam. The overall elements of the appearance conspired together, beckoning the passerby to at least glance at, if not venture inside, the tastefully designed establishment.

The front door was wide and welcoming, and was the only public entrance or exit for the Grille. Just inside was a tiny, dimly lit lobby that opened immediately on two sides to the bar area, with attractively decorated dining tables beyond.

Many a man crossed the Grille's threshold, and a good many, too, cursed its occasional flaw: a latch that at times, especially in cold weather, got stuck. Under the right conditions it could be a good deal harder to leave than it was to arrive at the Sunset Grille. Then the fun would begin. Some inebriated soul who had long since disobeyed his wife's instructions to "stop by the store for a loaf of bread and be home for supper" would weave his way to the door on a damp winter's night and encounter the infernal latch. The barroom would bellow with laughter. The harder the fellow pushed, the more the door seemed to resist, and the louder the crowd laughed.

I paused on the sidewalk just outside the door which, even on a Sunday, boasted a fair amount of traffic. By far the majority of those entering and leaving the Grille to-night were men, although now and again one would see a woman escorted by a man who was glancing about nervously, as if afraid of detection. Just now, two men approached, one appearing to lead the other. As they drew near, I could hear snatches of their conversation.

"I dunno, Bill," one was saying. "Mary Beth'd kill me if she knew..."

"Aw, come on, Terry," the other said, clapping an arm companionably about his friend's shoulders. "Loosen up! There's nothing in here to hurt anybody! Just a little peek now and then won't make any difference. Come on, you'll see what I mean...."

"I'm still not so sure—"

"Now, Terry," said Bill, his voice dropping to a conspiratorial murmur, "you don't want the boys at the station to think you're a pansy, do you?"

"I guess not," intoned Terry doubtfully.

"All right, then," laughed Bill. "Let's get on in there. Tell you what," Bill continued affably as he tugged open the front door, "I'll buy you a couple of cold beers to sorta help you relax. Then later we can get us a chicken-fried steak...."

I followed Bill and Terry inside. I discerned a rustling above Terry's head, and caught the merest hint of a voice whispering to him: "Don't. It's the first step downward that's the hardest; after this it becomes much easier...."

I sighed. Terry wasn't heeding. The Way of Escape was

there, just as he always is, urging this human to take the nearest exit from the broadening, descending corridor he was about to enter. But Terry had to take the first step. And he was choosing not to.

I looked about me at the main floor of the Sunset Grille, recalling what I had read in the dossier. There had been only one manager of the establishment since its creation, a white-haired gentleman by the name of William Robbin Detzer. To his regulars he was known as Billy Bobb, which suited him fine. He was never one for formalities. He wanted his patrons to think of him as their buddy, and he rarely forgot a face, or a bar tab.

He was a handsome man, a former ophthalmologist. He'd never married, and was always the life of any party. He rarely talked willingly about his life before the Sunset Grille, but if forced to explain why he left his medical practice an unspecified number of years ago, he would usually make some vague allusion to finding himself "unfulfilled" in his former line of work. Afterward he simply drifted, until the representatives of the Grille's ownership—the "suits," Billy Bobb called them—approached him somewhere about managing the Sunset Grille in Ellenbach. The notion appealed to the hedonist in Billy Bobb, and he arrived in town just as the last truckload of construction workers was departing. Since then, he had worked himself deep into the fabric of the local male culture. His name became synonymous with a good time, and he always had a smile and a joke for anyone who came through the front door.

The first floor was taken up by a bar and grill, decorated artfully by the manager himself. The visitor, upon his initial arrival, would look in upon a scene that resembled a twilit sylvan glade. Several papier-mâché "trees" appeared to grow right through the ceiling. Lanterns hung from their branches, casting a subdued, moon-silver glow on the patrons. And Billy Bobb had strewn about on the floor artificial leaves and bark and other bits of ersatz flora. The total effect was, I had to admit, quite striking—almost mystical, in fact. I half-expected to see a satyr dodging about in the shadows.

A long, richly carved wooden bar, fronted by red leather-upholstered barstools, lay along the wall to the left. And behind the bar, above the shelves of liqueurs and scotch and bourbon, was Billy Bobb's famous mirror.

More than a few people had made wild claims about the massive piece of beveled, leaded glass, and not all the claimants were drunk. Some swore they saw translucent, unfamiliar figures walking behind the normal reflections. Others wrote it off to party spirit. Some were concerned enough about their mental faculties that they never came back. Nevertheless, all of the stories matched. Those who saw it agreed there was something almost "living" about the mirror.

In the winter there was always a crackling fire in the corner hearth. And in the summer a cavelike coolness wafted through the windowless main room, as if arising from an unknown source deep down in the earth where mushrooms grow like wildflowers. The walls were a collage of plants and vines and pictures of people who nobody in town ever seemed to recognize. At least they weren't from Ellenbach.

It was a fairly ingenious setup. One could go into the Sunset Grille pretending—possibly believing—that all he intended was to hoist a few drinks with friends, or to enjoy one of Billy Bobb's excellent sirloins. And, for a while, he might be able to limit himself to that, to pretend that he wasn't secretly fascinated by the dark green double doors which opened onto the stairway leading down....

But all the clever decoration on earth couldn't disguise

the nauseating, sickly sweet odor of evil that assaulted me as soon as I stepped inside. The Sunset Grille stank of wickedness as a trap stinks of bait. The whole place was built to draw one systematically into the uncritical acceptance of all its offerings. As men entered the darkened Grille, silent voices whispered to them, cajoled them. Even now I could hear the sibilant, oily promises they made to those brought here by their inability to resist the fascination of darkness. Looking to my left, I saw Bill and Terry, seated at the bar. And I saw the shadowy, grinning form leaning over Bill's shoulder, muttering in his ear the phrases he parroted at his friend.

"Come on, Terry boy," they coaxed together, "nobody's got to know. Let's go on down to the second floor and see what the action's like. It can't hurt!" Even to my ears, the countering cautions of Terry's Way were now all but inaudible. Sadly, I knew that before he left this place, Terry would have gone through the green doors, down to the lower levels, in accordance with the real purpose of the Sunset Grille. He would, this day, be drawn deep into the pernicious, addictive worship of the human body—a carnival of the senses which promises so much, yet delivers less than nothing.

I felt myself bristling with indignation and crushed by sadness. It was infuriating to contemplate what the Foe had done to your kind by his deceptions and half-truths. You see, in Heaven, "nakedness" and "clothing" are irrelevant terms. There we—and one day, I hope, you as well—are both always naked and always clothed. Naked, in the sense that all things there are revealed, and displayed in open, unceasing praise to their Maker. One has no need of concealment in Heaven. One appears on the outside as one is on the inside. Yet we are also clothed, because everything there is sheathed, enfolded, penetrated, and permeated by the glory of the Supreme One.

He is our robe, our covering, and our crown. What need have we to fashion other garments?

In Heaven there is no shame, nor need of any. Shame was an invention of the Liar. He came to your most ancient parents in their open, trusting, unveiled innocence, and perverted that glorious, worshipful freedom into something vulgar, something awkward—something to be hidden. And ever since, man has both craved his nakedness and been embarrassed by it. It is a snare by which the Traitor has captured poets, philosophers, and kings.

I decided to observe the lower levels. The door to the basement levels was, like everything else in the Grille, placed with a diabolically discerning eye for human nature. It was located at the end of the corridor which led to the men's restroom, allowing one to reach the stairway unobtrusively. Many a Grille patron excused himself to "take care of business," and passed the green portal to the lower levels. Even the rudimentary constraint of others' knowledge had been removed.

Descending to the topmost of three below-ground levels, one found himself in a long, dimly lit aisle, lined on either side by black-painted wooden cubicles. Standing outside the booths, I could plainly hear the clink of quarters into slots, and the click and grin of projection equipment. I had little doubt as to the subject matter of the viewing.

Following the opening of the bar and grill above, this floor had been occupied earliest. The two levels below were only furnished later, in descending order—when the way had been prepared for them.

I went down.

If the enemy's messengers whispered and insinuated on the floor above, down here they were giggling and laughing aloud. I could hear them as they goaded their victims on: "Ooooh, yeah—look at that!...Just one more quarter—you're already in here, you might as well..." One human came out of a stall at the end of the aisle and walked past me toward the stairs. I nearly gagged when I saw what rode on his shoulders. A demon, in the form of a huge, glistening leech, had wrapped itself about the victim's neck and head. Its mouth-parts were fastened about the man's left ear—but instead of sucking out blood, this spiritual leech was force-feeding the human a steady diet of filth and perversion.

I refocused my eyes to see through the demonic manifestation to the human's face—and gasped. Larry Ravelle's visage stared out blindly through the enslaving coils of his personal tempter. Then I noticed the man's gait, rocking from side to side as he walked. The limp! This was not Larry, but his twin brother, John!

I sensed the leech-demon becoming aware of my presence. Quickly I faded into an empty booth, holding my breath. It would not do to be discovered here, so vastly outnumbered by the enemy's minions.

Don't misunderstand. My kind can't be killed—otherwise, what's the point in being immortal? And the ultimate course of the War was decided two thousand or so earth-years ago, when the Supreme One performed the act of glorious ignominy for which He is lauded forever. But in the skirmishes surrounding our human assignments, we can be hurt—badly enough that it may terminate our missions—or prevent our returning to the pipe. I didn't want to risk that at this stage.

Then something moved in the black-painted darkness to my left. I squared around, clenched my fists, and prepared to fight, which, even as a Trial, I am permitted to do in self-defense. But as I stood panting, my shoulders wedged against the wall of the booth, I was hoping madly that the noise was merely a creaking board. As I told you before, Trials have a fairly specific set of gifts—and hand-to-hand battle isn't one of them. That's more the province of the Ways of Escape.

There was a sound of heavy, deep breathing near the wall I was now facing. I sniffed the air, but detected no stench of the underworld. Yet the presence of whatever shared this booth with me was enormous, full-spirited, and ready to attack.

I heard my own breath coming in short, panicked nostril-bursts. I gathered a deep breath, along with as much courage as I could muster on such short notice, and sprang forward...at the same instant as my adversary! Our heads collided at the middle of the booth, and we both were knocked backward. I rose to defend myself again, but stopped short.

My unseen opponent had muttered something under his breath—and it wasn't the snarls and curses of one of the rebellious ones. I allowed my eyes to refocus, and the earthly darkness around me faded, melting into another type of vision. Across the booth from me stood a fellow angel—a strapping, broad-shouldered chap with a shining mail shirt and a long, gleaming sword strapped about his waist. A Way! He was rubbing his forehead with a grimace on his face. Then he looked up—or, rather, down—at me.

"Huh!" he grunted in surprise. "For such a little guy, you sure pack a powerful punch. What did you hit me with, anyway? A boulder?"

I grinned. "Not exactly." I pointed to the knot rising on my own noggin. "Although some folks have told me that my head was as hard as rock." I noticed the familiar pouch marked with a "W" hanging from the thong about his neck. "You must be my partner on this assignment." I stuck out my hand. "I'm called Skandalon."

He took my hand in his big paw, returning my smile. "Pleased to meet you. I'm Diasozo, but most folks call me Dias, for short."

"Good enough, Dias," I said. "I was just at the pipe, and your pouch was still unclaimed. When did you get earthside?"

Dias shrugged. "I'm not sure. I haven't quite figured out this time business yet."

Hadn't figured out time . . . ? "Is this your first assignment?" I asked him.

He nodded, a trifle sheepishly, I thought. "Yep. Yours?"

I nodded. I'm sure the disappointment must have shown on my face. I was under enough pressure as it was. I had so hoped my partner would be an experienced hand. . . .

"Say," Dias interjected, reading my mood, "don't worry, Stumble-on."

"Skandalon," I corrected.

"Oh, yeah . . . Sorry," he grinned. "Anyway, don't fret so! We were selected and sent on this mission, and you know the Supreme One doesn't hold much truck with coincidence. We're gonna sail through this thing with flying colors, just you watch!"

How very like a Way, I thought, before I could catch myself.

"Never mind," I said. "We'd better not stay in here much longer."

"Right," he agreed, looking around him. "Might wake the neighbors. Although—" I saw his meaty fist wrap around the hilt of his sword, loosening it in its sheath—"I can't say I'd mind a little scrap, just to warm up the ol' reflexes. . . ."

Looking at him, I felt again my secret envy for his kind. The Ways of Escape were the rulers of Heaven's playgrounds in what corresponds to an angel's child-hood. As a group they were known for their strength, their indomitable fighting hearts. They were big, boister-ous, confident. They were so many things I wanted to be, but would never attain.

"Well," I said, "we'd better get going."

"Let's go!"

We were up and out, moving through a colder, cleaner air. Free of the stifling obscenities of the Grille, we could not have suspected that the morning to come would reveal an ugliness taking place under these very same stars—an ugliness more hideous, if possible, than the perversions purveyed by the Sunset Grille.

THE TRAGEDY

THE ATMOSPHERE inside the Paradise Donut Shop crackled with tension and disbelief.

The usual early crowd was there: the local merchants and clerks who took their morning coffee with one of Cyrus Daye's pastry creations, the retired farmers enjoying a morning snack before making their stops at the bank and the post office, even an eligible widow or two, scouting out suitable prospects among the ranks of those just mentioned—Cyrus's donut shop was the place they all stopped this time of day. Donuts and coffee were only a fraction of what was dispensed here.

But this morning the usual joviality and good-natured ribbing was absent. Instead, the regulars sat with their mouths agape, wide-eyed with horror as the whispered phrases ran from table to table.

"Found her dead in a field last night..."

"They said her eyes were open, with the awfullest, most scared look..."

"Just last night, they said—near Baker's woodlot..."

"Had she been...?"

"*Yes.*"

"I just can't believe it. Here, in Ellenbach?"

"Yes. Emily Hansen—and she just turned seventeen..."

All eyes turned toward the door as a grizzled older man, his face stiff with shock, trod heavily into the shop, followed two paces later by his wife. Ad Cates looked around at the silent room, knowing they all knew: It was he who had the dark honor of discovering the violated body of the Hansen girl early this morning as he made his rounds with the mail on Route One.

With the muted, reluctant pride that often colors the carrier of the latest bad news, Ad seated himself wearily at the nearest small, round-topped table. Cyrus, knowing the mail carrier's habits by heart, silently placed a cup of black coffee by Ad's elbow, and a cup of beige creamed-and-sugared brew in front of Marge, Ad's wife.

Taking a slow, studied sip of the steaming coffee, Ad glanced up at them, and began.

"She was in the bar-ditch across the road from Baker's place—right by the mailbox. Nearly run over her arm with my right front tire. Good thing for headlights..."

One of the women gasped softly, covering her mouth with a fist-wadded napkin.

"Carlton said looked to him like she must have lost a lot of blood, while she wandered around awhile, in a daze like, after... after it happened." Carlton Smith was the county coroner.

Ad's eyes never left the ebony surface of his coffee as he narrated the horror in a dead, inflectionless voice. "Of course, once I seen her, I wheeled around and got back to town quick as I could. I called Sheriff Sweeney's place first—then Carlton. I figured they'd both need to be there."

Another slow sip. "She was all drawed up, curled up like... like a baby—"

Ad's eyes filled, the line of his lips blurred with the awful recollection. By now most of the women were sobbing softly into soggy napkins, and the men had the dour, wooden-faced solemnity usually associated with tidings of death. Jacob Hansen was well-known to all those present. In his own way, each commiserated silently in the unspeakable tragedy which had befallen the family, a tragedy which could hardly have happened in a less likely place than Ellenbach.

"I heard she was . . . beat up pretty bad," offered another man quietly. Ad Cates nodded silently, confirming the tale.

"Also heard they found some footprints in the ground not too far off: hers . . . and a man's . . ." The other voice trailed off into silence.

Ad sniffed and wiped his nose on the back of his hand, glancing up at them again, then back at his coffee cup. "Sheriff Sweeney said there was somethin' funny about those prints . . ." He squinted toward the window, slowly shaking his head. "But I cain't recollect exactly . . ." Again, the heavy silence. "Shore hard to figger," observed Ad quietly, when a few more seconds had passed, "somethin' like this . . . happenin' here . . ."

A few of his listeners nodded. The rest only bowed their heads in silence.

THE FUNERAL was delayed several days by the autopsy— required by the state in cases of violent death.

Cars and pickups filled the parking lot of the Ellenbach Community Church, overflowing along the curbsides for the entire block surrounding the building. The sanctuary of the Ellenbach Community Church was even more crowded than the parking lot. Nearly every family in town was represented at the service for Emily Hansen. In fact, Larry and several of the deacons had to scramble about in the Sunday school classrooms for enough metal folding chairs, placed in the aisles and the foyer, to accommodate all those in attendance. Several pews were almost completely taken by youth group kids, Emily's peers.

The hush deepened when the Hansen family filed in from a side door of the sanctuary. Jacob Hansen, a stolid, well-respected member of the community, struggled valiantly to still his quivering chin. He walked with one arm about the shoulders of his wife—who covered her face with both hands and leaned weakly on her husband as they made their way to the front pews reserved for the family—and the other arm wrapped around Luke, Emily's thirteen-year-old brother. Luke's face, normally ruddy and creased with a ready grin, was pasty-white, and his eyes were dark, round pools of numbed disbelief. Grandparents, cousins, aunts, and uncles followed the immediate family and quietly took their places on the front pew. Between them and the altar, the flower-covered casket rested.

When the family was settled, a woman stood in the balcony. Unaccompanied, she sang in a clear, lilting voice the painfully beautiful melody of one of Emily's favorite hymns:

> *Flee as a bird to the mountain,*
> *Thou who art weary of sin;*
> *Go to the clear flowing fountain,*
> *Where you may wash and be clean;*
>
> *Fly, for th' avenger is near thee,*
> *Call, and the Savior will hear thee,*
> *He on His bosom will bear thee;*
> *Oh, thou who art weary of sin,*
> *Oh, thou who art weary of sin.*

The poignant, minor-key strains of the ancient Spanish melody filled the sanctuary—and the heart of each one seated there—as water fills a basin to overflowing. As the song echoed into silence, Larry Ravelle rose to speak. He opened his mouth, then closed it again in a futile swallow, clenching his trembling jaws together in an effort to stem the tide of emotions clogging his throat. After a number of deep breaths, he looked out over the audience, and began.

"Brothers and sisters, the body in this casket is far too young." He drew a few ragged breaths, then continued. "Death is always a tragedy, friends. Even if it comes at the end of a long and useful life, it is the reminder that we live in a fallen world, that the original plan of Almighty God was marred by the deceitfulness of Satan. It is the hateful reminder of his pollution of that perfect relationship which existed between God and man in the beginning—the relationship God intended man to enjoy forever. A relationship which required the very death of God Himself, in the person of Jesus Christ, to restore.

"I want to bring words of comfort to you today, Jacob," he said, tears coming to his face as he regarded the weeping, suffering family on the front pew. "I want you and Carrie and Luke, and all the relatives and friends gathered in this place, to know without any shadow of a doubt that even now—while we weep and mourn and ask God and ourselves why such a hideous thing came to pass—even now, Emily is smiling up into the face of God, and hearing Him welcome her to a place where pain is less than a memory."

Jacob Hansen looked up at Larry then. And through the tears and redness of his wounded eyes, he managed the ghost of a smile, and a nod of the head. When Larry could tear his vision away from that of the bereaved father, he glared about the sanctuary with a stare as fierce as an eagle's.

"People of Ellenbach, can there be any doubt of the source of such depravity as that which claimed the life of Emily Hansen? Does anyone here still wonder where a person could gain such a distorted view of humanity that he could descend to the brutish depths of Emily's attacker?

"Let me be very clear about this, folks," Larry said, coming out from behind the lectern and standing on the dais above the casket as he continued. "I stood in this very pulpit a few days ago and issued a challenge. And in light of the tragedy that brings us here today, I want to repeat and reinforce that challenge. You see before you one pastor who will not rest or relent until the merchants of filth are banished from Ellenbach forever!"

His voice was still quiet, but increasing in urgency, demanding to be heard. "I don't ever want to preside over another funeral for a victim of unbridled lust," he said, clasping a fist into his palm. "And Emily is only the most visible victim, brothers and sisters. Because we're all victims. Every one of us has had something precious ripped away from us by this needless death. And the only way to reverse the theft of our peace of mind, our trust in our neighbors, our very souls—" He paused, pivoting slowly around, as if trying to look into every face in the pews and the balcony "—is to close down the Sunset Grille!"

THE START

Even for a seasoned tempter, Central Files could be confusing. For the novice it was positively intimidating. Pitch closed the door softly and glanced around. The room was constructed with flagstone from floor to ceiling. Along each wall, at ten-foot intervals, was a fireplace . . . ten fireplaces in all. Pulled up around each roaring fire were two or three chairs, a low stone table, and a small metal bookshelf. In the center, running the length of the room, were the files . . . great gray cabinets thirty feet high with hundreds of handles, labeled alphabetically. Ladders on tracks leaned against the files to give access to the upper drawers.

Pitch tiptoed across the stone floor to the far left side of the files. He was reaching for the handle on one of the drawers in the "R" cabinet when a voice startled him from behind.

"Rookie, wait your turn!"

Pitch wheeled around and saw a chest where a head should have been. There was a shiny, vertical scar starting in the middle of the abdomen, barely visible through thick body hair, and he followed its line past massive shoulder muscles until his eyes met those of a giant demon. Pitch said nothing.

"You *have* read the rules, haven't you?" the demon growled, glaring down at him as he pointed to a wooden board posted next to the entrance.

"Uh... I'm not sure..."

"Just as I thought," said the giant. "Stand aside!"

With that, the demon shoved Pitch out of the way and rummaged through the same drawer Pitch had approached until he found what he was looking for. Then he slammed it shut and walked away.

If there was a twinge of cockiness in him before he arrived here, then the egotistical pride welling up in Pitch at being pushed around quickly overwhelmed such a feeling. Muttering to himself about the "brainless stack of muscle" who had bullied him, Pitch yanked open the drawer with a loud bang. The scarred heads of several other demons turned toward the sound, but Pitch ignored them.

Ramirez... Rashid... Ratani... Rausch... Ravalli... There it was: Ravelle—Dr. Lawrence Paul Ravelle. The folder was slightly askew, having not been pushed all the way down by its last user.

He took out the file, found an unoccupied chair, and started reading. Sure enough, the file indicated that this Ravelle possessed the quirk alleged by the Head—not that Pitch had had any reason to believe otherwise, but it was always best to check one's sources where the Head was concerned.

Pitch began remembering what he had learned of temptation during his earliest days in Hell—those vaunted days when the first beachheads had been staked out in the world where the Enemy was fast proceeding with his insane project. Oh, the spirit of those times! The print on the file in front of Pitch blurred into a fog of reminiscence as he thought of the bold, confident dispatches being received from the field.

Have established contact with the Enemy's playthings . . .

Have begun program of counter-intelligence within ranks of Enemy's stooges . . .

Have successfully disrupted communications between Enemy and mortals . . .

Then, the riotous celebration that had broken loose in all of Hell when word came back of the Enemy's abandonment of his human pets! What days those had been! Days when anything had seemed possible—even likely! Days when one could almost forget the ignominy of the Retreat. When one could almost forget the shackles clamped on Hell's hordes, the vast chasm between what they once were and what they had become since their ouster from the kingdom they rightfully should have ruled—would have ruled, if not for their Prince's impetuosity—Pitch checked himself. Such thoughts and musings were occasionally discovered, with most unpleasant results.

Then that disastrous event occurred which yet reverberated in terror through the infernal princedom, an event so horrendous that it was never referred to anywhere in Hell, on pain of the most severe punishment: the Incarnation.

Pitch shuddered in distaste. Who would ever have entertained the possibility, even in his wildest fancies, that the Enemy would actually *become* one of the stinking, grinning, defecating, meat-laden beasts he had created? Basest treachery, this unholy marriage of the finite and the infinite, of time and eternity! The demons had howled in agony when they realized the Enemy's abandonment of his human toys had been but a ploy to ambush them all!

One of Pitch's cronies had been trapped on the earth in those days. He returned in disgrace to Hell, telling a chilling tale of a sudden eviction, and a stampeding herd of swine. The cliffs . . . the plunge . . . *horrible!*

And yet . . . if the Prince had had only a little more perception, paid a little more heed to those wild-haired, half-crazed humans called "prophets" . . .

Again Pitch willed himself to drop that line of thought. He forced his eyes back toward the Ravelle file. He flipped a few pages, looking for the family history of this human. Frequently one could pick up clues, indications of the best pressure points—ah, yes, here it was. There were some promising tendencies indicated by this twin brother. . . .

Again, memory wafted Pitch back to a day Before—in another, brighter existence, one he could barely recall. *Why now?* he wondered. Why should he be remembering . . . a twin? Something about a twin . . .

He pulled himself with difficulty back to the present. Where was he? Oh yes, the brother. Potential there, certainly. And the father . . . Pitch read of the Ravelle human's childhood and adolescence, and began smirking slyly. *Yes,* he thought. The Head, for once, had spoken truly. There was fertile soil here. . . .

A thin, narrow-shouldered clerk hurried up to the files, pulling open the "R" drawer. The demon dug frantically through the folders. He paused, cursing under his breath. Then he glanced back to where Pitch was seated, studying the file in his lap. He marched angrily up to the chair.

"Give me that file, you!" he demanded, thrusting an impatient hand toward Pitch.

Pitch looked angrily up at the clerk. "What's your problem, needle neck? I've been assigned to the field," he said, a trifle self-importantly, "and this human is my subject." A moment more he glared at the clerk, then returned to his reading. "So get lost," he finished, under his breath.

The clerk snatched the file from Pitch's hand with a loud curse. "I've got work to do, you fool!" he snarled. "I can't waste time with every prima-donna rookie in Hell!" Shoving a now-crumpled piece of paper into the folder, he flung it back at Pitch. "There's your file, you arrogant whelp! Choke on it!" He stomped off in the direction he had come, muttering loudly to himself.

Pitch stared murderously at the retreating back of the clerk. Then he gathered the now-scattered contents of the file, picking up the item added by the surly clerk. It was a memo—a very recent one. He read it, and felt fresh anger burning his insides. What cretins were on the ground in this Ellenbach place, that they would allow such a dim-witted thing to happen? Didn't they have the faintest idea of the tactics of temptation, any notion of strategy?

They had gone and inspired this rape to happen, and gotten a good portion of the town in a self-righteous uproar over the "smut peddlers"! Pitch wanted to bite someone, he was so provoked. His first assignment, and his own kind were fouling the nest! No doubt some junior tempter had seen an opportunity to get his human to indulge himself, and was so besotted by a little momentary iniquity that he stopped thinking.

Pitch crammed the papers back into the file and stood, leaving the folder on the chair. It was high time he went to Ellenbach and got started, before any more stupidity happened.

DIAS and I conferred all during the night, huddled in the belfry of the church. It was his first assignment earthside, and he was curious about the role of a Trial, so I pulled my orders from the leather pouch and read aloud to him:

To Skandalon, faithful member of the Legion, an Angel of Trial: On this day, begin to test the man's faith. Cease not until endurance comes. By way of harshest conflict, perfect him and complete him. Hinder not your foe, but rather allow your mortal charge opportunity for testing—for My strength shall come to him, if he will but ask, believing. And I have sent to him the Way of Escape, which he shall find if he shall seek diligently.

Stand strong, good and faithful Skandalon. And pray. Remember always these words: "Not my will, but Thine, be done."

Dias didn't say anything for a long time after I finished reading. When he did, the words came with a dark glance and a scowl. "Sounds like your whole job is to make mine harder."

I was abashed. The same thought had often entered my mind as I had received the Trial's charter. But for the sake of the mission, and Dias's understanding, I had to attempt an explanation.

"You and I are not sent here for the sake of each other, Dias," I began hesitantly. "We are to aid the accomplishment of the Supreme One's will for the humans to whom we are sent. So any talk of 'jobs'—apart from the realization of the Supreme One's goals for Larry Ravelle—somewhat misses the point."

He wouldn't look up at me. Instead, he toyed sullenly with the hilt of his sword. "Easy words for the one who doesn't have to face the blades of the enemy," he muttered. "I must engage the forces of darkness who will come for the soul of Larry Ravelle. I must look into their hate-filled eyes and deal them blow for blow in the contest for the man. And you—" he looked up now, a resentful frown kneading his forehead—"you will permit them!

You'll allow the pitfalls to open before him, and it's up to me to wade in and take my lumps along with him. And will you be doing anything while I'm putting my neck on the block?"

By now, frustration frayed the tether of his control, causing his voice to louden to a near-shout. "What's the difference between you and the enemy, anyway?" he yelled, his wrath finally reaching the boiling point.

I hung my head. I knew Dias was off the mark, but in my own confusion I did not know how to tell him so. "I'll do what my orders direct," I whispered. "I'll pray." My words were correct, but just now they seemed insufficient.

I remembered the analogy one of my teachers had used in the briefing for this mission. Having no better ideas of my own, I decided to attempt to use his.

"On earth, Dias, there are people called surgeons. Do you know what they do?"

After several seconds of silence, I heard him mumble, "Yes, I think I do. Aren't they the ones who treat sick humans when medication won't work?"

"Right. And do you know how they perform their treatment?"

A doubtful expression came into his eyes, and he shook his head.

"They cut them, Dias. Slice into their bodies with sharp blades and rearrange what's inside."

He looked at me in disbelief.

"It's true," I assured him "The surgeon has to wound his patient in order to permit healing." I looked carefully at him before continuing. "The difference in a Trial and the enemy is the same as the difference between a surgeon and a butcher. The one wounds in order to heal. The other slashes in order to destroy."

A thoughtful look began to slowly replace the angry one of moments before.

"And the difference in the outcome of my surgery, Dias," I mused quietly, voicing my own most central fear, "depends not so much on my incisions as the response of my patient. It is possible to cut carefully and still lose the battle."

For a time neither of us spoke, wrapped in our own inner strivings. Finally Dias broke the silence. "Sounds like you've got your work cut out for you, Stumble-on."

"That's *Skandalon*. Can't you at least get my name right?" I asked, a bit testily. "Now, how about you? What do your orders say?"

Immediately the defensive scowl flared again on his face. "Don't worry—I know what to do."

"I have no doubt of that," I insisted, "but I still think I should know the extent of your charter for this mission. It has a direct bearing on our efforts." My stare challenged his, until he dropped his gaze and reached for the pouch around his neck. Pulling out the parchment strip on which the orders were etched, he handed it to me without meeting my eyes.

"Here," he said. "Read it."

"You can simply tell me."

Again his temper flared. *"Read it!"*

I didn't know what to say, as the embarrassed silence softened his eyes and the corners of his mouth. After a while, I looked down at the parchment, and read silently:

To Diasozo, faithful member of the Legion, an Angel of the Way of Escape: On this day, begin to provide a path of deliverance for the man. Be not perplexed whether he chooses you or not. Only obey, and persevere. Guide him, and fight the good fight. You are his Way, Diasozo, created to give your all for him.

Our eyes met. He shrugged, and I grinned. It was time to get started.

ON THE edge of town, where babyboomers built their three-bedroom brick homes, and the highway came winding out of the grain fields, weak November breezes rattled in the dead-brown roadside grasses. Dried thistles danced in the accumulation of cigarette butts and six-pack plastic.

An old flatbed bob-truck whined westward through the last curve in the highway before Ellenbach and headed toward town, its payload leaning precariously. The man in the cab had driven all night, and was tired. Suddenly he lurched both ways on the steering wheel, jarred fearfully alert. A great gust of wind had come out of the west, hitting the grill head-on. The truck shivered and slowed, as if held back by some unseen hand.

The heater-knob was turned to the top notch, so the driver never felt the unearthly cold which accompanied the blast. Neither did he notice that the roadside weeds, whipped so violently about by the sudden wind, had just as suddenly ceased their movement. A look in the rear-view mirror would have shown calm fields as far as the driver's eye could see....

Pitch had arrived in Ellenbach.

II.

THE BARBECUE

PITCH picked his way gingerly across the barren field, wincing as he walked. The terrain of earth pained him with each step, and he was reminded of the penal logic behind those despised words, "On thy belly thou shalt go!" He understood for the first time why the Head sent others to do his work. In fact, he had suspected for a long time that the Head was far less powerful than he acted. After all, how much *real* power could one possess whose only forays into this world were supervisory by nature? Brainwork was nothing. Why, anyone could slip into a body for the sake of giving orders for a while. But to actively contend with the angels of Heaven... now that was another matter.

Pitch was trying to reach a dark, abandoned building at the edge of this field he was traversing. A large concrete loading dock fronted the building—an abandoned packing house. Pitch wished fervently to reach the relative comfort of the smooth concrete, and quit this plowed field, each loamy clod of which was exquisite torture to the soles of his feet. Each step served notice that the ground he traversed could not be thought of as ordinary dirt and rocks. It was made of words...enormous, lasting, monosyllabic blasts of irresistible creative force.

Let there be Earth!

And there was earth. With the rest of the spiritual host he had witnessed the dire spectacle, as the Enemy summoned being from nothingness. Even in the caverns of Hell they cowered beneath the thunder of his mighty forge, as he built a universe to suit his own incomprehensible purposes. *Let there be Earth*—and there was earth.

And earth was punishing him now. The very rocks were crying out in alarm at his presence. The winter wheat in the field behind the packing house looked particularly uninviting. Its tender green blades, swaying gently in the wind, would shred the bottoms of his feet if he blundered into them just now. He turned left, out of the field and onto a dirt road, which he hoped would make walking less torturous. "Got to practice navigating in this cursed place," he thought to himself. For even among the demons, a faint echo remains of what they once were. By diligent drill, Pitch, like the other demons sent earthside by the Head, could summon to himself a modicum of his celestial density. He could learn to walk upon the earth—but a certain level of concentration was always required.

He tiptoed the last ten feet to the edge of the loading dock, and lifted himself up. This was perfect, he thought. What better place to butcher a lamb than a former slaughterhouse? He would make the pastor pay for every stab of pain he incurred on this God-stained globe of clay.

Pitch rolled back the door with excruciating agony and did not bother to reclose it. Inside, he found what he was looking for...shadows! They would be useful in his work later on. Right now, he longed to curl up on the floor and sleep—the fatigue of his journey had caught up with him.

"About time you got here," growled a gravelly voice from the darkest corner of the loading bay. Pitch stared into the blackness, and saw two burning holes returning his gaze.

"Who are you?" Pitch asked, taken aback.

"I'm your partner on this blasted errand," grated the other, stepping into the faint moonlight which trickled through the open door.

It was the scar-chested behemoth from Central Files! Pitch began to grin. This was quite poetic, he thought—for, as primary tempter to the Ravelle human, he had the position of command on this mission. This ape had to obey *him*!

"So," Pitch asked, nonchalantly turning his back on the other, "how long have you been here?" He could fairly hear the muscle-bound moron's teeth grinding in useless rage. He grinned secretly. "Speak up, you!" he added, allowing an edge to his voice. "I asked you a question!"

"Got here just before you walked up," the other demon mumbled.

"And I suppose you've read the file, have you—by the way, how are you called, anyway?" Pitch was enjoying himself.

"Stool," croaked the other.

"How... appropriate," drawled Pitch, drily. "Now, as I was saying—have you read the file on this mission?" Pitch knew quite well Stool had. He only hoped the broad-chested monster had enough memory to recall whom he had insulted as he fetched the folder from its drawer in Central Files.

"Yes, I've read it—" Stool began a trifle impatiently,

then stopped. He stared closely at Pitch, and his jaw slackened in sudden recognition. Pitch grinned sarcastically, and stuck out his hand.

"I'm called Pitch," he smiled, looking up into the rotted teeth of the other demon, "and I'll be filing the mission report with the Head." He gave Stool a look of mock concern, adding, "I certainly hope everything goes smoothly, don't you?"

Spinning on his heel, he sauntered toward the dark corner where Stool had been waiting for him. "This corner looks to be the most comfortable spot in here," he remarked lightly. "I'm tuckered out from the trip, Stool, old boy—think I'll catch a quick nap." As he settled himself into a resting position, he roused once again. "Oh, and—Stool," he called, "you'd better stand guard, keep watch, that sort of thing. Wouldn't want to get caught unprepared, would we?" He yawned, then smiled to himself.

Presently, he drifted into the demonic equivalent of sleep, dreaming sweet dreams of revenge.

Dias and I met our opponents for the first time in the pastor's backyard.

In a corner of the patio sheltered by the house from the early winter breezes, Larry was cooking steaks on the grill: beautiful pieces of meat, each with its own marbled design and distinct shape. They were a special treat for the family, and called for an outdoor cooking regardless of what season the calendar said it was.

I watched as Larry tossed the first of the steaks on the grill, and heard him say to the smallest cut, "You, little one, are for Annie." His daughter, bundled up in a bright blue jacket and playing with a doll by the kitchen doorstep, heard him too.

"Leave the fat on, Daddy," she pleaded.

"Okay, Annie Rose."

Larry also assigned the others, holding each one up to show Annie before tossing them on: "Here's Peter. Here's Mommy. Here's Daddy," he said with a smile, while Annie laughed.

"Make one for Lord Byron, Daddy."

"Good idea! L. B. needs to celebrate, too." Larry cut a piece of raw meat from his own steak and set it to the side.

"Whose birthday is it?" asked Annie.

"It's nobody's birthday. It's Support Daddy Day."

"What?"

"It just means Daddy's work is getting tougher, but we're still gonna have fun at home."

"You already have a tough job."

"Yes, I do ... yes, I do," nodded Larry.

The wind blew smoke in his face. He coughed and backed away from the barbecue.

"You're in charge of the Sunset Grille, aren't you, Daddy?"

"No, Annie," Larry laughed, rubbing her head and pulling her close. "I'm in charge of closing it down. It's a very bad place."

"Why?"

"Because it hurts people."

"How?"

"Well ... they get sick when they go there."

"Do they have bad food?"

"No, not exactly. Why do you ask that?"

"Jonathan Haskins says it's just a restaurant."

"Well, Jonathan Haskins doesn't know."

Annie looked into the fire.

"He told me his father says you're crazy."

"Nope, the name's Larry." He smiled at his girl, and Annie looked up and grinned back.

Just as he reached out to turn the steaks, a flame shot up between the meat and he jerked his hand away just in time. He stuck it in his mouth anyway and sucked it for good measure. I noticed his smile begin to fade.

"Look at his eyes," observed Dias.

Through the smoke he looked tired. Since the funeral Larry had worked nonstop, campaigning against the Grille. Many in the town seemed behind him . . . tentatively, at least. Still, he couldn't help noticing the times when one or two of them had ducked their heads in passing, feigning unawareness of his presence. They seemed embarrassed. And some—especially the Chamber of Commerce members—were downright angry at what they perceived as the pastor's meddling in civic affairs. Larry worried over the number that might fall in this second category.

As I watched, I wondered what he was thinking.

Larry let his eyes wander down the hill that sloped toward the center of town. Here and there they settled on different houses he could spot between the trees. And I felt him saying to himself, "Do they side with Jonathan Haskins and his dad?"

"Dearest Heaven! How can he be thinking such thoughts?" I asked myself, aloud.

"Maybe he can't stop them," said Dias. "Maybe they're not completely his thoughts. He's worried, Skandalon, That's why we're here."

Then I saw the two of them: dark spirits, talking in low tones by the shed at the back fence. They didn't seem anxious to start anything. My partner and I sat on the woodpile with one eye on the demons, and the other on the steaks Larry was cooking.

In the distance sat the Sunset Grille, as if on cat haunches, peering back across the woods at Larry, waiting for the last ray of day to depart. The Grille's western wall burned in the face of the setting sun. Larry's cheek twitched, and his shoulders shivered at the nip in the air.

The two spirits walked across the lawn toward us. One of them at first glance could almost be called handsome. The other, foul words could not describe. This one walked with a more pronounced limp than his smaller partner, stopping once or twice to calculate how much farther he had to go, and all the while cursing under his breath. He was as big as he was ugly.

With the practiced casualness of a fighter, Dias eased himself to his feet. I fell in behind him as we paced slowly to meet the foe. We met in the middle of the yard, by the cast-concrete birdbath.

"Greetings from Hell," said the better-looking one.

I said nothing, but took in his smooth, well-proportioned face, his dapper air, the braceleted wrist of his proffered left hand—but stayed on our side of the birdbath, ignoring his gesture. I could smell the evil on him.

The ugly one said nothing, but only shifted from side to side. His scarlet eyes were nearly closed. His thin-pressed lips showed a distinct line of drool, seeping from the reservoir beneath his tongue. His hands hung at his side, with nails that seemed to quiver against his thighs. On his chest was an imposing scar.

Dias's eyes were wide open and alert, as was his stance. He folded his arms across his chest, looking every bit the part of Heaven's warrior. His face was carefully neutral— the look of one who doesn't wish to provoke his opponent, but who is more than ready to answer any threat offered. I could tell by the tensing of his sinews that he was itching to tear into the big demon, given the slightest provocation.

"It's a pity our comrades don't hit it off," said the smaller one, "but perhaps that will change in time."

Again I said nothing.

"I'm Pitch," the demon continued. "My partner is Stool." Stool did not seem at all pleased at the introduction. He was obviously the subordinate.

"I am Skandalon," I replied.

"An excellent name! If I remember my Greek, it means 'Stumbling Block'—correct?"

"Correct."

"I don't mean to be rude, but isn't that my job?" he asked, taking pleasure in his words. "I don't suppose you're trying to make things easy for me already, are you?"

"Could we adhere to business?" I said in a flat voice. I didn't want to let this Pitch know he was getting under my skin.

"By all means," answered the demon. "Surely, though, we have not strayed so far apart that you must doubt my intentions. After all, we *are* both of us angels."

"Of different tribes!" bellowed Dias. He took a step toward the birdbath. Stool responded. They were nose to nose in an instant.

"I remember you," Dias hissed. I stared at him, wondering what he meant.

Stool stared at him too, with a grin that showed his rotten teeth and putrid tongue for the first time. "How could you forget?" he yapped.

"I should have finished you then!"

"Yes . . . but your boss prevented that, didn't he?"

"His final blessing upon you, no doubt," said my partner, clenching one huge fist.

"Boys! Boys!" interrupted Pitch. "This should be a happy occasion. How can there be such quarreling when you haven't seen each other in such a long while? Besides, Stool was just kidding. Isn't that right, Stool?"

The big one was quiet again, but his chest heaved with barely bridled anger. He took a step back and kept the glowing slits of his eyes fixed on Dias's throat.

"There, that's better," said Pitch.

"Your intentions with the pastor? What are they?" I asked.

"My intentions? Of course. Let's just say that we are like-minded when it comes to our desires for changing the man."

"Change? How so?"

"For his own good," said Pitch. "What else did you think?"

"Then you're all for his endurance?" I asked, naively.

"Endurance? My Scratch, no! I should say not! He's had enough of that. Why, endurance has played the devil with him. What Larry needs is a little rest, don't you think?"

I looked at Larry tending the smoking barbecue. He did look tired.

"Have you really considered the man?" asked Pitch. "I mean, have you *really* considered him?"

"Of course."

"Then you know his weakness?"

"I have some idea of it . . . yes."

"But no real facts, eh? I mean . . . what I mean is . . . you *have* done your homework, haven't you?"

"Yes! I'm ready," I replied curtly. But I was feeling less and less ready the more he talked.

"Good!" Pitch exclaimed. "Then I'll say it again. Rest! That's my intention for him. Rest from this moral inquisition he puts himself through. If you ask me, that should be your intention also. Where's all this grace your higher-ups are always spouting about? Couldn't this man use a little of that?"

I sighed.

"Lovely family, aren't they?" Pitch observed smoothly, looking toward the humans gathered near the barbecue grill.

"What's that? Yes...yes, they are." I looked at Larry again. Peter was at his side explaining how he had sunk ten-for-ten free throws in the school gym that day. Larry listened halfheartedly to his son. He could not get his mind or his eyes off the darkening shape on the horizon. Rose had come out and was talking with Annie.

"Yes. They are a lovely family," I repeated.

"You could help them," wooed Pitch. By now he had stepped alongside me, and placed his arm around my shoulder.

"Rest, Skandalon. All he needs is a little rest."

I stared at the bracelet which hung in front of me. Pitch's long, black fingernails nearly tickled my chest. For a moment, I pondered the demon's prescription. I turned and looked in his eyes. They were warm, amber holes, like the inside of a woodburning stove...inviting one to come rest before the fire. Rest. Rest. Rest. Heaven knows, the pastor needed some.

Suddenly, the wind blew cold through the yard. The oak trees on the rim of the lawn shifted and swayed. Those nearest the house batted the siding with a hiss and a spank. And I remembered my explanation to Dias about the charter of the Trials.

Hiss... Spank. Test him! moaned the trees. *Scrape... Rattle... Hissss.... Tessssst himmmm!*

I glanced at Dias, standing behind, looking warily from me to Stool. Would he ever understand?

"No, Pitch," I said at last, shrugging his arm from my back, "We will put him to the test. It's the way of endurance."

"You're making a big mistake," shouted Pitch above the wind. "The man needs rest. He'll crumble! He'll crack! Watch and see!" said the demon with increasing excitement.

"That's not our concern," I replied. I tried to ignore Dias's questioning eyes.

Pitch was plainly agitated by now, but he kept his composure. His partner, on the other hand, was not at all composed. The wind had stirred up a great deal of trouble for Stool, and he was limping and running about the yard, dodging falling leaves and any other errant debris that posed a threat. Nevertheless, even above his yelps and Dias's laughter rose a new sound.

"Larry!" came Rose's voice. "Larry! The meat! Be careful with the meat!"

Everybody stopped to watch the suddenly flaring flames eagerly licking at the steaks. Even Stool slowed his mad racing to investigate, and was knifed in the back by an oak leaf for his curiosity. None of the humans heard his howls of agony.

In his daydream Larry had lost track of time. When he finally got the fire out with the garden hose, he stared down at four lovely cuts of meat...blackened beyond recognition.

The wind stopped abruptly, and light rain began. Stool dashed for the shed, screaming curses at the drops of water pelting him from the sky. Pitch just nodded, and with a smile he said, "There. Now do you believe me? The man is a bundle of nerves. Call off this Sunset Grille business and he'll be the picture of health in no time."

"Not a chance, Pitch," I said, with a sigh.

"Then I'll have to exercise my rights."

"And what at those?" I asked.

The demon narrowed his eyes and stared at the pastor. "I have a right to do my own testing. Will you permit it?"

I looked at Dias. He shrugged once.

"I...I suppose I must," I answered. Pitch looked a great deal more frightening than he did a half-hour before. I knew he had no genuine concern for Larry...only hatred.

"You'll see," said Pitch. "This good man of yours won't

look so good when he loses his following. Why, anyone can champion a cause when he's got enough cheerleaders." He grinned and continued in an oily voice. "But a cause with no applause comes quickly to an end."

"Run along now," said Dias, fidgeting with the hilt of his sword, "before I lose my patience with you."

Pitch moved away, then collected his partner from the shed. *"You'll see . . ."* he called back at us.

We watched them vanish into the gathering dark.

Over by the barbecue, Larry was apologetic.

"I'm sorry, everybody. I don't know what got into me."

"That's okay, Dad," said Peter. "We can eat spaghetti."

"Spaghetti suits me fine," announced Rose. She smiled and kissed her husband on the cheek, then headed for the kitchen.

Annie stood with her head down and arms folded. Larry unfolded an umbrella that he kept on the patio for such occasions and held it over his daughter. He let the rain fall on his own head.

"You disappointed?"

"Yeah. Sorta."

"Me too."

Annie was silent.

"Don't have steak too often around here, do we?" said Larry.

"Nope."

"What are you thinking, Annie?"

Annie thought for a second. Then she replied, "I think we should all get in the car and go have a steak at the Sunset Grille."

Larry looked up at the blinking neon above the trees.

"That's enough of that talk, Annie," he said, his voice gaining a hint of sternness. "Run inside. I'll be in shortly."

Annie did as she was told. But Larry stayed out for a

good long time, watching the dying coals and thinking. Eventually, Rose called him in to test the spaghetti and take a phone call.

Dias and I talked in the backyard until midnight. I'm sure neither of us would have admitted it, but I think we were both held there by the smell of earth's autumn at nighttime. There is mystery in that season...a damp, posthumous riddle. Some might think it strange for an angel, who has never tasted death, to be so intrigued with the smell of it. But after all, there is no fall in Heaven.

Presently, we retired to the belfry, but not before I asked Dias one last question.

"You said you remembered him."

"Who?" asked Dias.

"Stool. You said you knew him. How?"

"Oh, that," he nodded. Then he mused for a while. Finally he answered.

"Have you forgotten we were all together once?"

"No, I haven't forgotten," I said. "But I don't think I've seen his ugly face before. And I know I've never met that Pitch fellow."

"Think again," mumbled Dias as he flew off ahead of me.

"What? What's that?" I asked.

"I said think again!" he shouted over his shoulder. "He was wearing a bracelet just like yours!"

THE BRAINSTORM

THE EVENING grew late, but a light still burned brightly in Larry's study in the church's education annex. Outside, a bitter wind was blowing, and occasional pellets of sleet pecked ominously at the windows.

Inside the study, a tightly drawn circle of people huddled around a small, square coffee table, which Larry normally kept in the corner for the purpose of sunning plants. They were gathered to launch the church's campaign against the Sunset Grille. The study lamp from Larry's desk illumined the tabletop and little else, giving the scene the appearance of a council of war—an atmosphere Larry had cultivated intentionally.

An old radiator against the wall chuffed and moaned out its heat, steaming the windows. A teapot simmered on a hot-plate beneath the bookshelves, which were lined with tomes on subjects frequently found in a pastor's study: theology, homiletics, biblical archaeology, pastoral counseling. The Regulator wall clock near the door chimed nine times.

Larry was wearing his favorite corduroy jacket, the one

with the collegiate elbow-patches. He was intent upon being a good host, and he kept jumping up and manning the teapot whenever a cup was half-empty.

To the left of Larry sat Fig Pemberley and Patrick "Gunner" McGuffy. Fig was roundish, fiftyish, and a great fan of Larry Ravelle. Her full name was Katherine Alison Pemberley, and she was the never-married, slightly eccentric daughter of one of Ellenbach's founding families. Due to a childhood fancy for Victorian literature, she fell into the girlish habit of telling people, with a sniff and a shrug, "I don't care a *fig* for __." As is so often the case with an unfortunate affectation, it evolved into a nickname, gleefully applied by the boys of her peer group. The name adhered, and very few in Ellenbach still remembered her given name. She had even come to think of herself as Fig. She was an early-morning regular at the Paradise Donut Shop.

Seated beside Fig was Gunner—the current mayor of Ellenbach. He was a retired schoolteacher whose wife of forty-odd years had passed away some seven years before. He, too, was a regular at the donut shop—hence the proprietary way Fig hooked her arm in his as they sat around Larry's table. Gunner was an Ellenbach native who had moved away toward the allure of the horizon, only to return for the peace and quiet. Gunner looked old, partly because the face-level glow from the lamp cast the lines on his face into sharp relief . . . and partly because he *was* old—or felt it. He was tired, too, and not at all certain that he was up to "tearing down strongholds" and that kind of thing. His presence tonight had a lot to do with his sense of duty to "civic decency," as he put it.

On Larry's right sat Roger Allen, an unapologetically portly lawyer. The wages of his sins covered the folding chair in which he sat, with quite a bit of attorney left over on either side. But everyone in Ellenbach knew him as being a good-hearted sort—if sometimes a little bombastic. At least that was how his clients put it. To the opposing lawyer, he was just plain loud.

When the tea was all gone, there came a short knock on the door.

An older gentleman entered with a blast of cold air. "Sorry I'm late, folks," he apologized as he took off his coat and hung it on the back of the door. The first thing the others noticed about the newcomer was the unauthentic head of hair—jet black, as was his goatee, his glasses, his trousers, and his shoes. He had a careful, studious look, and a cautious way of moving that made Gunner mistrust him instantly.

"Nigel!" Larry exclaimed. "Do come in and sit down! This is a surprise. I figured you'd take at least a week to settle into the job before joining a committee. I've yet to meet your wife. How is she?"

"Happy as a lark . . . and looking forward to being back in the country where she belongs," replied Nigel as he seated himself with the group.

"Fig, Gunner, Roger," Larry said, motioning around the group gathered at the table, "this is Nigel Hendrickson, our new church custodian." After introductions, Larry looked at Nigel. "We've known each other for the greater part of three days or so, since I met him on . . . what was it? Last Friday morning?"

"Correct. Bright and early," said Nigel. "And I'm sorry to say I haven't been very useful here yet. We've been pretty busy unpacking."

"No, no. That's quite all right," said Larry. "We've made it through an entire fall without keeping a janitor for more than three weeks. We're just glad to have a man of your caliber. Surprised, actually."

"Doctor Ravelle, you promised," Nigel blushed.

"What's the harm?" said Larry. Then he turned to the group. "Nigel, here, is a retired . . . what was it?"

"Psychiatrist."

"Yes, psychiatrist...from Charleston...with degrees a mile long. I'm almost embarrassed to let him clean the floors. But he's got the job...if he wants it."

Fig was obviously impressed. She leaned in front of Gunner to shake Nigel's hand enthusiastically. The look in her eyes made Gunner roll his.

"Of course he wants it!" she said. "I find it quite admirable when a man doesn't quit just because he's sixty-five." Gunner gave a not-quite-inaudible moan.

"Being a janitor is a far cry from being a psychiatrist, Mr. Hendrickson," said Roger.

"That's *Doctor* Hendrickson," Larry corrected.

"Oh, I don't mind—Roger, is it?" asked Nigel. Roger nodded as Nigel continued. "As this lovely lady across from you has alluded, I'm just glad to be anywhere at my age."

Fig was beside herself at the compliment. Gunner twisted a corner of his lip upward in an expression that could have been a half-smile or a half-sneer. "Well, I'm all for it," he grunted, "if he can shrink the dirt around here as well as he shrunk heads."

"Really, Gunner! You're impossible!" shot Fig.

"Okay, you two," soothed Larry. "Let's not scare our new member away before he gets started. Anyway, Nigel, we are honored to have you on the team. And I know you're already aware of the serious nature of this meeting."

"Well aware...yes, well aware," nodded Nigel, hesitantly.

"Good. We were just getting into some brainstorming, so we'll carry on."

"What's there to know about this guy who runs the Grille, anyway?" asked Roger.

"William Detzer is his name," said Larry. "He's from a

big city originally... Detroit maybe, or Buffalo. I'm not sure. But he's not from here."

"And he manages the place, right? Doesn't own it?"

"That's right, as far as I know. Of course he's there all the time, from what I hear. I've never actually been to the place or met the man. But I don't think he owns it."

"What difference does it make?" said Gunner impatiently. "Where's this leading?"

"It's leading to the big boys, that's where it's leading. Is that what you're getting at, Roger?" asked Larry.

"Bingo!" said Roger, firing a thumb-and-forefinger pistol at Larry. "And those are the folks we have to pressure."

"So what does it all mean, then?" asked Gunner. "Are we talking about picketing, and that kind of stuff? 'Cause if we are, you can just count me out."

"Now hold on, Gunner," said Larry. "You knew things might get rough when you came to this meeting. Don't pull out before the first shots are fired. Relax."

"I just want to know up front if I'm gonna be carrying some sign that makes me look like an idiot."

"The way you're acting now," said Fig, "the sign might be an improvement."

"Please!" Larry interrupted. Fig and Gunner glared at each other, then subsided.

"Picketing would be only a very small part of what needs to be done," put in Roger, redirecting the subject. "It might help to boycott the retailers who support the place."

"You mean the beer folks, and that type?" said Nigel.

"Yes, I do... and the food suppliers, and so forth."

"What are you going to do about the barley and wheat people?" Nigel asked. "The ranchers? They're not going to take this lying down, you know."

"If you ask me, they'll just have to paint or get off the

ladder," said Roger, his face reddening. "Plenty of them say they're behind us. We'll just have to see what happens when their jobs are on the line. But the 'big boys,' as Dr. Ravelle calls them, aren't involved in all that stuff."

"Who are the 'big boys'?" asked Gunner.

The room got silent. Everyone looked at Roger, but it was Nigel who answered. "He means the smut lords, don't you, Mr. Allen?"

"Call me Roger. And yes, that's exactly who I mean. The pornographers."

"Okay," said Gunner, standing abruptly. "That's all I need to hear. I'm leaving."

"Sit down, Patrick McGuffy!" shouted Fig.

"Fig!" blurted Larry. "Allow me." He looked up at the mayor and spoke with easy assurance. "Gunner, please relax. There's no need for panic. I'm sure the same fears have been raised in all of us. We simply need to identify and discuss them."

Gunner shrugged and sat back down. "Then I'll start," he said. "I know exactly what I'm afraid of. I'm afraid of pain. And I don't mind if everyone knows it."

"Pain? There's not going to be any pain," responded Roger. "At least not the kind you're thinking of. Nobody's going to wire our cars ... I don't think ..."

"No. No, of course not," said Fig. "That only happens to nuts who interfere with the wrong crowd ... like the organized crime outfits. The ones who do *that* are the real activists. We're not like them. We're just ... we're just part-time. We're as normal as everybody else." She sounded unconvinced.

"Before we talk ourselves out of this," said Larry, "I probably should tell you that Nigel here has been involved in social-action causes before. He says the key is mobilizing public opinion—right, Nigel?"

All eyes swung to Nigel Hendrickson. The retired psychiatrist sat hunched in his chair, picking diffidently at his fingernails. "Well, yes," he admitted, a trifle uncomfortably. "And that brings up an important question: How many people do you really think would get behind this?"

"Do you mean . . . people in this church?" asked Larry.

"Sure, for starters."

"Let's see . . . uh . . . I'm sure many would be . . . well, there's always the elders to remember too."

"Yeah," observed Gunner drily, "and I don't see any of them here tonight."

"True . . . but the people . . . they're faithful attenders and tithers. And . . ."

"How many, Larry? Right now—today!"

"To be exact?"

Nigel waited. Larry looked embarrassed when he answered. "Four total." He gestured helplessly around the table. "You're looking at them."

"Good," said Nigel, though his tone of voice contradicted him. "Then what you're going to have to provide," he said decisively, "is proof positive that the Sunset Grille is detrimental to the individual and to the community. How to do that, I can't tell you. This is your town. But I do know this," he said, meeting their eyes squarely for the first time as he raised a finger in warning. "To get more people involved, you must have more proof. Otherwise, in the public eye, you'll never be more than a small group of complainers who are against free enterprise. Because that's the first argument the Grille people— and maybe the farmers and ranchers—will hit you with."

The radiator let out a groan, but all ears were tuned to Nigel.

"We need media coverage," he went on. "We need research on zoning laws. We need backing from other pastors, other churches, other groups—" Nigel hesitated. "I'm sorry for coming on so strong, being the newcomer to the group. But believe me, I've been involved in this kind of thing before, and I know all the ins and outs."

"I know some media people over in Laird," offered Fig. "The Kurt Stedley Show might be interested." Gunner gave her a jab with his elbow.

"Now, Gunner," chided Larry.

"Stedley's an ambulance chaser, that's all," said Gunner. "I just thought we could do better... maybe find someone with more class."

"But our discussion tonight is all green-light thinking," responded Larry. "You know—brainstorming. Nothing's carved in stone. Let's just let the ideas flow."

Fig triumphantly offered another suggestion. "We could try to come up with some ordinance that's tied in to the liquor licenses. They do serve liquor at the Sunset Grille, don't they?"

"Excellent idea," said Roger. "Now we're thinking."

"I've got an idea," began Nigel slowly, "and I hope this doesn't sound too harsh: We need an example, a scapegoat if you will—someone who's been so badly influenced by the place that his case will convince the church and the town to join the cause." Nigel's mind tasted the idea and savored it. His voice increased in volume, riding the crest of his fervor. "We've got to get a stampede started, folks, because four won't cut it. We need lots of people involved, and this is the best way I know to get it done. You show them a glaring example of what the Sunset Grille can do to a supposedly upstanding citizen, and—" he shrugged—"the place won't stand a chance."

"One question, though," cut in Larry. "Where are we going to get a legitimate scapegoat? I mean, we don't want to frame anyone here."

Nigel leaned back in his chair. Roger raised his head and thought for a moment. Then he began, "Well... I've been an attorney for fifteen years. I've dealt with a few private detectives in my time."

"Would one of your contacts be willing to do some work at the Sunset Grille?"

"I think so," answered Roger. "If the price was right."

After a pause, Larry looked around the group. "Any objections? Anybody got a better idea how to proceed?"

Nigel, his chin cradled thoughtfully in his hand, opened his mouth, then closed it with a slight shake of the head.

After a few more ideas had surfaced, along with a few more flare-ups between Fig and Gunner, it was agreed that the basic three-part strategy was in place: Explore the idea of a city ordinance to clamp down on the Grille, try to line up media coverage to broaden support for the campaign, and watch for a scapegoat.

Roger Allen closed the meeting with a short prayer.

THE ORDINANCE

ELLENBACH'S town council met at seven the following Monday night in the city hall. The council members were seated at a linoleum-topped folding table at the front of the room, beneath the obligatory pictures of Washington and Lincoln, with an American flag draped from a pole standing at the end of the table. An unexpectedly large attendance was crammed into rows of rattling, squeaking folding chairs. Women brought their babies and their *Ladies' Home Journals*, men brought their sporting goods catalogs and outdoor magazines, and all of them waited for the gavel to strike. Particularly prominent in the crowd was the turnout of farmers and ranchers, many of whom lived a half-hour's drive or more out in the country.

As mayor, Gunner motioned and everyone in the room noisily rose for the pledge of allegiance and the invocation. The first order of business was typical of most council meetings. It seemed that a few residents were upset at Sonny's Septic Service, whose trucks—laughingly referred to as "honey trucks" by the locals—had been plagued with leakage. The audience was greatly amused at the red-faced council member who couldn't bring herself to say the word 'waste' in describing an accident at Staple's Creek Bridge, and who eventually resorted to saying that the vehicle had "inadvertently spilled some of its . . . its . . . honey," which brought peals of laughter. Even Gunner couldn't help himself.

Another twenty minutes was devoted to the increasing problem of stray dogs. Then Bea Halloran complained about the two-hour parking limitation on the north side of the railroad tracks downtown. She claimed it hurt her sewing machine business—located in that vicinity— particularly since she was trying to remodel, and she couldn't afford to have the carpenters running off every little while to move their trucks.

After discussing both these matters—with much quasi-parliamentary wisecracking from the gallery—the council agreed to defer action.

Finally, at a quarter past eight, Gunner proceeded to the main topic on the docket. Looking up at the audience, then at the council members, he drew a deep breath. His eyes found Larry, seated toward the back of the audience. The pastor nodded slightly at him, and Gunner began.

"Seems to me that somewhere along the way these last few years, this town has dozed off!"

The audience nodded in agreement. They weren't always certain as to what he was saying, but they all agreed that Gunner made things interesting. They were willing to go along to find out what he had on his mind.

"And while we were sleeping," Gunner continued, "somebody went and gave us a civic lobotomy!"

"What's he mean by that?" whispered an old woman on the front row to her neighbor.

"Give him a minute, Maude," the other elderly lady replied. "He'll make it all clear sooner or later."

"Seems like we've all been a little ignorant as to what's really going on down at the Sunset Grille," Gunner concluded. "And fortunately for our sakes, the pastor here has brought it all into focus for us." Gunner pointed to Larry, who was seated at the back of the room. Larry half-stood to acknowledge everyone with a smile.

"Larry," said Gunner, "I don't mean to put you on the spot or anything, but do you mind giving a summary of the situation?"

"Not at all," answered Larry. He worked his way to the podium near the front of the room so he could face the crowd. As he opened his mouth to speak, a sudden, terrifyingly vivid memory rushed at him from a blind corner in his mind.

It was dark, and he was scared. What if they got caught? What if Dad found them? What would he do to them?

"Come on," John said, "I've got a flashlight."

The pictures frightened and fascinated him. They stirred something in him that was secret, unimagined—and delicious. . . .

Larry stirred, and looked around. Gunner was peering at him curiously, and the people in the folding chairs were murmuring to one another. Hastily he gathered himself and launched into the remarks he had rehearsed.

"I appreciate all you good people coming out tonight," he began. "Shows a lot of community spirit. Not every town could say the same for its citizens. What I'm really here for tonight is to inform you folks about the ordinance I am proposing to the council concerning the Sunset Grille."

"Give it to us straight, Larry!" a voice asked loudly

from the middle of the room. "How much time has she got?"

A round of laughter went up at this comment, not intended to ridicule Larry, but as an expression of the townfolks' ease around the popular pastor. Their relationship to him was a blend of respect, friendship, and familiarity.

"The answer to your question," said Larry, smiling as the laughs died down, "can only be determined by how you respond to what I've got to say. Now...where was I?"

"You were at the Grille!" came the same voice. More laughter followed. Only Gunner noticed the way Larry's neck turned slightly red.

When silence resumed, Larry went on.

"As you know, Frank's place has been gone for about five years now. The Sunset Grille, which may well have the best food in town, took a while to catch on. But now it's, uh...how should I say...almost a landmark. Don't ask me how it happened so fast. I never saw Ellenbach move that quick about anything else." Larry smiled, and added, "I've been back here twelve years now, but some folks still ask me how I'm liking it *so far*...."

Larry joined in the laughter this time.

"We generally take faster to a man who says 'y'all' instead of 'you guys,'" someone shouted.

"But in your case," said another, "we had to make an exception."

Gunner banged the gavel, but he had a grin on his face. "All right! That's enough! Let's have some order here," he said.

"Anyway," continued Larry, "It seems like the gentleman who manages the Grille has sort of expanded the entertainment over the years, and I'd like to see it stopped before it goes any further."

The room was silent.

"How far has it gone already?" hesitantly asked a woman with an infant in her arms.

"I don't mean to offend anyone here tonight," said Larry. "So if you've got young children with you..." And he gestured for them to cover up the little ones' ears. "Uh...I'd say three words pretty much explain the whole situation: money...sex...and power." He ticked them off on his fingers as he listed them. "There's no doubt the place makes plenty of the first. Lately, rumor has it, there is no shortage or restriction of the second. And finally, by the sheer numbers of people flocking in here from other counties, I'd say there's getting to be a great deal of the third."

"Get to the ordinance part, Larry," interrupted Gunner. "I'd say pretty much everyone here agrees that the place is bad cinnamon." The rest of the council seemed eager for him to get on with it, too. They kept glancing at their watches and nervously shuffling papers together.

"I'm not so sure, Mayor," observed Larry, shaking his head. "I made the announcement from my pulpit, and I've hardly seen a finger lifted since." His gaze panned the room, encountering mostly lowered heads. "Sure, folks are talking about support. But so far it's mostly talk, and not much support."

"Well, support is one thing, and involvement is another," said an older woman on the front row.

"Let's put it to the test, Gunner," said Larry, suddenly. "How many of you folks here tonight think we need to do something about the Sunset Grille?"

A wave of hands rose silently.

"Good!" said Larry. "Now, how many of you are willing to speak out against it publicly?" There was not a movement in the room, other than the slow, self-conscious turning of heads to glance from side to side.

"Anyone willing to go on the record?" Larry persisted. Total silence.

"Help with the phone? Participate in a boycott? Picket?" His eyes roved the motionless room. He shook his head. "I didn't think so."

"Now, Larry," said Gunner uncomfortably, "you're being awful hard on your friends here."

"Maybe so," Larry agreed. "Maybe so. But I'm sure there's not a person here who would want to see their sons going into that place. Or their daughters working in it," he added darkly.

"You've got kids, Gunner!" the pastor said, turning to the mayor. "Sure, they're grown. But think about it: Would you want your little girl working, say, in the second basement?"

"Let's not turn this into a personal thing between you and me, Larry!" said Gunner with a note of embarrassment in his voice. "You know how I feel."

"But it *is* a personal thing!" shouted Larry. Then he wheeled on the audience. "What's wrong with us, folks? Everyone's *for* me, but nobody's *with* me! This is a family community, for heaven's sake! What are we all willing to do to help out?"

Another voice boomed from somewhere in the rear: "What did you do to help us when the bottom fell out of the grain market?" It was Tom Jordan, a farmer from the north end of the county.

"I stayed up till four in the morning, counseling some of you," answered Larry. "I talked with your wives and kids, prayed for you . . . I tried my best to help you all."

"Well, your help wasn't enough," Tom said. "Billy Bobb's place came along and made a difference. That's why I ain't volunteerin' for no social-action job. I know whose hand's been putting the bread on my table."

"Do you really?" shot back Larry, his eyes bracing Tom with a hard stare. "Are you so sure about that?"

There were a good many other grain farmers present, and they looked from their colleague to Larry, shook their heads, and mumbled under their breaths.

"Actually," said Larry, "the ordinance won't necessarily affect you farmers and ranchers. I mean, it's not like it says the Sunset Grille can't serve drinks. What it does say, though, is that any place that serves alcohol cannot have entertainment of this nature."

"That's hogwash, Larry!" said Tom. "You know good and well that if you cut out the girls, you cut down the gross—"

There was an uneasy murmur. This was the first open admission tonight of the nature of the Grille's "live entertainment." The debate took on a new level of discomfort.

"And that means you don't need as much booze," Tom shouted above the noise of the crowd. "I can't make a living off of my chickens, Larry. Like it or not, me and the other farmers need the Sunset Grille. And Ellenbach needs us."

As the discussion went on, opinions from both sides flowed back and forth. At times Larry seemed to be standing alone on the sand, waiting for the next wave of opposition to break upon him.

"Yeah," came a voice. "We all need the Grille!"

"Like a hole in the head!" Larry responded.

"Like a boost to the economy!" retorted Charlie Vaughan, a local businessman.

"Economy!" Larry shouted, turning to face the man. "We're discussing the moral disintegration of this town, and you're thinking about the economy?"

Charlie, who was younger than Larry, rose slowly to his feet.

"Look, Dr. Ravelle. I don't mean to sound disrespectful, but you may be a little behind the times on this issue." Heads nodded all over the room. "First of all, I don't believe anything gets too far out of hand down there. And even if it did, we've got to think about people's constitutional rights. That's the bottom line, as far as I'm concerned."

"The bottom line is pornography!" insisted Larry.

"Are you sure it's that bad?" someone asked. "Are you willing to go see for yourself?"

The question landed hard—more so than it should have, Gunner thought. Larry had a dazed, unfocused look on his face.

Larry looked out at the faces, trying to see who had asked the question. It seemed to have come from the middle of the crowd and as Larry looked, he was met with a roomful of curious stares.

"All right, all right," said Gunner, tapping his gavel. "We've gotta call it a night here pretty soon, folks. We haven't even read the proposed ordinance yet. Now, we could read it twice and get it over with, but it sounds like there needs to be more discussion."

Larry shot an irritated glance at Gunner, but the mayor was looking down at his legal pad and didn't notice. "Tell you what," Gunner said, glancing at the other council members for approval, "we'll give 'er the once-over tonight. Then you can all go home, and think about what you've heard. We'll listen to more testimony next meeting, and then vote."

Larry grimaced, but Gunner sternly ignored him, and pressed on. The ordinance was read once. And the meeting was adjourned, exactly two hours after it began.

As Larry trod wearily out of the room, he noticed the small space that opened spontaneously around him as he wound his way through the crowd. No one spoke aloud to him, and few even nodded.

It figures, he thought. He was alone, exhausted, and upset at the foot-dragging of his supposed ally, Gunner McGuffy. This meeting had not gone at all well. He needed that ordinance passed—and soon!

THE STORY

KURT STEDLEY took a slurp of the coffee in his mug, and grimaced. Cold. He got up, pulling a cigarette from the pack on his desk and sticking it, unlit, between his lips. He headed for the break room, intending to dump this cold coffee in the sink.

Just as he reached the doorway, his phone rang. He spun around, leaned over the desk, and yanked the receiver from its cradle. "Yeah," he snapped, the cigarette waggling between his lips, "this is Stedley."

"Kurt, I got a little old lady from over in Ellenbach who wants to talk to you about some brouhaha they're having over there." It was Pam, his unflappable secretary.

"Pam, I'm on deadline!" he exclaimed. "I haven't got time to talk to every old gal that—"

"Her name is Fig Pemberley," Pam interrupted. "Sound familiar?"

Stedley carefully set down his mug and began massaging his temples, a grimace crawling across his face. "Not that goofy broad whose daddy died and left her holding a twenty-five percent interest in our company—"

"That's the one," said Pam. "Wanna talk to her?"

"Like I got a choice," muttered Kurt. "Yeah...gimme about three minutes, then put her on."

"Gotcha."

Stedley moaned as he picked up the coffee mug and went to the break room. He poured himself a full cup of black coffee, lit his cigarette, and took a long, deep drag. He'd need all the fortification he could muster to deal with this Fig character. Reluctantly, he went back to his office, set down his coffee, picked up the receiver, and pushed the blinking button.

"Hello," he said in his best on-the-air voice, "this is Kurt Stedley. How may I help you?"

"Hello, Mr. Stedley," came the effusive voice at the other end. "I'm so glad I caught you."

Yeah, right, Stedley thought, rolling his eyes.

"I called you about...about an idea I had—for a show."

I can hardly wait. "Oh, is that right? Well, listen, I'd really love to hear your—"

"Oh, good!" she gushed. "I just knew you'd be interested!"

Pantomiming a pistol placed to his head, Stedley sank into his chair, leaned forward on his elbows, and settled in for a long siege.

"Well," said the woman on the other end, "here it is: You see, Mr. Stedley, Ellenbach is a quiet, family-type town; has been since—well, since forever."

"Uh-huh." He pulled the trigger on the pistol.

"And then, about five years ago, this big outfit from out-of-state comes into Ellenbach..."

"Is that right?" *Wonderful. Another one of those big-bad-business-putting-all-our-home-folks-out-of-work sob stories. Boring, boring, boring...*

"...and sets up this—well, it's impolite, but—"

105

"Please, go on." *Please, go away.*

"I don't know how else to put this: They build a strip joint. Right here in Ellenbach!"

It wasn't news to Stedley. But a tiny tingle of interest tickled the tips of his journalism receptors. Nothing sold air time like sex and controversy. And if the controversy was about sex... "Now, tell me—Mrs. Pemberley, is it?"

"*Miss* Pemberley," she said firmly.

I'll bet! "Sorry, Miss Pemberley," he said. "I was going to ask you—what are folks over there wanting to do about... about this place you're talking about?" He reached for a pencil and searched for a blank space on his desk blotter.

"Well, it's called the Sunset Grille," Fig began, feeling very pleased with herself. "And by the way, I watched that series of reports you did on the proposed toxic waste site in Cook County, Mr. Stedley, and I must say, I was *very* impressed. The way you took on those big corporate moguls right in *front* of the *camera*—well, when I thought of it, I just *knew* you were the man to call!"

Kurt was remembering the flap surrounding a house of ill repute in some one-horse town in Texas—back in the sixties, was it? Why, the reporter who blew the lid off the place even got himself written into a Broadway show! The ratings calculator built into Kurt's brain was starting to click. He was mentally sketching program ideas, promotion proposals, and interview schedules, even while he continued to feed Fig a steady line of questions.

Fifteen minutes later, he hung up the phone, leaned back in his chair, and blew a stream of cigarette smoke at the ceiling. He smiled, nodding his head. This thing in Ellenbach could be big. He could feel it.

THE DEAL

K URT stood for a second at the front door of the Sunset Grille, blowing on his hands in the cold air, and looking up at the building's pleasant exterior. *Not bad*, he thought.

He lowered his head and was about to enter when he heard someone pounding on the other side of the door and struggling with the handle. He could hear muffled cursing from whoever was trapped inside, followed by a final hard shove.

The door flew open, barely missing the end of his nose. He jumped back, and found himself staring down at two workmen sprawled across the threshold with a beer keg—thankfully empty—on top of them. Somewhere in the background, a voice shouted at them.

"Easy on my front door, you knuckleheads!"

The men scrambled to their feet, mumbling and swearing, and picked up the keg with the dolly from which it had tumbled. The men shoved past Kurt toward the curb, where a beer truck was parked. They loaded the keg and drove away. Kurt closed the door behind him.

"Anybody home?" he called, as his eyes adjusted to the perennial twilight inside the Grille.

"Always am," came a reply.

Kurt walked toward the voice. He saw a man seated at the bar, sipping beer from a long-necked bottle.

"Mr. Detzer?"

"Nope," said Billy Bobb, taking another sip.

"Oh—I'm sorry. I assumed you were the fellow who—well, anyway. Can you tell me where I can find Mr. Detzer?"

"Yep." Another swig of beer, and a sidelong glance. "Mr. Detzer died about fifteen years ago."

Billy Bobb allowed the stranger's confusion to deepen a bit further before grinning and sticking out his hand. "But I'm his boy, Billy Bobb. Maybe I'm the one you're lookin' for."

Stedley gave a wry smile, and shook the manager's hand. "Yes, I guess you are the one I'm looking for. I tried to reach you by phone—"

"We don't always answer it."

"Yes. I figured that out." He took a quick glance around the dark but attractive interior. Then his eyes focused on the mirror behind Detzer.

"What's your name, son?"

"Oh, yes. Sorry. Stedley. Kurt Stedley."

"What can I do for you, Mr. Stedley?"

Kurt believed in getting straight to the point, so he plunged ahead.

"You can sit back and watch me make a lot of money for you, sir."

"Don't 'sir' me, boy," said Billy Bobb with a scowl. "I work for a livin'." Again the playful grin, as he waved at his half-empty bottle. "Wanna beer?"

"No, thank you," answered Kurt. He had expected a greater show of interest. In fact, he was surprised Billy Bobb didn't recognize him.

"What would you say if I told you I could get you sponsored by one of the big breweries?" he asked, probing for an opening.

"I'd say there had to be a catch," parried the manager. At last he set his bottle down on the bar, squared around, and stared Stedley in the eye. "What are you getting at, son?"

"Truth is, Mr. Detzer, I work for the TV station over in Laird, and I'm interested in using your place here for a show."

"Is that right?" exclaimed Billy Bobb.

"Yes. In fact, we want to cover this whole preacher-versus-the-Sunset-Grille thing I've been hearing about."

"Well, I'll be! Why didn't you just say so?"

"Then you're interested?"

"No. I never said that." Billy Bobb again reached for his bottle, and took a swallow.

"I see," said Kurt, grinning to himself. *These good ol' boys are so predictable* . . . "Well, then . . . name your price." *That ought to get him going. . . .*

"I'm not for sale, son," the manager smoothly replied. "Not for money, anyway. Besides, I don't think you could pay what I'd be askin'."

Kurt reflected a moment on this remark. "Just out of curiosity, Billy Bobb . . . what are you asking?"

"*People,* Mr. Stedley!" Billy Bobb answered immediately. "All I want in life is for people to come and enjoy my place here."

"Money has nothing to do with it?" asked Kurt in a disbelieving voice.

"Son," said Billy Bobb, "before I ever started this business, I had bucks coming out of my ears, and it ain't slowed down since. What would I want with more money?"

Kurt was confused and frustrated. This egg was harder to crack than he thought.

"Then it's advertisement you want?" he asked.

"Maybe." Billy Bobb turned the bottle up, draining the last sudsy swallow of beer into his throat.

"Well, that's no problem," Kurt said quickly. "I mean, we couldn't say anything about what goes on downstairs, but..."

"How do you know what goes on downstairs?" asked Billy Bobb quickly.

"I thought everyone around here knew."

"Just a whole lot of hearsay, my friend," said the manager, a tiny smile playing about his wrinkled cheeks.

The conversation was becoming very confusing to Kurt.

"You mean...?"

"I mean, the only folks who know what goes on downstairs are the ones who take a look for themselves—and they ain't the ones doin' the squawkin'. That's what I mean." He leaned toward Kurt conspiratorially. "And you're welcome anytime, Kurt," he smiled. Again he pointed toward the empty bottle on the bar. "Sure you don't want a cold one?"

"No, thank you. I'm sure," said Kurt. He sat down on the stool next to Billy Bobb, feeling weirdly uncomfortable to have the mirror at his back, and said nothing for a while. Again he looked out over the tables and the papier-maché trees. A fish tank behind the bar gurgled softly in the background. Muffled sounds of traffic filtered through the front door.

"I just have one more thing to ask you," said Kurt after a moment. "Then I'll get out of your hair."

"Shoot," said Billy Bobb.

"Is there any truth to that preacher organizing a boycott against your place?"

Billy Bobb paused thoughtfully, scooting his empty bottle around in the circle of moisture in which it sat. Presently he looked up at Kurt.

"I believe so, son. It's a shame, isn't it?"

"Is it?" replied Kurt. "Lots of folks in town say this place is the worst thing that ever happened to Ellenbach. They say you ought to be closed down, and the sooner the better."

The manager leaned back on the stool and laughed. "Oh, they say that, do they?" he chuckled, shaking his head. "I'd give a hundred-dollar bill to look them in the eye and watch them say it to my face." He chuckled a bit more, then fixed Kurt with a stare that belied the smile on his lips. "Most of them are only saying that 'cause they're out there—" he pointed at the door—"in the light of day, in front of God and all their churchy friends. But some of those same folks sing a different tune when they come in here...." Billy Bobb uttered a little chuckle that had nothing to do with mirth. Kurt felt the short hairs on the back of his neck standing at attention.

"And anyhow," the manager continued in a lighter tone, "fact is, you'd see just about the same amount of skin as downstairs if you were over at the Lion's Club pool in July or August—don't you think? I mean, have you seen some of the swimsuits these gals are wearin' nowadays?"

Kurt felt the room getting just-perceptibly hotter. "That's a good point," he agreed, not sure why. He had the urge to loosen his tie, but resisted.

"Look, Mr. Detzer—I mean—Billy Bobb," Kurt said persistently. "I want to do a show here. And you said you want more people. You give me what I want, and I'll bring in more crowds than you can handle. It's as simple as that. We're talking national TV, potentially."

Detzer raised an eyebrow. "You sure you can back that up?"

Kurt nodded, slowly at first, then with more conviction. "I think it's a very real possibility, if we play this thing up right."

"That simple, huh?" said the manager.

"Let me put it this way. This town isn't big enough for you and the preacher. One's got to go. If you let me do my program in your place, I can guarantee two things. I'll put you on the map, and I'll put that preacher on the streets. Deal?" He held out his hand.

Billy Bobb ran his hand through his white hair, and rubbed his smooth-shaven cheeks. Then, to Kurt's surprise, he shrugged, grinned, and grabbed Kurt's hand.

"Sounds like it could be fun. You got a deal, son."

THE FLIGHT

FROM the moment Larry's plane left the ground at the regional airport in Laird, he felt the weight of his dilemma weighing on him like a leaden vest. He felt like a cold, emotionless lump, a man-shaped stone in seat 21-C, sharing a journey through the air with people who appeared so light, so free of care.

Of course, Larry knew why he felt that way. He was going to a church conference in Sioux City, where pastors and leaders from congregations all over this part of the country would be gathered. There would be the usual glad-handing and hail-fellow-well-met greetings. And there would be colleagues from seminary days there, as well. Some of them had heard of the confrontation in Ellenbach, and they would want to talk to Larry about it. They would ask him questions which would make him feel this stony emotion a thousand times stronger. And though he would answer well, with the right catch-phrases, and mouth the proper formulas, he would be lying.

Even now Larry could feel the lies forming on his

tongue. But he was helpless to prevent them; they were the price he had to pay for preserving the image of himself that he still wanted others to see.

They would say something like, "It must be quite a spiritual struggle...your war against pornography." He would answer, "Yes, it is." They would ask, "What are the keys to winning this war?" Then he would pontificate, like a stone lecturing birds about flight. And he would feel ten times heavier after speaking than before.

He was glad for the hour-long flying time. There was some solace in not being "known" by anyone as he hurtled through space. To the flight attendant he was merely "the ginger ale in the window seat." To the airlines he was "a fare." Soon, however, he would land and be known again as Dr. Larry Ravelle, "the man who is closing down the Sunset Grille."

Already he was receiving calls and letters for advice in other cities—so many that Rose joked the other day, "Pornography must be as big a franchise as McDonald's." She was refreshingly naive, Larry thought. She was always the last to know the truth of her humor.

Indeed, there was a sea of Sunset Grilles beneath the wings of this aircraft. They squatted in profusion across the nation, and were called by various names. He imagined as he looked out the window that somewhere down there was a huge thing...a corporation, of sorts...to which they were all connected, in a network like a thousand-armed octopus. Though unseen, he felt it staring back at him. And he felt its tug, as if it sought to pluck him from the heavens.

A thought shot through his brain like a well-aimed arrow. *He would be anonymous in Sioux City*. Larry tried to ignore the thought, for he knew what thoughts came after. Yet, try as he might, the thought remained. And it grew stronger...

No one will know, it pounded. *No one will know . . .*

Larry was grateful for the two empty seats in his row. He could not have held up his end of a conversation. And he certainly could not have told anyone what he did for a living . . . not today . . . not the way he was thinking just now. . . .

From the front of the passenger compartment, Dias and I had our eyes on Pitch and Stool, who were crammed between narrow armrests across the aisle from Larry.

Pitch moved closer to Larry, whispering into the pastor's ear. Then he turned back to his oversized companion: "The Head was right about one thing, at least: Just because a man knows how to pray is no guarantee that he'll actually do it." Pitch was enjoying this job.

"How'd you like the way I sidetracked him at that town meeting, Stool?" remarked Pitch. "Just one little carefully chosen memory, and he nearly folds up like a cut flower! I wonder how those goody-goodies from the other side liked that little bit of work?"

We said nothing.

In his seat, Larry began thinking of the way Rose had looked this morning when he kissed her goodbye. The thought of his family back home in Ellenbach waiting faithfully for his return brought a sudden tightness to his chest. "Lord God," he prayed silently, "please protect my family while I'm gone! And . . . Lord . . ." He paused long over the next words—afraid to utter them for fear of insincerity, but just as afraid to leave them unsaid. "Lord . . . help me," he finished weakly.

In a blinding, painful flash of light which seemed to them to erupt from nowhere, Pitch and Stool reeled in their seats. Standing above them, glaring down with a clench-jawed smile, was Dias.

"Hello, boys! Mind if we join you, since we've just been invited?"

Stool growled, shaking his head.

I was now beside the pastor, with my arm around his shoulders, whispering into his ear. Pitch was enraged. "You have to give me access to the human," he said to us in a whining, accusative tone. "You know the rules! You can't shield him from me completely!"

Dias's lip turned downward, and his big hands clenched into fists.

"You have to!" roared Pitch, defying the implied threat in Dias's stance. "Ask your partner if it isn't so!"

Nostrils flaring in distaste, Dias cast a glance over at me.

I looked back at my partner and gave a sad little nod.

Larry yawned and closed his eyes. Pitch was at his ear in an instant.

"That's it! *Rest!* Rest, and I'll enter your dreams . . ."

The constant rumble of the jets lulled Larry into a fitful sleep full of fleeting images of TV cameras, bright lights, and rooms crowded with people. He was surrounded somewhere by angry farmers and ranchers. "You did it to us!" they were shouting. "You put us out of business."

Then he found himself inside the Sunset Grille. Billy Bobb Detzer was standing in front of him, leering and holding out a glossy-paged, full-color magazine with female flesh splayed shamelessly on its cover. The lights were bright, the cameras rolling, and the crowds of people looked on smugly. "Come on, boy," he was saying as he brandished the magazine. "Just a little peek. You like it—you know you do!"

He wanted not to look, told himself to keep his eyes away...

John was there too. "Come on!" his brother was saying. "I've got a flashlight. He won't find out! You're not a sissy, are you?"

The lights were hot and bright.

Come on!... Just a peek... Come on!...

With the bump of rubber on tarmac, Larry woke in a sweat. He waited impatiently for the airplane to taxi to the gate, then stood shoulder-to-shoulder with the rest of the passengers as he gathered his carry-ons and quickly exited the plane. He walked straight to baggage claim and retrieved his suitcase. Then he hailed a taxi, which took him to the hotel. Once in his room, he lay back on the bed.

I saw Pitch sitting in the corner armchair, smiling and scratching his chin. Stool studied the little box on top of the TV until he found the adult channel.

"I think the doctor would be very interested in that kind of programming, don't you, Stool?" asked Pitch, grinning.

"Ask Mr. Stumbling Block," Stool suggested. He jerked his thumb toward the door, where Dias and I were standing.

"Well?" asked Pitch, looking expectantly at me.

Test the man's faith... by way of harshest conflict... The words of my orders echoed mercilessly in my mind. "Permission granted," I said, wishing desperately I could say anything else. I began to pray immediately. Dias, on the other hand, prepared to fight.

"Come on, Larry!" he said as he eyed Stool and began to loosen his sword in its sheath. "Give me one good shot at his ugly mug. That's all I ask."

Stool backed away from the TV, smiling and squaring off for the fight.

"*Okay, Larry,*" said Stool. "Come on and turn this knob right here. I've got just the channel for you. And it's all ready to go."

Larry looked up from the bed at the TV. He rose and walked over to it. Dias stumbled as he circled Stool.

"Hold on, Larry," I prayed. "Know that the Spirit of the Holy One will help you."

Larry read the directory on top of the television. It said, "Adult films...Pay-4-TV...First three minutes *FREE!*"

"*See?* You can get a preview," coaxed Pitch. "And nobody at the desk will know. It won't cost a thing. You're far from home—who's it going to hurt?"

My prayers became suddenly very practical. "Unplug the set, Larry!"

Then Larry took action, drawing on the Spirit's strength within him. As Pitch wheedled, Larry bent over the television—and grasped the power cord! With an angry tug, he yanked it out of the socket. Then he turned the set toward the wall.

Stool wavered as Dias moved toward him. My partner delivered only one blow—nevertheless, it was impressive. Stool took it square in the chest, and flew backward through the hotel wall. When I looked out the window, he was sprawled on the parking lot three stories below. Pitch exited quickly, and Larry took a nap.

The meetings that evening and the next day went well. Larry, one of the presenters for a panel discussion on the counseling needs of rural and small-city churches, closed the session with a beautiful, heartfelt prayer. And upon returning to the hotel that night, he instructed a bellman to remove the television set from his room altogether, telling him simply he was addicted to late-night talk shows and couldn't afford to lose the sleep.

I was in fresh awe of what a man can do when he lets the Spirit have His way, and proud of Larry's victory.

The night before his departure for home, Larry tossed and turned until the wee hours. Finally he got up and showered. And in the shower, something changed inside him. When daylight came, he shaved and dressed quickly, packed his few belongings, and paid his bill at the desk. As he walked toward the exit, I smelled something wrong about him. Dias and I followed him closely as he got into the cab, waiting for any slight opening to encourage and support.

But his mind was closed to me. He was depressed as he sat in the backseat of the taxi on the way to the airport. He hardly conversed with the cab driver—and certainly not with the Supreme One.

In the terminal he began to act agitated. Looking about him as if afraid he might be recognized, he checked his bags and located his gate. Finally, when he was sure he would not miss his plane, he walked to the magazine store by the deli and made a purchase. I saw Pitch riding his shoulder coming out of the shop, and he was grinning at me in triumph.

THE
SLAUGHTERHOUSE

AT THE Ravelle home, the phone rang in Larry's study room. Rose, who had been invited by the church's teen-age group to be a guest speaker at one of their weeknight Bible study meetings, was sitting at Larry's desk with a few of his commentaries spread out before her. She picked up the phone.

"Hello?"

"Oh, uh . . . hello, Rose. This is Roger—Roger Allen."

"Good afternoon, Roger! How are you today?"

"Fine, I guess."

Roger's voice didn't sound "fine" to her; he sounded distracted, disturbed.

"Is Larry there?" he asked.

"Yes, Roger, but he's asleep. He got in just this morn-ing from that conference in Sioux City, and was so worn out he just set down his suitcase and fell into bed."

"Oh . . . I see . . ."

Rose's forehead wrinkled. The listless tone of the usu-ally ebullient attorney was beginning to worry her. "Roger, if you really need him, I'm sure he wouldn't mind my waking him."

"Oh, no! Don't do that... Just tell him to give me a call at the office when he wakes up. That'll do fine."

"All right, Roger—if you're sure..."

"Yes, that'll be okay. Have him call me as soon as he wakes up. Thanks, Rose. We'll see you Sunday, huh?"

"Sure, Roger, Goodbye." She hung up the phone, staring at it for a long time.

LARRY sat on his bed and yawned as he dialed the number for Roger Allen's office. If it had been left up to him, he would have waited until he was good and awake. But as soon as she heard him stirring, Rose had come in and insisted he call.

Hearing the buzzing on the line, he waited for an answer.

"Law office," came the efficient, crisp voice of Roger's receptionist.

"Hello, this is Larry Ravelle. I have a message to call Roger."

"Yes, Dr. Ravelle. I'll put you through."

He was stifling another yawn when he heard the rushed words, "Hello, Larry?"

"Yes, Roger. How you doin'?"

"Not so well."

Rose wasn't kidding, he thought. "Roger—what's wrong?"

There was a long silence. "Larry, my detective friend brought me a report today."

Larry drew a deep breath. *Get a stampede started... show them a glaring example...* "Okay, Roger, I understand you. What'd he say?"

"Larry... it's Gunner."

This time Larry drew a sharp breath, as if he had just been splashed with ice-cold water. His eyes felt as if they

121

were straining at their tethers. "Roger... are you—are you sure?"

"Yeah, Larry. Yeah, I'm sure." Another long silence, then, "My guy took pictures. They're fairly explicit," the attorney added needlessly. "Larry," he continued in a voice flattened by dejection and remorse, "I never thought it would come to this. Never in a million years. I mean—it's *Gunner!*"

Larry felt his face slackening with shock. Almost in the next instant, he felt a hot fire of anger bursting to life within him. Now he understood! The wariness at the first meeting—the delaying tactics in the town council... Larry began to see a picture developing, a portrait of deceit and hypocrisy. He felt his jaw clench and unclench, his teeth grinding together as he contemplated the way Gunner had given them all the runaround.

"All right, Roger," he managed at last, "I understand. When can I come by your office and view the... the evidence?"

"Larry? This is *Gunner* we're talking about! Have you thought about what this could do to him? To the town?"

"Roger," Larry replied in a steely, even voice, "I hear you, and I appreciate your concern. As Gunner's pastor, I share your apprehension. But—" his voice hardened a notch—"I also have a responsibility to the church, and to the community—and to God." His voice hardened even more. "I regret Gunner's involvement with this... this evil business. But my personal regard for the sinner doesn't mean I'll ignore his sin. Do you understand me?"

"Well... yeah, I guess..."

"Fine. Could I come by tomorrow—say, right after lunch?"

"Uh... sure. That'll be—that'll be okay," Roger said doubtfully.

"All right, then. Goodbye, Roger." Larry hung up the phone, his nostrils flaring.

He strode to the dresser and grabbed his car keys and wallet from the valet. He stalked down the hall, passing the doorway of the study where Rose had returned. She glanced up curiously at his stormy pace.

"I've got to get out for a while, Rose," he called back to her. "I'll be back by supper time."

"Larry! What's—" the front door slammed—"wrong?" She sighed, staring up from the desk for a moment, then resumed her study.

Why am I going back there? Larry asked himself as he drove. He had cruised aimlessly for a while after receiving Roger's call, stewing on the betrayal of Gunner McGuffy. Then, for some inexplicable reason, he had decided to go back to *that* place.

He remade the decision several times on his way. Once, when he pulled his car to a halt at one of the intersections in town, he considered turning right and picking up Peter when school was out. Instead he steered left and drove north. Then again, at the signal on the north end of town, he told himself that he really should say no to whatever it was that was urging him out into the country. He even played a little game: If the light turned green before he counted to fifteen, he would return home.

In the backseat of Larry's station wagon, Pitch and Stool were rumbling with delight.

"Did you see how I gigged him, Stool?" grinned Pitch. "How I played to his vanity, his fat-headed ego?"

Stool smirked. "Just let them see someone else enjoying a sin they want to commit, and they go all ga-ga!"

The demons roared with laughter. Pitch glanced outside, then leaned forward. "Go straight here, Larry. Just keep on driving north."

There was a ringing in Larry's ears, and his head was beginning to hurt. The light changed at thirteen, and Larry pulled through the intersection headed north, even while telling himself he had been counting entirely too slow, and that if he had used his watch, he would have reached fifteen with time to spare. But he drove on.

And then he was there. Larry stared through the dusty windshield at the dilapidated, corrugated-tin building. It was an old slaughterhouse—abandoned for almost two decades. He pulled up in the weed-grown parking lot, stopped the car, then got out and started walking.

This was his second stop of the day at the vacant, rusting building. The first had been earlier this morning as he returned from the airport. For some reason beyond logic, instead of continuing south into town and his home, he had pulled off the Laird highway, down a quarter-mile dirt road, and into this place. He had parked the car in just about the same place as now: in the farthest corner of the parking lot near a thick stand of poplar and chinaberry trees that blocked any view of his car from the highway. He had then taken the magazine out of the glove compartment, walked quickly across the two-acre gravel lot, climbed on the packing plant's loading dock, and flung the thing, glossy pages flapping in the air, through the open doors of the old building. He thought he was casting it from his life forever. But now he was pacing slowly across the weed-infested lot toward the dark opening through which the thing had disappeared. ...

Dias and I stood on the loading dock, watching him come toward us, hearing the distant murmurs of the two unwelcome passengers in the backseat of his car. Then

Pitch and Stool got out and followed Larry toward the slaughterhouse. I looked down to Larry, wanting desperately to reach him, to raise some flicker of resistance to the onslaught of temptation for which Pitch had brought him here. But by now the way of escape was far behind him . . . lost somewhere in a confused cloud of guilt and self-justification. The path he now walked was smooth and wide—and descending.

It had been a freezer-burned day, and was just cold enough now for Larry to notice the ends of his toes against his loafers. He zipped up his jacket against the cold wind as he stepped closer to the slaughterhouse. Thoughts of Rose tapped timidly at the door of his mind. But he shut the curtains, turned out the lights, and pressed on. "I'm just going to glance at it," he told himself. "I've got to find out—got to see what it is that traps men like . . . like Gunner." He knew he was lying to himself. But now he couldn't turn back.

Though it was midafternoon, Larry felt himself oddly afraid of walking alone—in this place at this time. He had the mad perception of someone—or something—just behind him, matching his walk step for step. He found himself wishing a train would pass on the tracks not far away, and drown out the sound of the imagined intruder's infernal plodding.

Behind him, a winter-shriveled chinaberry fell from its bare branch onto the hood of the car. The sudden noise sent an unwelcome surge of adrenaline through his body. Then he realized it was not noise he was wishing for after all, but the presence of a friend.

His mind was befuddled by the sorcery of peripheral vision. On his left, some small pieces of rotten lumber in a reckless pile, topped by a board with a knothole, became a rotten man lying in wait, with one eye watching him. On his right, a piece of garbage bag fluttering from a corner of the building became a shirt sleeve, undoubt-edly attached to some ragged form reaching out to grab the passerby. Larry considered dispelling the images by looking square at them, but the thought of turning his back on a rotten board in order to face up to a fluttering bag, and thereby risking attack from behind, was too terrifying for him. Like the little boy going to the bath-room in the middle of the dark night, he knew there were really no monsters dogging his steps—but the knowl-edge in his brain did nothing to quiet the pounding in his chest.

He made his way onto the loading dock, crossed it halfway, and peered through the dark doorway.

To his fevered, guilty imagination, each shadow of the vacant, creaking building concealed a ghastly row of zombies. The harder he tried to ignore them, the more they leered their toothless grins. So he looked straight ahead, to where the magazine lay crumpled on the dusty concrete of the loading bay floor.

Then he turned away. He put the dark interior of the slaughterhouse to his back. Stepping back to the lip of the dock, he gazed out wistfully across the surrounding countryside. He saw some of Hank Willis's Hereford cattle, moving slowly, nose-down, through the fenced-off hayfield in which they grazed, living out their lives daily and methodically. To the north, an emerald-green section of winter wheat rolled in the strong wind, first one way, than another, its shiny blades glittering in the weak winter sun. A white spot at the head of a dirt-red line appeared in the distance and advanced until it be-came a truck, traveling along one of the myriad dirt roads that crisscrossed Johnson County. For a moment Larry wished madly it would slow, turn toward the packing plant, and give him an excuse to leave this place which was, for him, so full of haunted, weird impressions. But the truck passed on without slowing, a dirty red cloud in tow.

A meadowlark flashed its yellow underbelly. A rust-clad tractor rested forever beneath a winter-bared elm. The scene should have been one of peace, rest. But Larry's insides were anything but quiescent.

It had been that way for him as long as he could remember. Hurried. His secret life would not let him be otherwise. To move slowly meant to think. And to think meant to throw wide the curtains of the soul and awaken slumbering conscience. He much preferred to let that tired wretch sleep.

This day, however, Larry lingered on sin's cornice long enough for that part of him which he cursed so regularly to open at least one eye and squint about at the world. "Consistency" was what his conscience saw in the wind, and the wheat, and the wandering cattle. He paused and drew conclusions. On the gusty wind, these words came to him:

That which is born in man's field will end up on his table.

That which rests too long under God's sky will be clothed in ruin.

And that which seems most securely anchored will be mowed down at harvest....

I heard the confused, sad, befuddled thoughts falling from the lips of Larry's soul. I raced to his side, at the entryway to the slaughterhouse, and I shouted at him.

"For all these, Larry, there is no choice. But for you...!" Might he not even now walk to the car, get inside, and drive back to his wife and family? Might he not choose whether or not he picked up the magazine?

"Choice is such a difficult thing," muttered Pitch into Larry's ear. "So difficult...so conditioned by the past. Just think of the past, Larry! Think of the choices that were made for you...by your father, for example..."

The smell of the hay, the thick clouds of dust threatened to choke him, to strangle him. John and he had been bad—or so Dad had said. It was easier to anger Dad after Mom died, it seemed. And so he had shut them up in the barn, with a surly order to "think about what you've done, and I'll come let you out when I think you're ready!"

The eyes of the owls in the rafters glowed in the near-dark —twenty pairs of round, yellow discs shining down on them in their terror. Then he and John were pounding on the door, screaming for Dad to let them out, please let them out; they wouldn't do it anymore, honest . . .

And then, in the shadows, John had stumbled across their father's secret cache. Stacks and stacks of glossy, full-color photography . . . So strange . . . so wrong . . . so irresistible . . .

Later they invented the ghosts . . . or 'bony men' as John had called them, as with the minds of boys they had fantasized about the bodies behind the yellow eyes peering down on them from the darkness above. To Larry, the faces of the bony men were all the same: Dad's face. And the magazines they studied in the twilight of the barn became talismans of dark fascination—bound with horror and anger.

He and John were nine. That was easy to remember because of the nine unlit candles on two cakes. Other things were easy to remember . . .

Dad shouting over the telephone—"Tell Dr. Watkins to meet me there!"

A screen door banging.

Father carrying Mother, her arm hanging limply from his desperate grasp.

The funeral. The murmuring of the adults . . .

Half-empty bottles of Scotch—then more and more . . .

John singing . . .

drumming with a wooden spoon . . .

"Happy birthday to us! Happy birthday to us! . . .

Happy birthday, John and Larry!"

Unlit candles, and Dad passed out on the couch . . .
Two cakes . . . unlit candles . . .

Larry turned and faced the wide-open doorway of the slaughterhouse. "Stop it!" he screamed to the haunting of his past.

He stepped inside the entrance, then slid the door shut behind him, first making sure there was no lock on it.

He entered the dimness of the main cutting floor. All around him were the mechanisms of butchery, now silent and useless. He fancied he could still hear the bleat and bawling of animal alarm.

He looked above, at the rail where carcasses had been suspended for the dressing operation. Now the steel hooks hung empty, rusting in the darkness.

To the rear was a dark, spacious area used by Hank Willis to store hay. The room was stacked with bales, to a height of thirty feet. Slivers of light squeezed through the gaps in the tin and danced in the dusty layer hovering close to the ceiling. Larry crossed the room and sat down on a bale. Without realizing it, he had picked up the magazine from the floor of the loading bay. He held it now, staring at it, as if it were a viper or a magic lamp.

His heart pounded in his chest, and his hands trembled . . . no, shook . . . as he tore open the cover. Larry's breaths were shallow by now, as if he thought the sounds of his normal breathing might somehow tip the town of Ellenbach as to the whereabouts of its favorite pastor.

Larry wavered. He turned his wedding ring slowly. He thought of flinging the magazine behind the hay and running back outside to his car. Someone would find it later and blame it on some prurient farmboy. *I'm above this,* he told himself. *I'm educated . . . I . . .*

I saw and heard Larry teetering on the brink of decision, feverishly dallying with his options. He weighed them all, and made his choice. He turned back the cover and looked inside. The rush of clandestine behavior swept over him. His mind darkened as the afternoon wheeled slowly past.

A blackness moved across the cutting floor. Stool approached as neither mass nor vapor, but, rather, a vague sense of void. Dias and I crouched behind a pile of bales toward the rear of the room. My partner drew his blade and threw back his long hair, gathering it with one hand at the nape of his neck, and tucking it down the back of his mail coat.

"They attack," he spoke in whispered steel, "and this time with power we have never seen in them before. I'll stand with him."

I wanted badly to lift my hand to help. But nothing of that sort would change things.

"I'm sorry, Dias . . . I mean . . . sorry that you have to fight alone."

He looked at me.

"And what will you be doing?" he asked with a smile.

"Standing and praying," I answered. As a Trial, it was the only answer I could give.

"Then pray well, Skandalon," came Dias's strong voice. I turned again to him, but he was gone.

Through the darkness, I could barely make out Larry. He was hunched over his reading like a starving man over a bowl of stew. When I thought of Dias out there on the floor, facing blows from Stool over this pitiful man's soul, contempt sent a cold chill down my spine. But then I looked again, and saw Larry as he truly was—a weak, weary mortal, suspended between two worlds he was woefully unable to see. And I loved him, and prayed all the harder that he would wield the Spirit's sword:

Fight, creature, filled with lust,
fight the fires raging!
Fight, or else be left to smoulder
in your mortal caging . . .

The "void" stood out in the room, black as tar in a tunnel. All the earthly darkness around it seemed as light by comparison, and it moved like a spider in the bottom of a barrel. Stool, or this 'thing' he had become, hunkered back against the wall waving an ebony shadow before its face. Dias leaped onto a bale of hay with his back to Larry.

Even now, as Dias faced the dark void, neither he nor I saw any longer a hole with a sword extending from its midst, but rather a black dog—no, ten black dogs, spreading out in crescent fashion, moving closer with each step toward Larry.

The end dog was so close to me I could have separated its head from its shoulders—if I had a blade. Instead I prayed harder. Dias backed up until his heel would have been against the side of the pastor's shoe. Ten sets of demonic hackles stood on end. Forty paws clicked forward on the wooden floor. Dias found the lead dog and held its eye. With its head close to the floor and black orbs boring into the angel, it spoke in a gravelly, cursing growl:

We mongrels from Hell,
a dozen shy two,
circle the sword from Heaven.
Stand aside,
or we'll tear your hide.
Give up, and we'll call it even . . .

The lead dog's eyes burned red with the fires of distant furnaces. Dias stood with his feet apart, and though the point of his sword wavered while he calculated and recalculated the odds of this uneven battle, he would not stand aside.

With a sweep of his sword at the leader's head, Dias drowned all other options. The demon dog bobbed out of reach. The pack moved in. A yellowed set of teeth sank deep in his heel . . . another just behind his knee. The pain drove him downward. He knew that in an instant they would be upon him. His sword clattered to the floor, and he let it lie. Using it would only cause the black spirits to alter form. He spun toward an opening in the circle, pulling the nearest dog on top of him. With the beast writhing against his chest, Dias grasped a waving front paw with his left hand and ran his right arm under the dog's snapping jaws, clenching a patch of matted hair between its ears. Then he pulled with all his might until he heard an awful snap. All along his arms and legs he felt the rip and tear of flesh as the savages darted in and out, taking pieces of his heaven-suit with each assault.

Dias scrambled backward, clutching the dead dog to his breast, until he reached the wall of hay. Then he braced himself against the dusty backdrop and pushed up with his aching legs. A single dog charged from the shadows. Dias swung the corpse like a club, striking his attacker square in the ribs. It went yelping off into the dark to join the chorus of the others.

The eerie presence of the nine filled the slaughterhouse, as Dias huddled by the hay and I prayed with all my might. The dead dog sprang to life at his feet where Dias had let it fall, and for a moment bared its fangs as if to attack again. Then it, too, melted into the shadowy circle. Once more there were ten.

A burst of wind whistled across the metal roof, and then silence settled over the slaughterhouse like a dark blanket. A low growl began somewhere above Dias's head, and then came the terrifying sound of cattle careening around the room, loose from their chutes and pursued by the snapping jowls of Hell's apostates.

Dias looked ceilingward and caught in his face the full bulk of the snarling attacker. The ten dogs had reunited into a single, vicious malevolence, bent solely on wreaking irreparable harm to my partner. He tumbled back, wrestling with the beast, then flinging it from him even as he fell backward, exhausted, onto the concrete floor.

Hell's beast drooled as it stared toward my partner. I hid behind the bales and doubled my prayers. Dias was radiant, even now. His eyes met the stare of the opponent with poise, daring the Stool-dog to approach near enough to sink its black teeth into him.

Out of a dark mouth hissed more poetic threats:

> *Heaven's fool*
> *snapped in twain . . .*
> *Indeed a handsome sight.*
> *I dedicate*
> *these teeth of pain*
> *to punctuate your plight.*

Beyond hope, I felt my prayers catch a tenuous hold in Larry's heart. Suddenly, he staggered to his feet like a man at last realizing he has drunk far more wine than he should have. The black dog turned from Dias and lunged for the frightened pastor.

A sudden, unreasoning fear rattled Larry—as if the bony men were descending from the rafters of the slaughterhouse, stumbling toward him on decaying legs. He shook from hair to heel. He wanted out—he must get out!

But still the force held him—he felt its intoxicating power. It compelled him to look inside the magazine just once more.

"No!" he begged.

It tugged harder. "Enough!" he said. "Please!" It clamped down tight, with an exquisite, certain knowledge of the precise point where pressure was best applied . . .

"O God, *please!*" shouted Larry.

The walls reverberated . . .

Dias saw his chance. He bolted toward the main sliding doors. The dog yowled curses, seeing what his opponent intended, yet unable to reach Dias in time. My partner strained every pound of muscle against the metal door, mounted on a rusty track . . . and it moved. A shaft of light—the fading red glow of sunset—shot through the opening. The shaft became a shower of amber as the hole widened.

A Hell-howl filled the slaughterhouse. The mongrel broke with a shriek into a thousand shards of blackness, each with its own discreet nature. Rats and snakes and millipedes and scorpions and bats scuttled and flapped in every direction, shrieking tiny cries of alarm.

With horror, Larry heard a violent blast of wind shake the entire building, and saw it lift the door from its old sliding track, opening it a good three feet. He rushed across the slaughterhouse floor, out the door, and onto the dock. Then he jumped to the ground and ran as hard as he could toward the station wagon.

The sandy gravel of the packing plant lot became a beige blur as he raced to reach his car. A few early stars in the east jiggled like the ends of July Fourth sparklers. As he ran on, his own car bobbed up and down in the narrowing distance.

For a moment, he felt as if he were a madman in a funhouse corridor. He heard the cursed intruder shadowing him again. Same footsteps. Same wheezing. He knew they were his own, yet knowing that only added to the terror.

He lost a loafer in a rut in the darkening lot, but kept going. He reached for his car keys, and missed his pocket, which was tight against his thigh as his legs pumped up and down. He fumbled again and found them. His index finger slipped through the cold key ring, and he grasped it tightly.

But now his pursuer was upon him, within him. It pounded on his sternum and reverberated down to his groin. Predator and prey united for one brief moment as Larry slammed into the car door and grasped the handle. When he swung the door open, he was conscious of an automobile approaching on the quarter-mile road. It was speeding his way.

Larry got in and fell back against the seat. It was freezing. The windows were frosted over all the way around. His breath came in quick, visible puffs. His left foot wore a dirt-caked sock that drooped to the ankle. A corner of his mind told him he'd need a story for that by the time he got home. He closed the door and started the engine. The lights of the approaching car lit the rearview mirror.

He floored the accelerator, slinging loose dirt behind him as he sped out of the slaughterhouse lot.

ON THE dock, just outside the doorway, lay a still form. I rushed to Dias and did my best to lift his hulking shape into my arms. His mail shirt was badly damaged, but not irreparably. There was a large tear in his left side. His life-essence oozed steadily—but not in a gush—from the wound. Bite marks covered his legs. He opened his eyes and looked into mine.

"Our friend Larry doesn't choose the Way easily," panted Dias.

"No," I replied. "No, he doesn't."

My partner took a deep breath and looked away.

"We fought well," he said.

He shivered and I pressed his head against my thin shoulder. I was afraid, and quite ashamed of being so. The evil I feared was far from the slaughterhouse now, trailing a station wagon in the form of a silent swoop of blackbirds.

One bird, a larger one, remained behind. It perched a few feet away from me on the edge of the dock. And though it said nothing, its thoughts might as well have been words, for they were Pitch's thoughts. I had no difficulty discerning what the tempter wanted to express.

"*May we sift him?*" the thoughts asked. The bird gazed at me with big yellow eyes.

"Go," I muttered....

THE AUTOMOBILE pulled off the highway, jogging and bouncing along the rutted path leading to the slaughter-house lot. It pulled into the lot, and stopped.

Billy Bobb got out of his car, shoved his hands into the pockets of his fleece jacket, and strolled about the lot, whistling tunelessly to himself. His foot stumbled across something. He stopped, looked, and stooped to pick it up.

It was a shoe—a loafer. Its lining was still warm.

He stood, peering back down the road in the direction taken by the car he had just passed.

Fella must have been in a big hurry, he wondered, *to go off and leave a shoe on a cold evening like this.* Shrugging, he tossed the shoe through the open door of his car onto the front seat, and strolled on toward the loading dock. As he walked in the gathering dark, he pulled a pocket-sized flashlight from his jacket and flicked on the white beam.

If the ordinance on live entertainment passed the town council, he was going to have to relocate the Grille. And this old packing plant could be the place, since it was

136

outside the city limits. He was here to get a feel for what it was like in the darkness.

He walked back and forth for a while, looking at the front of the building, then climbed the steps of the loading dock, shining the light inside. Something lay on the floor. He walked over to it. It was a magazine. For a moment he peered at the portraits of the nude women—not really seeing them, but wondering why a person would come all the way out here to look at dirty pictures, then leave in such a hurry that he left a shoe lying on the ground.

It was getting colder. He carried the magazine back to his car, tossing it atop the abandoned shoe. Then he got in and drove back toward Ellenbach.

THE ARGUMENT

"**A**RE you okay?" asked Rose. She addressed the question to her husband who, at the moment, was hunched over the kitchen sink staring out into the dark backyard. He had driven as fast as he could to get home for dinner. Now, he was hardly aware of the warm water washing over his hands, or the bar of soap which he wrung increasingly thinner between his reddened fingers. He looked into the dark as if in a trance. The back porch light had recently burned out, so he could see only as far as the light falling through the kitchen window—to the swingset, and no further.

"Hmm?" Had Rose said something? "Oh—yes, dear. Just thinking."

"I'm interested in your thoughts," said Rose. She had been peeling potatoes, but the knife lay still now and she sat with her hands folded on the counter, waiting.

Larry had liked that about her at one time. So inquisitive . . . so adoringly enamored by his words. It had made him feel wise back then. But his impatience with her longing to know his heart had grown in proportion to the number of secrets he had accumulated recently. Phrases like "How was your day?" or "Tell me more... I'm interested" were like annoying search beacons to Larry—prodding him along, pinning him down, dragging him from the shadows. He turned off the water and paused, leaning against the sink. His forearms rested on the Formica. His fingers drip-dried above the garbage disposal, and his eyes looked down into the small, black hole. At the bottom of the disposal, sprawled across the blades, was a greasy, dark banana skin. It looked up through the opening and in a voice meant not for the ears, but for the soul, spoke to the pastor.

"She is the enemy."

That was all it said, and all it needed to say, for when he heard it, Larry didn't question its origin, but thought of it as his own. He embraced it... wrapped feeling around it... then acted upon it. He chose the most benign words possible, and proceeded.

"Where are the children, dear?"

Rose sat motionless, her gaze fixed on her husband for at least some sign that he was not going to ignore her question altogether. Larry felt her eyes, and he could not face her. Does she know? Could she? Was his afternoon wandering so evident?

"Well?" Larry repeated when he decided she wasn't going to reply. "I was just wanting to know where the children were. If you don't want to talk, I understand."

Rose could feel the subject shifting, moving away from the center. She decided this time to grab hold of it and not let go. She took a deep breath and said what she was feeling.

"Larry," she began, "I do want to talk. I'm scared. Where have you been this afternoon? Is it so wrong for me to want to know about the man I love? Something's happening to you, since all this Sunset Grille business started. Won't you at least let me help? Let's start with that phone call from Roger, for example," she persisted. "What was that all about? Why did you storm out of the house, and just now get back?"

"Rose, it's late. This is hardly the time . . ."

"And when *will* it be the time, Larry?" she said firmly. "Tonight? Will that be the time? When I'm lying in bed, and you're doing who knows what in your study till all hours of the night . . . will that be the time?" Larry said nothing. "How about tomorrow morning? When I crawl out of bed at seven and you've been gone already for two hours . . . will that be the time? Or when I call you down at the church and you're not in . . . will that be the time?"

Larry's eyes were fixed in their gaze down into the disposal. Rose kept on.

"The fact is, *dear* . . . there has not been time for days. There's never a time!"

Rose's words would have sunk deep had they not collided with another message that floated up from the black hole in the bottom of the sink: "There's never a time" met with *You don't have the time,* and the second overrode the first. *She doesn't appreciate you* followed. Then, *She never will appreciate you.* And finally the knockout punch: *You don't need this—you don't deserve it; look at all the pressure you're under!* Larry took a step away from the sink and turned toward his wife. He mimicked the gurgling suggestion as if he had thought of it himself.

"I don't need this!"

"And neither do I!" she retaliated, her eyes flashing fire.

Larry could hardly believe his ears. He had never heard Rose talk like this. Deep down he probably knew there would come a day when she would, but not now . . . not when he was falling apart.

All right, then. So she wants to know—fine. Tell her a little something to get her off your case.

140

"Well, if you *must* know," he began, his voice dripping with patronizing overtones, "the call from Roger was in regard to the fight over the Grille."

"I assumed that." She wasn't mollified in the least.

"And," he went on, "Roger had some very disturbing news for me. Concerning someone we both know—or knew—quite well. Even trusted."

A shadow of concern had partially replaced the defiant, demanding expression on her face. "Well?" she asked. "What was it?"

Larry fixed her with a significant, hurt look. "Gunner has been frequenting the Grille—and I don't mean the restaurant."

Her face opened in surprise, then distress. "Gunner! That's . . . that's awful!" she said, shaking her head.

Larry nodded wisely, with what he hoped was a noble expression on his face. "Yes—that's exactly what I thought," he agreed. "Naturally, when I found out, I was very upset—"

Suddenly, Rose's eyes snapped back into focus, with a suspicious set to her jaw. She locked gazes with him, and interrupted, "How did you find this out—by trailing him down there? Spying on him?"

Larry was open-mouthed, caught flat-footed. "Why . . . Rose! Of course not! I wouldn't go into that place—"

"Then how?" she demanded, her nostrils flaring. "Did Roger follow him down?"

"No . . ." His mind was spinning furiously, seeking some path out of the dilemma. "No, we—that is, the committee—we . . . hired someone."

"Hired someone to what?" she half-shouted.

"Hired a detective," he mumbled, staring in great concentration at the laces of the shoes he had changed into before coming into the kitchen. "We hired a man to

141

gather... evidence. For the effort against the Grille..."
Even in his own ears, the words sounded paltry, guilt-laden.

"Oh!" she scoffed. "So now it's an 'effort,' is it? And I guess the end justifies any means—is that it, Larry?"

"I ... well, I ... I asked Roger Allen to hire a good detective," Larry began. "How was I to know the mayor was a pervert?"

"Pervert? Is that all you think he is? Did you remember he's a friend? And a longtime member of the community?" By now, her voice was loud enough that he was concerned what the children were hearing. He had never, in all their years together, seen her this angry. "Did you ever stop to consider what this could do to the man you've known since your childhood?"

"I never—"

"That's obvious," she snapped. "So what happens now? Do you get the *Gazette* to publish pictures of Gunner in the Grille, or just tack them on the bulletin board at church?"

"Listen, little lady..." He pointed an accusative finger at her.

"No, you listen, Mr. Preacher! I'm stronger than you think!"

They both drew up short as these words fell onto the table, she no less shocked by her boldness than he. Then she drew herself up straight, unwilling to back away from what had just been uttered.

Even in his anger, Larry was beginning to see the point: Rose had her own mind, her own opinions about— about lots of things. She wouldn't always be going along meekly with whatever Dr. Ravelle wanted her to do.

"So what are you saying, Rose?" he asked softly.

"I'm saying ... I didn't marry a man who treats people— lifelong friends—like cannon fodder. And I'm saying I want back the man I *did* marry."

They were both quiet again.

"Please, Larry," she said, a note of her accustomed tenderness stealing back into her voice. "Be honest with me. I told you before, you don't have to go through this thing alone." She rose from the table, pacing slowly to him and laying a hand on his arm. "I think you're taking too much responsibility for this project. Let others carry some of the load," she beseeched, peering into his face for some sign of agreement, some echo of tenderness, of compassion.

He stared stonily at the opposite wall, unwilling to meet her eyes. *It's no use—nobody understands.* Though his back was turned to the disposal, the thoughts still twined themselves seductively about his brainstem.

The phone rang and Larry yanked it from its cradle.

"What?" he said irritably. "Oh, I'm sorry, Roger. I'm pretty beat...Uh-huh...Sure, Roger, I'm well aware of the risks...He said what?...No! I don't think...Uh-huh...Sure. Look, Roger, can we discuss this sometime when I'm not so tired? Sure—no, that's all right, you didn't know...Okay, then...Yes. Bye." Then he hung up the phone. Rose was still standing in the same position, but he had moved away from her while conversing on the phone. Larry started back in where he had tried to go at first.

"So...where are the kids?"

She looked at him, tears brimming in her eyes. "You aren't going to let me in, are you?"

He looked away. "This thing won't go on forever, Rose. When things settle down—"

Rose walked from the room and Larry stared after her, his phrase falling to the floor like a broken kite string. His brain felt like it was tightening against his skull, and he was aware of a deep, churning ache in his stomach.

Apparently dinner wasn't going to be served. So he

made himself a sandwich and resigned himself to the fact that he would be spending the evening alone. He reached inside the icebox for a package of cold cuts and, just before he closed the door, noticed the glass vase on the counter by the sink. He looked at it for a long while. It was empty. For the first time in twelve years he had forgotten.

Guiltily, he considered his alternatives. Even in his self-absorbed state, he could see that the cord of Rose's endurance was fraying. He should do something—but he felt helpless. What would he say to one of his congregation if they came to him with a similar situation? He tried to remember the platitudes he had mouthed in cases like this. Pray... Talk it out... Be patient... Seek counseling.

Maybe that was it. Maybe he should talk to someone, to another professional, someone who would understand.

THE
UNCOVERING

THE NEXT morning, after a quick phone call to set it up, Larry got together with Nigel Hendrickson. The old psychiatrist-turned-janitor agreed to meet him at the church for a one-hour session.

They met in Larry's office, where they could talk freely without the possibility of being overheard. With the window shades pulled down it was dark and quiet—perfect for an intimate conversation, with a sort of natural soundproofing built into the bookshelves in the form of Larry's extensive library. Dim secrets whispered here would remain safe. Larry thought of the many slow, halting conversations he had held here with suffering members of his flock. In this room he had witnessed grown men weeping like little lost boys, and sedate, outwardly serene older women dissolving into quivering lumps of raw emotion. The books in this room had heard many secrets, seen many confidences divulged. And they had never betrayed any of them. But this time, Larry thought with an inner shiver, the secrets, the confidences would be his own. That seemed to make a great deal more difference than he had ever thought it would.

Nigel sat in Larry's chair with his knees crossed, while the pastor sat uncomfortably at one end of his couch, looking at the clock, looking at the books. Nigel began the session.

"Relax, Larry. This is not a test," he smiled.

"I'm sorry, Nigel. I've never done this before. I'm usually seated where you are—*doing* the counseling, not receiving it."

"That's quite all right. I'm just going to ask you a few questions."

"I'll tell you right off," joked Larry, "I was potty-trained at two and my mother had all the warmth a boy could ask for."

"Good! What more is there to say?" laughed Nigel. He leaned back deeper into the chair. "Tell me though, truthfully... were you close to one another?"

"My mother and I?"

"Your mother... your father..."

"Mom died when we were nine, and after that, Dad..." He couldn't force himself to say more.

Nigel nodded to himself. "Larry, I couldn't help noticing—you said, 'when *we* were nine.' Tell me about your siblings. You do have siblings, don't you?"

"One brother."

"Just one brother. I see. And you were close?"

"Oh, heavens, no." Then Larry checked himself. "Well... I don't know. I suppose we got along about as well as most. We're twins—"

"Um-hmm," encouraged Nigel. "And where is your brother now?"

Larry paused long before replying. "Ah... He's here. In Ellenbach."

"You don't say! I don't think I've ever seen him—"

"No. You wouldn't. He...he doesn't come into town much."

"Hmmm," mused Nigel. "I see...But, of course, I thought perhaps at church—"

"Hah!" scoffed Larry. "Church would be the last place you'd see him."

Nigel looked thoughtfully at Larry for a long while, then made a quick note or two on the pad in front of him. "Well, then...back to my original question: Were you and your brother close?"

"Maybe at one time—when we were pretty young. You know, we played together, got in trouble together—" *Yellow eyes...the bony men...the luscious, forbidden pictures...No! Forget that!* "Just the usual stuff, I guess. I don't know...Is that close?"

"What do you think, Larry?"

"I think I'm going to hear that question a lot." They both laughed again.

The old radiator caught the joke, and let out a loud bellow. Then it got very quiet in the room. The clock ticked out its monologue. Larry gazed down at the carpet.

Nigel let the silence go on for a while, then asked in almost a whisper, "Is there something troubling you, Larry?"

Larry thought about the question. He closed his eyes and wondered what it might be like to open a door which he had kept locked from the inside for so long. How much might come spilling out, even through the tiniest crack? Was he strong enough to stop it, or would it get out of hand?

"If it's guilt, Larry," said Nigel, "then it cannot benefit you. Forget about it, that's the thing to do. I'm not a theologian, of course, but I believe guilt can be very destructive...Don't you?"

147

Larry was staring blankly into the air before his face. With difficulty, he brought himself back to the conversation. "What's that? Guilt? Yes," he said doubtfully, "sometimes that can be the case. Yes, of course. That would be the case here," he said, almost hypnotically.

"How's he going to find the Way of Escape with that kind of advice?" demanded Dias, staring angrily at the black, toupéed head of Nigel Hendrickson.

I had to agree. The older man was trying to be helpful, but this type of help could turn out to be harmful to Larry. True, there is a useless, self-absorbed kind of guilt that can eat a hole in a human's stomach, and this is one of the best-honed arrows in the Enemy's quiver. But there is also the kind by which a human is directed beyond himself, by which he is blessed...even saved. And who should know the fine line between the two better than a Trial? To completely remove guilt from the human spectrum of emotions would be like taking out the brain of a man who complains of a headache.

Nigel was speaking again.

"You've got a lot of guilt, don't you?" the older man asserted quietly.

Larry, seated on the couch, didn't know how to respond to the question. It felt true. Yet it felt false. Good. And bad. Larry considered this as he sat there on his own counseling couch, and finally saw it as an acceptable way to get past the surface stuff with Nigel.

"Some," Larry said, a shamed sound in his voice.

"Some?" asked Nigel.

"Yes. Some."

"Are we playing twenty questions, or what? Come on, Larry. What is 'some'?"

"'Some' is 'some'! I don't know. 'Some' is everything. It's the way I feel. I don't know!"

"Sounds like 'some' is a lot."

"Okay. 'Some' is a lot."

"I told you this wouldn't be easy, Larry."

"I know. I know."

"What was life like at nine, Larry?"

"Nine? Nine what? Nine o'clock? Nine years?"

"Nine years old," said Nigel.

"Why do we have to talk about that right now?"

Nigel put down his pencil and looked sternly at Larry. "Dr. Ravelle, I want very much to help you unburden yourself. But if you are so intent on obstructing my attempts, I have to question the advisability of proceeding."

"I'm sorry, Nigel," Larry said, rubbing his eyes. "I . . . I guess I'm not nearly as good on the couch as I am in that chair." He looked up at the bespectacled other man, smiling weakly. "That was a pretty traumatic time in my life, though. I may have to take it kinda slow."

"Fine," said Nigel, smiling gently. "I have no problem with going slow—as long as we're going forward." Again he picked up his pencil. "Now. In your own words, and in your own time, tell me about your life, beginning at nine. Close your eyes if that helps. In fact, I suggest it. There. That's good. Close them and relax."

Larry closed his eyes and propped his feet up on the couch.

"Now," said Nigel softly, "Whatever comes to your awareness, feel free to share it. Don't make it be a word or a picture or a memory. Perhaps a silly tune or a sensation or a smell . . . really, anything is all right. Don't censor it for my sake. Touch down gently on each, like it was a cloud, and then see where it takes you. Drift freely."

"Isn't this a little strange?" asked Larry. "I mean, it sounds . . . you know . . . sort of hocus-pocus."

"Trust me, Larry," Nigel reassured him. "All we're doing here is allowing your mind to associate freely. There's nothing mystical about it."

There was silence for a long time. Finally Larry spoke. "The clock."

"The clock?" asked Nigel. He glanced at the polished walnut case on the wall.

"I hear it ticking."

"Freely drift, then. The sound. Let it go all the way around you. Imagine the sound getting closer and louder . . . until the pendulum is swinging right next to your ear."

"It seems very loud," said Larry.

"Yes. And it's saying something to you. Back and forth. Back and forth . . ."

"I had a clock like that once."

"Relax, Larry. You think too much. Let the ticks do the thinking for a while."

"I'm not going anywhere. This is silly. Why can't we just . . ." He started to sit up.

"Larry. Please relax and trust yourself," insisted Nigel.

Larry lay back, uncertainly. There was more silence.

"That ticking just keeps coming back!"

"Will you let it be your friend, Larry?"

"Let it be my friend. Let it be my friend. Okay. Okay."

"What do the ticks say, Larry?"

"Nothing!"

"In a moment, I'm going to count to three," Nigel said quietly. "And when I reach three, an imaginary cuckoo is going to pop out of that clock and tell you what that back-and-forth cadence might be saying to you. Relax for now. That's good . . . Lean your head back on the couch . . . Float . . . And drift . . ."

Larry let his body go limp. It felt good to lie on that couch in the middle of the day. It was relaxing. He began to let down his guard.

"When I reach three, Larry, feel free to say what the ticking is telling you. One . . . Two . . . Three."

"Fairy."

"Fairy?" repeated Nigel, his forehead wrinkling.

"Fair . . . eee. Fair . . . eee. Fair . . . eee."

"Allow yourself now to see that word 'Fairy' as a cloud, Larry. Walk all around it. Touch it. Feel it. And in your own time, when you're ready . . . ease back into it. That's right. Go ahead. Lie down. Good. Now let it take you where it wants to take you. And when it lands again, tell me where you are."

Another long while passed.

"I'm in my house," said Larry. Then, he swallowed hard.

"And now—right where you are standing in that house—if you were to turn right and walk straight ahead, what room would that take you to?"

"The den."

"Describe the den."

Larry was quite relaxed by now, so much so that he didn't even hear his secretary's voice when it came over the intercom, announcing some phone call. Quickly Nigel thumbed the "mute" button on the intercom. His eyes went back to Larry, who was beginning to speak again.

"Toys . . . round rug . . . toys everywhere . . . there's a lamp on in the corner . . . very warm . . . someone's lying on the couch . . ."

"Someone?"

"Yeah. Someone," said Larry. "I can't see his face."

"But you know it's a 'him'?"

Larry nodded.

"And where are you in the room?"

"By the TV."

"And Mom?"

"Gone. Dad's gone, too."

"He'll turn his face away from the back of the couch in a moment," said Nigel. "Now he's looking at you."

"He called me 'Fairy.'"

"Who?"

"John."

"John? John is on the couch?"

"He's my brother."

"What else is in the den?"

"Books."

"Books?"

Larry still appeared relaxed, except for his hands. By now, his fists were clenched at his side.

"He made me read them. He said he'd beat me up if I didn't. He said I was a fairy if I didn't."

Nigel sat back in his chair and looked thoughtfully at Larry. "What sort of books are they, Larry? You're looking at one of them now, right?"

Larry nodded, his brow curdling in confusion and distress.

"Calm down now, Larry," Nigel soothed. "It's only a book—ink on a page. It can't hurt you."

"But it's bad!" whined Larry, his eyeballs leaping about beneath his closed eyelids. "It's wrong to read about these things—nasty..."

"What are you reading, Larry?" pressed Nigel. "They're only words—not right or wrong—only words. Tell me the words. What are they about?"

Larry jerked his head to one side, like a horse refusing the bit. "It's...about men and women...doing...doing bad things."

Nigel nodded in satisfaction. "I see. The books are about sex, are they, Larry?"

Larry nodded. "John made me read them. He said if I didn't he'd beat me—"

"It's quite all right, Larry," soothed Nigel. "Sex isn't bad. It's . . ." The psychiatrist searched for words that would pierce the resistant shell of Larry's anxiety. ". . . it's a God-given pleasure, Larry. He invented sex."

"Not this way," fretted Larry. "Not the things they do in the books—"

"Now, Larry," Nigel said in a calming tone, "don't be so scared. The things in those books can't hurt you. In fact, you need to face up to your greatest fears . . ."

This had gone on long enough! I reached out to Larry, probing for a link with the little boy who knew, far better than the man, when to be frightened at the approach of evil.

"Take the Way!" I prayed on Larry's behalf. "The Spirit of the Almighty will show you the Way! Flee, Larry! You'll find no help here!"

Larry fidgeted on the couch. "I'm not sure I want to continue," he said. "Can we resume tomorrow? Maybe over lunch?"

"Just a few minutes more, Larry," wheedled the voice of Nigel Hendrickson.

Then Stool was in the room, standing between me and Larry. He growled at me.

Dias stood, and edged toward the slavering spirit by the couch. "Back off, Stool," he warned.

Stool tossed his head and grinned. "What's the matter with that little twerp?" he said, pointing at me. "Can't he fight? You'd have me two-to-one—or maybe he's the real fairy here."

I kept praying. But his words stung.

"Don't listen to him, Skandalon!" warned Dias, turning to me. "He's trying to—"

Stool had dived into Dias, at once lifting him in a bear-hug and pinning him against the shelves, then butting him with his own stone-hard forehead. When Dias's head slumped forward, the spirit sank his fangs deep into his skull. I saw the muscles in the demon's back and neck bunching, and he was just about to rip backward when Dias's hand, reaching blindly along the shelf above him, raked a sheaf of papers off the shelf. The pages fell in a haphazard shower, straight toward the spirit's face.

Shrieks filled the room. Each leaf of paper sliced Stool like a scimitar. He clawed his face. He roared. He swung wildly, blindly, trying to reach his opponent.

Larry stood up, glancing toward the bookshelf where a breeze from the heater vent had disturbed a pile of sermon outlines.

"Nigel, I think it's best to call it a day. I'd like to stop now."

"I understand," Nigel said, sounding disappointed. "But we were uncovering so much . . ."

"And it will still be there to uncover tomorrow."

"Well, if that's how it must be. We'll finish this later." Nigel stood to leave.

"Yes," said Larry, rubbing his face. "Maybe later."

After the door had closed behind Nigel, Larry went behind the desk, and began gathering and stacking the sheets of paper which had fallen off the shelf. As he worked, the thought occurred to him that he and Nigel should have started the session with a prayer. He always began his pastoral counseling in that fashion. Odd that he hadn't thought of suggesting it. He shrugged, and replaced the outlines atop the bookshelf.

THE
EXCOMMUNICATION

GUNNER knocked once on the heavy wooden door to Larry's office, then waited for an answer. The pastor had been so insistent yet so evasive about why this meeting was necessary in the middle of the week.

After what seemed an endless period of shuffling his feet and looking up and down the hall, he heard from behind the door the words, "Come in, please." *Why so formal, all of a sudden?* he thought.

He went in. The office he entered was warm—and dim. The shades were pulled down, and the ancient radiator blasted its heat silently from behind Larry's desk. The coffee-maker gurgled in the corner. To Gunner's surprise, the church elders lined the room's perimeter, all ten sitting with arms folded, staring at him. In the shadows cast by the lamp on Larry's desk, Gunner couldn't clearly see their faces.

"Hello, Gunner. I apologize for the short notice. Please take a seat," came a voice in the direction of the heat. It was Larry, seated behind the massive desk. "How are you today?" The tone was familiar, and yet foreign.

"Uh, fine, Larry... just fine," he replied doubtfully as he peered around the room. The others maintained their silence. "Shouldn't somebody open a window shade?" Gunner continued. "I can't see a thing in here." The thin lines of winter brightness between the shades and the window frames added just enough backlighting to conceal, rather than illuminate.

"Why don't you have a seat over here, beside the desk," responded Larry. Gunner shrugged, shuffling toward the indicated chair. He seated himself, wondering madly why he and Larry were doing all the talking in a roomful of men they'd both known most of their lives. His anxiety was growing by the second. He wiped his palms on his pant legs and squirmed in the straight-backed chair.

"I've known you for quite a long time," said Larry from behind the desk. "As has just about everyone in the room, I suppose..."

"Yes, I guess that's about right," said Gunner.

Larry continued. "I know that having all these eyes upon you must be terribly uncomfortable. But there's really no other way. That's how we function as a governing body, here at the church."

Another man spoke. "Gunner, something's been brought to the attention of the elders."

"And what is it, Richard?" said Gunner, his tone revealing more than a hint of hostility. He resented the atmosphere in the room; he felt like a heretic at an inquisition.

"That you have some behaviors in your life that are immoral," said Richard, without further ceremony. "Do you have anything to say?"

Gunner felt a sudden sense of claustrophobia sweep over him, not unlike he remembered as a schoolboy when being questioned by the principal. At the same time, anger bubbled up within him. What right did they have to call him on the carpet like this?

"Immoral? Well, now, I don't exactly know. Do beer and poker count?" He no longer troubled to conceal his irritation.

Richard was taken aback. Another voice jumped in the fray.

"I believe drunkenness and gambling *do* count, Gunner. But this is no joking matter!"

"Well, what is it, then?" Gunner shot back. He was on full defensive alert.

"How about debauchery?" said another. "Lust . . . lewdness . . . whoremongering?"

"Debauchery. Now there's a word I haven't heard for a while." *So that's what this is all about!* His chest began heaving as he wondered fiercely who had been telling tales out of school. *What is this—the KGB?*

"Haven't you been going to the Sunset Grille, Gunner?" asked Larry.

Gunner turned toward his friend. "I've been there once," he replied sullenly.

Richard entered back in.

"We've been told by someone outside the church that he saw you in the bottom level—and that you go there quite often."

"How would you know what's on the bottom level?" demanded Gunner. "You been down there, have you?" The heat from the radiator was becoming unbearable.

"Certainly not!" hissed Richard. "So," he pressed, "you don't deny frequenting the bottom level?"

Gunner said nothing. He had already told them he'd gone there. They had their minds made up anyway—anything he might say would only be twisted and used further against him.

"So you do frequent the Sunset Grille?" said Larry.

Gunner held his tongue. He could hardly believe the words coming from the lips of his friends.

Larry continued. "As you know, this type of thing, especially from a professing Christian, calls for discipline."

Now they're getting to it, he thought. Gunner wasn't even sure he was a Christian anymore, much less a professing one...unless, of course, the only prerequisite for being one in this church was to show up on Sunday.

"We're left with one recourse," said a new voice. "We're asking you to leave the church until you publicly rectify the matter."

"I'm sorry, Gunner. That will be all for today," said Larry, whose voice by now, along with the others, sounded to Gunner like an irritating mix of gurgling coffee, clanging radiator, and self-righteous condemnation.

Suddenly the whole thing was over, and he was out in the hallway, breathing better air and feeling a great deal less warm.

Gunner McGuffy returned home from the meeting in Larry's office an excommunicated man. Surprisingly, he didn't feel that much sense of loss. On the contrary, he felt free...free to tell his friends that what he'd suspected of the church all along was true. They were hypocrites to the core, false shepherds with no real love for the flock. *If one little slipup was enough for them to turn on one of their own, then who needs 'em?* he thought. Of course he would leave out the part about the Sunset Grille. There was no need for anyone to know about that. Besides, it was only one time...at least, here lately...

* * *

Back at the church, Larry waited until his colleagues had all left the office and gone home. Then he hurried down the hallway to the restroom, threw open the door to one of the stalls, and vomited until the emptiness in his gut matched that in his soul.

THE
NEGOTIATION

IT WAS Saturday, the day Larry usually spent with Peter and Annie and addressing Rose's "honey-do" list. But today was different. There was "someone he had to see over at the office," he had told her. He promised to be back by lunch. She shrugged, and took another drink of coffee. Since the previous Sunday, when he had read from the pulpit the letter announcing withdrawal of fellowship from Gunner, Rose had hardly spoken three words to him.

He walked out. How long could he go on? How long before someone saw through his carefully cultured facade, to the rottenness beneath? But when these thoughts crept into his mind, he sternly shut them out. *Got to tend to business,* he told himself. *Got to get that place shut down.* It was all he thought about anymore—as if by closing the Sunset Grille he could atone for the darkness in his own soul.

Perhaps a week and a half had passed since the experience in the slaughterhouse, and during Larry's increasingly infrequent bouts of self-honesty, he could admit that the guilt of that evening—and the need to conceal it—was what drove him on. And yet with his next breath he could fool himself into thinking of yet another defense: If he could just see the Grille fall, the rot in his soul would go down with it, and his healing would be accomplished.

He headed to the center of town, where he hoped to find the man for whom he was looking—without running into too many other folks on the way. It was about seven-thirty, but in front of the Paradise Donut Shop only two cars were parked. Larry pulled up behind them. Across the street, the red-brick, windowless Grille squatted. Larry took a deep breath, got out of the car, glanced up and down the street, and crossed to the other side. It was time to declare his real intentions, to look the other man in the eye and say, "I'm going to close you down."

He opened the door. Unaccustomed to the darkness inside, and unsure if Billy Bobb Detzer would even be at his place of business at such an early hour, he knocked on the door that he was still holding open.

"Come on in," said a voice from his right. Larry cautiously let the door close, and entered the darkness of the Grille.

"Howdy," said the voice. Larry saw a white-haired man seated at the bar. "Place isn't open yet, but come in anyway." He smiled, then did a double-take. "Why... it's ... no, wait a minute," he mumbled, staring intently at Larry's face.

Larry shifted uneasily from one foot to the other under the gaze of the Grille's manager. He stuck out his hand. "My name is Ravelle—Larry Ravelle."

Billy Bobb slapped his leg and chuckled. "Sure, that's it! I knew I recognized your face!" He grabbed Larry's hand and shook it heartily. "You're the preacher fella, right?"

Larry nodded, puzzled. "Yes, but ... I don't recall seeing you in church—"

"Not me, fella!" laughed Billy Bobb. "Oh, excuse me ... I mean *Reverend*—"

"Just call me Larry," the pastor suggested. "Everyone else does."

"If you say so—Larry," Billy Bobb said, just as Larry's eyes were momentarily distracted by a movement he perceived in an enormous mirror behind the bar.

"Say," Billy Bobb suggested, "why don't we move back to my office?" He indicated a doorway at the end of the bar. Larry shrugged, and the two men moved to the walnut-paneled suite of rooms which served as the manager's office—and his sleeping and living quarters, as well.

"Yeah," Billy Bobb grunted when they were both settled in leather-covered armchairs, "this is much more comfortable." They were seated facing a desk and the wall-to-wall bookshelves behind it. Larry found himself caught off guard by the manager's congeniality.

"Well, now, Larry! I'm delighted you've come to visit," chuckled Billy Bobb, who sat casually in his chair, one leg draped over the arm nearest Larry. "I do hope you can stay awhile. It's such a good time for a man like yourself to come, Larry ... with all the customers gone, I mean."

Larry nodded, smiling tightly. "Yes, I guess you're right, ah—Billy Bobb, is it?"

The older man nodded.

"I'm curious about something, Billy Bobb."

"Fire away!" grinned the manager, with an open-armed gesture.

"You acted like you recognized me—and yet I don't recall ever seeing you before."

"No, Larry, I didn't recognize you, actually. In a manner of speaking, though, your face is quite familiar." He grinned expectantly.

Larry looked at the manager for several seconds before the answer came to him. John! His twin brother must be a regular here.

Billy Bobb saw the realization dawning across the pastor's face, and began nodding. "I think we're on the same wavelength now—right, Larry?"

The clock on the manager's wall chimed three times.

"I'm going to close you down, sir," said Larry. He looked straight in Billy Bobb's eye when he spoke.

"And you still have your manners!" said Billy Bobb approvingly, not missing a beat. "I like that about you, son. Most folks lose their politeness when they go on a crusade." He smiled and gave a sad little chuckle, shaking his head. "Well," he said, looking at Larry from the corner of his eye, "I guess you gotta do what you gotta do. Let me ask you just one favor—all right?"

"What's that?" Larry asked guardedly.

"Just make sure the newspaper stories spell the name of this place right." As Billy Bobb grinned at him, Larry felt his skin prickling with a premonition of evil. The manager went on.

"You know, a face-off like you and I are about to have will generate a lot of heat and light. And publicity is the lifeblood of a place like this, Larry. Publicity and curiosity."

Larry had no reply.

"Folks will be asking themselves, *Wonder if it's really as bad as that preacher fella says?* They'll stew on that awhile, and swish it around in their minds, and they'll up and decide to come have a look-see." Billy Bobb chuckled at Larry's chagrined, doubtful look. "Yes sir, Reverend, I might just do enough extra business out of this little flap of ours that I could *afford* to shut the place down."

"Then you won't oppose us?" asked Larry, an irrational hope starting within him.

"Oh, of course I will," said Billy Bobb, dismissing Larry's budding optimism with a wave of the hand. "I've never been the sort to take something like this lying down. I've also never been the sort to be without an ace up his sleeve." He rubbed his nose, and smiled slyly at Larry. "I've even been getting ready for a possible shut-down. I found a new location."

"Oh?" said Larry.

"You didn't expect me to just pack up and change careers, did you? This stuff sells! And you'd be surprised who's buying! Of course, you've already heard about your brother."

Larry's jaw tightened. Detzer continued, knowing he'd hit a nerve.

"Yeah, John and I have gotten to be pretty good friends. You know, he comes here nearly every night except Fridays. The girls downstairs say he's a good tipper, too." Billy Bobb leaned back in his chair, smirking at Larry's troubled expression.

Larry thought of a way to change the subject.

"We'll start all over then, Mr. Detzer," he said. "We'll close your new place as well."

"Not unless Ellenbach is talking about expanding its borders. No. Uh-uh. You can't touch me out there," Billy Bobb said smugly. He lit a burl pipe he had retrieved from a jacket pocket.

"And where is this new location?" asked Larry.

"A great place. Outside the city limits. I believe the 'suits' will like it, too." And as Billy Bobb spoke, Larry's eye caught something on the shelf above the manager's head—and he shuddered. It was a dust-covered thing... a cordovan thing... familiar, yet until this time never so important. It was the shoe. *His* shoe. And he realized it must have been Billy Bobb's car approaching that night at the slaughterhouse. Billy Bobb must have retrieved the shoe and brought it here. *Does he know?* Was this the reason for Billy Bobb's grin—for the overdone good-old-boy act? Did Billy Bobb plan to reveal what he knew—or suspected?

So intent was Larry on this frenzied line of reasoning that he didn't hear a word of the manager's explanation until the older man said the word, "shoe."

"What?" Larry asked, suddenly snapping back to the conversation.

"The shoe," said Billy Bobb. "That's where I found that shoe." He pointed to the loafer and looked at Larry. "It was peculiar, as you might imagine, to find it out there. I don't expect too many people have seen the place in a long while."

Larry hoped desperately that his expression was adequately puzzled. "Where is 'there'?" he asked.

Billy Bob laughed. "Have you been following me at all, Reverend?"

"Of course," Larry answered. "I just…"

"The slaughterhouse, Larry. The old Morton place out on the Laird highway. It's not being used for anything. I figure I might as well take a look at it. And you know what else, Larry?"

"No—what?" asked Larry absently.

"I found this out there, too." Billy Bobb got up and walked around behind his desk. He opened the lap drawer, rummaged around a while, and came up with a glossy-paged magazine. Larry recognized the risqué cover all too well, though he strove with all his might to keep the familiarity off his face.

"I figure the same fella that lost the shoe left this out there, Reverend," said Billy Bobb. "If the kids are used to goin' out there for a little thrill, I imagine it wouldn't be

too hard to get them to come out for a *real* good time—
what do you think?" Billy Bobb was clearly enjoying the
discomfort on Larry's face—although Larry hoped feverishly he didn't understand its true source.

"I don't know about that," said Larry in a daze. He
couldn't get his mind off the shoe . . . and every time the
manager looked away from him, he glanced at it.

Larry felt sick. He thought for a moment this meeting
was a nightmare and that he would be waking up soon.
Then he would gladly find that no discovery had been
made. His reputation would be safe again. He would be
free and clear.

But the longer he sat, the more he realized that things
around him were tangible, and that his hand against the
cushion felt as far from dreamlike as it possibly could. He
began to think and act like a man who is trapped. He
considered angles and alibis. The realization that Billy
Bobb had not only found his shoe, but come across the
magazine as well, became an obsession. *How could I have
been such a fool?* he thought.

"Are you all right, Reverend?" asked Billy Bobb.

"I'm fine, thank you," Larry said quickly. He wiped his
forehead. "It is a little hot in here," he added. Then he
tried to make a joke. "Maybe I'm just not used to the
surroundings."

"That must be it," agreed the manager. "After all, a
man of your profession would have no real reason or
desire to be acquainted with such things." Then Billy
Bobb slapped his forehead with an open palm. "Now I've
gone and done it! I've stuck my brogan in my mouth
again!"

"What do you mean?" asked Larry.

"There! See? You *have* been offended. I knew it. I knew
I should have bit my tongue. But, of course I went on.

166

And now...now I've offended you," Billy Bobb said, shaking his head solicitously.

Larry stammered, "But I am not in the least...Whatever gave you the idea that..."

"Naturally," said Billy Bobb, "there's no reason why you shouldn't be just as virile as the next man...as any layman, even. And here I am, making out like a preacher-type wouldn't have any interest in the goings-on downstairs. I sure am sorry, Larry!"

"Well—"

"Say no more, Larry...except to forgive me for insulting your manhood."

"But—"

"Confound it, Reverend! Quit trying to make it easy on me. It's my mouth that gets me into trouble, and it's my mouth that ought to get me out of it. Please...just accept my apology!"

Gratefully, Larry latched onto the manager's proffered apology as the escape for which he was looking. He nearly fell over himself forgiving Billy Bobb—happy to get the focus off himself. "Don't worry about it," he said, "most people don't realize pastors are humans, too."

"You're too kind," said Billy Bobb. "It's a pity we're on opposite sides of the fence about this place. I think I could learn to like you."

The pastor and the club manager shook hands and walked from the office across the dark, abandoned floor of the Grille.

"Listen, Larry," said Billy Bobb when they reached the door, "don't be a stranger around here." At Larry's admonitory look, he hastily added, "Now, I don't mean during business hours! Mercy sakes, I would never expect that! No, I mean—like today. When it's just the two of us."

"Well, Billy Bobb," said Larry, smiling a little, "I guess

that invitation could go both ways. I've visited your place of business—why don't you come visit mine?" He waited for the white-haired man's response.

The manager grinned, knowing he'd been had. "Well, I guess fair's fair. But—" he held up a cautionary forefinger—"not during business hours!"

Larry laughed, hoping his outward ease was concealing his apprehension about the shoe. "Like you said," he replied aloud, "when it's just the two of us."

Billy Bobb opened the door for his visitor. "There you go. Bye, now!"

Larry nodded, and the two men parted ways.

Billy Bobb closed the door. "Come back now," he sneered, then laughed aloud, the sound rattling like the crack of a whip around the empty room.

I WATCHED Larry walk away, more worried than ever. His guilt was a screaming alarm, and I knew Pitch, in heightened power now, was only too eager to exploit Larry's anxiety for his reputation—not to mention the pathology which the pastor carried with him from childhood. The tempter stood beside me on the sidewalk, smirking as Larry drove away from downtown, back toward his home. He turned toward me, saying in his maddeningly familiar voice, "Look up there." He was pointing to the roof of the Grille. "Recognize my partner?"

I shaded my eyes and looked up at the roof. On the ridge, along the gutters, and atop the chimney were dozens of blackbirds. They were unusually large for their species, and their eyes were a sort of jaundiced yellow. Their feathers were not the usual glossy blue-black, but more the dull color of dung. And not one of them (at least as long as I was watching) ceased fluttering up from his perch and then back down...only to take flight all over again—as if the contact of its feet with something solid caused it pain.

Pitch erupted in laughter. He held his sides as if by pressure he might be able to keep it in his belly. But it came spilling out all the same, causing him to fall off the curb into the street. He was nearly run over by a pickup when it rounded the corner and sped south. I thought the near mishap might sober him, but he only got worse. With palms flat on the pavement and legs sprawling, Pitch threw back his head and laughed.

It was then I noticed for the first time his teeth. They flashed in the sun like a knife that has been finely sharpened. The angle of his head let me look along their edge as a craftsman might when inspecting his work. And if he has done his job well, when he holds the knife up to the light there will be no discernible reflection where the two sides meet...only a line of black. Somewhere in Hell, there was one who knew his craft.

The birds took wing and followed Larry. Pitch got to his feet.

"My dear Stumbling Block, I hate to run so soon, but I've got to stick with my partner...uh, that is...partners." This nearly started him laughing again, but he caught himself. Then he followed the birds toward Larry's house.

Larry fumed and fretted all that day, ceaselessly coming back to the worrisome presence of the damning shoe in the manager's office. He played and replayed everything Billy Bobb had said, looking for some clue, some indication of how the affable man at the Grille might deploy his trophy.

Sleep evaded him that night. He got up three times

and paced the house. By morning he had a plan, for he remembered in particular one comment Detzer had made. He recited it to himself over a solitary bowl of breakfast cereal: *You know,* Billy Bobb had said, *he comes here nearly every night except Fridays.*

THE PLAN

LARRY was beginning to feel like a lad who has skated out onto the thinnest part of a frozen lake, and finding himself in such a predicament, decides to fling aside his blades and dance.

Things were starting to move too quickly, in too many different directions.

He'd been notified that the television interview for the Kurt Stedley Show was coming up in less than two weeks. Meanwhile, the prospect of his shoe being found inside the Grille, and the devastating admission such a discovery would entail, was driving him to distraction. He needed to focus on his preparation for the TV debate—for that was how the confrontation was being hyped, he was almost certain. Further, the rumor mill at City Hall had let it slip that Sheriff Sweeney was getting close to making an arrest in the Hansen case. Larry wanted to have everything in place to capitalize on the renewed public furor when the accused man was brought in.

There was also his knowledge that the publicity being

generated by the effort against the Grille was striking a chord within many churches in many communities. Larry knew well that the success or failure of this issue, even in little Ellenbach, would have far-reaching implications—for himself professionally, as well as for other communities.

And then . . . there were the difficulties at home. Peter and Annie could sense the friction in the air above their heads, and began, in their individual ways, to act out the frustration and fear they could not verbalize.

Peter became sullen and withdrawn—almost rebellious, at times. He had begun talking back, making sarcastic comments under his breath when asked to do almost anything. Nothing pleased him these days, and his customary expression was one of dissatisfaction looking for a target.

Annie, on the other hand, had become clingy and more vocal. She whined more and more, and about things less and less consequential. She would hardly let her mother out of her sight. The stress of the Grille campaign would have been bad enough, but with a nagging, complaining six-year-old thrown in, life at the Ravelle household became a daily gauntlet.

And of course . . . Rose. Larry had to sigh when he thought of the differences in his wife, even from a few weeks ago. She looked haggard—there was no other way to put it. But she wouldn't talk to him. At times—he had to admit, to his shame—he was relieved that this was so. He didn't know how to converse around the nasty hole in the center of his conscience—she would be sure to spot the falseness in him, if she hadn't already. He told himself that when everything was over, he'd sit down with her and work through the painful issues. He hoped that wouldn't be too little too late.

Despite all the pressures and counter-pressures twisting his soul into a pretzel, his paranoia over the shoe and the magazine was the preoccupation that ruled his days and nights. It was the weak spot, the Achilles' heel that he most feared. It gave him no rest; it inhibited his efforts to effectively prepare and coordinate. Each time he had a few moments of quiet, all he could think about was what Billy Bobb might know, what he might be preparing to do. And so it became imperative to him to put his plan into effect sooner, rather than later.

LARRY lied to Rose, telling her he had a late committee meeting at the church. He felt bad about it, he really did. But despite his firmly squelched remorse, the stench of the lie rose from him in a plume of guilt that, to one with my vision, was as evident as a muddy bootprint on a white tile floor. He felt bad about lying to her, even congratulated himself for having "a tender conscience" —but he lied to her all the same.

Dias and I sat on the kitchen counter listening to the whole thing, and we agreed we had never seen him so distraught. Of course, Pitch was only too eager to help Larry with this bit of falsehood. He stood with his lips near the pastor's ear, mouthing the optimal words to effect the deception. Then Stool and he took turns accusing and excusing the man. It was all my partner could do to keep himself planted firmly on the Formica, as he watched the demons at work.

Stool's words were gibberish, mostly. He was so consumed with filth himself that he was obscenely delighted at others' evil . . . to the point of frenzy. Even so, in his mad whipping about, and his frothing, and his inarticulations, there were sensible phrases here and there.

"You lied!" he shrieked. "See! See there!" Then he would fly off into rapid profanity and nonsense.

"See there, indeed, Sir Stool," said Pitch. "But see

here, too. After all, he *is* going to a meeting of sorts, isn't he? I see no real problems with his story."

"He's lusty, lusty, lusty! A lusty liar! That's all! That's all!" shouted Stool. Foam appeared on the demon's lips as he leaped onto the kitchen table, stabbing his foot on the stem of a banana, yet ignoring his wound. Stool's mania for Larry's weakness seemed to make him forget his terra firma curse.

"Oh, come now, Stool. He's not as awful as you paint him," soothed Pitch. "You forget, he's a preacher!"

"He'll preach all right! In Hell! Yes! Yes! Yes! We need one like him! He'll do! He'll do!" gabbled Stool, jumping up on the kitchen range, where one of the burners had been left on by mistake.

Larry massaged his temples. "Honey," he said to his wife, "I've got a headache all of a sudden. Could you get me some aspirin or something?" Rose returned with some aspirin and a glass of water, along with his coat. She moved listlessly, as if one set of motions was as good as another. Larry swallowed the aspirin while he leaned against the sink. And he stared at his brother's picture. . . .

"Why don't you pray?" I whispered to Larry. "Pray in the Holy Spirit!"

"No fair! No fair! No fair!" screamed Stool, who squatted on the stove with his heels smoking. He grinned and grimaced alternately, as if he couldn't make up his mind whether to pay attention to his pain.

"He's right," said Pitch. "No coaching. Tsk-tsk . . ." He gave me a sarcastic, admonitory look.

"So help me," growled Dias. "If Larry so much as utters an 'Our Father,' I'll . . ."

"Yes. We all know the outcome," sighed Pitch, studying his own hooked fingernails. "You'll beat the daylights out of me and my partner, and we'll have to pack up and move back to Hell. Bore, bore, bore," he said, shaking his head. "Aren't you tired of the whole setup? I mean, tell me...how much fulfillment can there be in a job that depends totally on the feeble petitions of a—" he chuckled—"a 'saint' like Larry here? Don't you ever get to flex your muscles on your own? Wouldn't that be more like it?

"Come to think of it," Pitch continued with a smirk, "you must be in terrible shape for an angel your size, what with such a lack of prayer among the 'brethren.' Why, I'd bet I could lick you myself! Come on down from there, Dias my boy, and spar with ol' Pitch." He grinned and shadow-boxed at the refrigerator.

Dias stiffened next to me. Stool sat cross-legged now on the red-hot burners, laughing, even as the stench of burning demon filled the kitchen...

Larry set his glass of water in the sink and slipped on his coat.

"I'll be back pretty late, babe," he said. "Don't wait up. I may be awhile—Rose? What's wrong?"

Rose had an anxious look on her face, and she had placed both her hands on her abdomen. "I...I don't know," she was saying. "All of a sudden, my stomach..."

Dias was on his feet in an instant, striding angrily toward Stool—who had come down from atop the stove and was hugging Rose around the waist, rolling his eyes about in his head in an obscene parody of ecstasy.

But before my partner could reach Stool, Pitch leaped across the table and began pounding the larger demon savagely in the face with his fists. Dias and I looked on in astonishment.

"Let go of her, you imbecile!" Pitch cursed, as Stool

began to cower under his blows. "Don't touch, don't touch, don't touch!" he screamed at Stool, punctuating each word with a blow to the jaw. "I've told you a thousand times since we've been on this case, but you just can't keep your paws off the lady, can you?" Stool fell back on the floor.

Pitch brought his bared fangs within inches of his partner's quivering cheek. "Our object here is not to coddle our cravings with some pathetic, watered-down human female."

I heard Dias's teeth grinding together, but he stayed back.

Pitch sunk his claws into the loose flesh of Stool's chest and banged the hairy giant slowly and repeatedly against the floor as he went on. "I will set the strategy for this campaign—I and I alone!"

Dias and I had a momentary glimpse of the hierarchy of the ranks of the rebellion. Pitch's expression was that of one in complete and knowing mastery of a contemptible inferior. And for his part, Stool was nearly shriveled with fright. He was clearly aware of something in his smaller counterpart that was blacker, fouler, and stronger than I had imagined, until now.

"Do you want me to call the doctor?" Larry asked.

"No . . . I'm fine," she said, "really. It's passed now. But there for a moment . . ." She laid her hands on her abdomen and probed about lightly. "It's gone now."

"This has been hard on all of us," Larry said. He went to Rose and held her. "I'll make it up to you. I promise."

"When, Larry?" she replied in a tone devoid of hope. "When will that be?"

The two of them sighed . . . the exhausted sigh of two boxers, leaning on each other in the final round, both too tired to land another blow. Rose rested her head on his shoulder.

"Do you really have to go again tonight?" she asked in a voice that already knew the answer. Larry nodded his chin against her head. He patted her back once, twice, three times. Then he pulled on his coat and walked out the side door, into the night.

THE
RECONNAISSANCE

Larry went to the church and into his office, switching on the light he knew Rose would be watching for from the living room window of the parsonage across the way. He stayed there, mentally rehearsing his plan and fidgeting nervously, until he saw the lights go out in his house. Fifteen minutes later, he crept out of the church, leaving the office lights on. Huddling as far as he could into his coat against the cold night wind, he began walking toward the downtown area.

He reached the flashing neon of the Paradise Donut Shop, across the street from the Grille. He glanced up at the sign's light, its bright cheer ringing hollow, somehow, against the dreariness of the winter. PARADISE DONUT SHOP, it proclaimed in bright blue, with "Open Early & Late" underneath in smaller letters.

Larry looked around carefully to see if anyone was watching, then went inside. He was relieved to see that Cyrus, the proprietor, was in the back when he came in, and hadn't heard the door open and shut. Larry wasn't in the mood for conversation. In fact, the fewer people he

178

talked with, the fewer who would have cause to wonder why the pastor was wandering about downtown at such an hour. There was a dark corner by the window which gave a view of the Sunset Grille. Larry slumped into a chair and tried to become invisible, keeping one eye on the front door of the Grille, the other on the on-and-off glow of the sidewalk under the neon sign of the donut shop.

Across the street, the door to the Grille thumped open and a man staggered out. Larry sat up a bit straighter, then settled back into his seat when he realized the man wasn't the one he had come to observe.

The fellow across the street first looked right, then to the left, then stepped quickly into the street. As he crossed toward the Paradise Donut Shop, Larry could see the man's breath puffing out in front of him in the cold, neon-lit air.

He entered the donut shop, his feet clumping noisily against the pine-planked floor, and turned to close the door. He untied his scarf, letting it hang loosely over the lapels of his overcoat. Then he chose a seat at the farthest remove from the direction of the Sunset Grille, and sat with his back to Larry, his shoulders sloping in fatigue— or dejection.

Larry caught a glimpse of the man's face in the light of the donut shop sign, and couldn't believe his eyes. It was Todd Blakemore! In his mind Larry pictured Todd sitting in the third pew from the front of the left side of Ellenbach Community Church, with his wife and three children ranged beside him. He was a regular attender— was even being considered for a deacon's position! *Todd . . . a patron of the Sunset Grille?* He huddled deeper in his coat, hoping more fervently than ever to avoid notice.

Cyrus Daye had heard Todd's entrance, and came out of the back—dusting flour off his hands, as usual.

"Evenin', Todd," said Cyrus.

"Evenin'."

"Coffee?"

"No. I just wanna sit. Thanks, though."

"You're welcome," replied Cyrus, looking thoughtfully at Todd for a moment. "Mind if I get some of this stuff cleaned up while you're sittin'?"

Todd shook his head.

Cyrus peered at him a half-second longer, then went about his work. He showed no sign of realizing Larry's presence.

The kitchen door swung open and shut on its hinges as Cyrus cleared the trays in the display, and the mixer hummed an electric testimony of tomorrow's goodies. Larry wondered how the baker did it: He had never come into the donut shop at any time, day or night, when Cyrus wasn't here dispensing coffee, pastries, and conversation. How did a fellow as old as Cyrus have the stamina to run a place—singlehandedly, as far as anyone could tell, and for five years—that stayed open so many hours? Even in a little place like Ellenbach, a man had to have some time to rest.

Larry could see Todd trembling. Every so often, as if being dragged by a magnet too strong to resist, Todd's eyes would rise to peer out the window of the donut shop—toward the Sunset Grille. Then he would drop his gaze again to the tabletop on which his elbows leaned.

The pastor didn't dare make a sound. He told himself he didn't want to embarrass Todd, but a small portion of his mind whispered a less noble reason for maintaining anonymity.

The mixer wound down slowly until it, too, rested in silence. Through the windows in the swinging doors, Larry could see the baker covering the bowl with a large piece of cheesecloth. The old man switched off the kitchen lights, and walked slowly out into the main room.

"You gonna sit all night, Todd?" he asked.

A long silence. Then, "I would if I could." Todd's voice was lifeless.

"Well, can't I at least get you a cup of coffee?"

"No, Cyrus . . . I'll be moving along in a minute."

"Take your time, son . . . really," said Cyrus. "I'm in no hurry. You wanna talk?"

"You wanna listen?" asked Todd.

Larry slumped further into the back corner booth of the shop. When Cyrus took a chair from an adjacent table and slid it over next to Todd's, Larry could have sworn the baker looked at him—but no. Cyrus turned the chair backwards and straddled it, resting his elbows on the chair's back. For a moment, the two men were silent, Todd staring blankly at the tabletop, Cyrus studying Todd's profile.

"Why aren't you home with the family, son?" the older man asked, finally.

"Same reason I wasn't two nights ago," came the haunted, guilty voice. Todd shrugged weakly and said, "It's not that important."

"Maybe not," said the baker, "but looks to me like you're only sayin' that from the teeth out."

Todd didn't answer. He ran his thumb along the edge of the table and stared out the window.

"You been there again, son?" asked Cyrus, pointing out toward the Sunset Grille.

"Look," flared Todd. "Cut the 'son' stuff, okay? I'm a grown man. Same as you."

"All right, Todd, all right," agreed Cyrus, quietly. After a stretch of silence, he persisted. "But if that's so, then why're you hidin' out in the dark . . . like you was afraid to go home or somethin'?"

"I'm not afraid." Todd's words contradicted his demeanor.

"What's eatin' you then?"

"You already know!" shouted Todd. The shop echoed with his voice. "It's the same thing we talk about all the time," he finished in a miserable croak.

"*You* talk about it," said the baker. "Your eyes and your hands do the talkin'. I just ask the right questions, now and then."

"I guess I don't need to say a single word to you, then," pouted Todd. "I don't need you—and maybe I don't need anybody..." His voice was whispery—hoarse and constricted. "I wish I'd never been born." He started shaking, with his head in his hands. Cyrus kept quiet for now.

The electric Coca-Cola clock rattled and ground on the wall. Larry turned to look out again across the street. On the sidewalk in front of the Sunset Grille another man made his way to the door. Larry instinctively leaned closer to the window, risking being heard and seen by Cyrus and Todd. Then he was certain. It was him—the man he'd come to see.

Across the street, John Ravelle was tugging on the cold-jammed latch of the Sunset Grille.

Cyrus had seen him too. He jerked a thumb toward the window, and spoke quietly to Todd: "You want out of that place just as bad as that fellow wants in, don't you?" Todd turned to see what he was pointing to, and watched as the form of John Ravelle finally entered the Grille.

Cyrus leaned close to Todd's ear. "You know...there's a way out, son," he said in a whisper.

Todd cringed, and suddenly stood to go. Then he looked again at the baker. "Maybe so, Cyrus. But somehow, I get lost on my way there..."

Larry wanted to see what his brother was wearing. He

182

squinted hard through the glass. The yellow light above the Grille's entrance distorted the color, but Larry recognized immediately his brother's work clothes. Then John disappeared behind the wooden door. As it closed, Larry heard footsteps behind him, and the sound of Cyrus's door opening. In the flashing neon light, Larry watched Todd step out onto the sidewalk in front of Paradise Donuts. The man hurried away into the dark.

Cyrus glanced at him, as if seeing him for the first time. "Excuse me, sir," he said, "I didn't see you—oh! Hello, Larry!"

Larry flushed with embarrassment, though there was really no need for it. "Howdy, Cyrus." After a few seconds of awkward silence, he added, "Sounded like a pretty serious discussion you were having. I didn't want to butt in."

"Oh, well . . ." the baker said, staring into the vacant air to his right. "Me 'n' him—we talk a lot. That's all. Always tryin' to figure out the world . . . solve its problems, you know. He comes in here a lot."

It was silent again.

More people filed out of the Sunset Grille. Cyrus glanced at them.

"Glad you're doin' what you're doin'," said the old man, nodding toward the Grille, "about *that* place, I mean."

"Yes. Thanks. Of course, we're really just barely under way . . . just drawing-board kind of stuff so far. Not much else."

Cyrus looked back at the pastor. "If you ask me—and I don't know that much, you understand—but if you ask me, I think most folks could walk out of there and never go back, if it wasn't so easy to walk inside in the first place. I may be wrong. Heck, I'm just an old man."

"Sounds like you know plenty, Cyrus."

"Of course, what I really notice is this—that is, if you care to hear more," said Cyrus shyly.

"Yeah," said Larry, in no hurry to return to his home after being out this late. "What's on your mind?"

"What I really notice is them folks who stop in here every day trying hard not to cross the street. Oh, it works for a while. Sort of a... whatchamacallit... a deterrent, I guess is what it's called. And then about the second week I see 'em coming and going from that door over there like it was a reward for all their hard work and self-control, and what not. You with me, Pastor?" Cyrus sauntered over to the corner by the swinging doors, where a broom leaned against the wall.

"Yeah," Larry replied, disturbed by the old man's perceptive words and his hedged-about, gleaming eyes.

"I talk too much," said Cyrus, slowly sweeping the pine planks in front of the counter.

"No! No! Really... you're absolutely right. Go on."

"Then I should say," continued the baker, like he had hardly even paused for a breath, "I should say that it's all there in the Good Book for 'em to see. Isn't it, pastor?"

"Yes..." Larry said, not certain where Cyrus was headed with this.

"I mean, the part where the good Lord was tempted on and on in the wilderness," Cyrus explained. "It's all there," he said as he wiped flour from his hands onto his apron. "It weren't till the fortieth day that the devil really came around making such a racket that you or I woulda just caved right in. I imagine we woulda been so proud of bein' good for so long, that we mighta sat down and had us a stone sandwich with the devil himself. An' that's the trouble here with these folks," the baker said, punching a floured forefinger in the air between words for emphasis. "Those—like young Todd, there—who wanna get out are too proud. They ain't countin' on the devil

184

workin' on the forty-first day. Of course, you know that, pastor," Cyrus said, shrugging and turning away. "I ain't teachin' you nothin'." He leaned on his broom, peering thoughtfully out the window.

"But you're saying plenty about the need for humility and accountability," said Larry quickly. He felt the flush in his cheeks. And it seemed to him that the neon light kept catching highlights in Cyrus's eyes—as if the wise old shop owner knew far more than he was telling. Finally, Larry could no longer look directly at him.

"You'd be amazed at the folks who go in there," said Cyrus quietly, continuing with his sweeping.

"How do you know they're not just going for supper?" asked Larry, perhaps a bit too quickly.

"'Cause it don't take anybody four hours to eat," scoffed Cyrus. He held Larry's eye a moment, then turned back to his task.

"Do they look ashamed—when they come out?" asked Larry, after an abashed pause.

"Some," said Cyrus, nodding. "But you can't always tell. I've seen folks doin' some mighty strange things outside that door. And I tell you," he continued, "the smartest thing that Detzer fella ever did was to put a menu on the wall there next to the door. You see it?" Cyrus pointed out the window, and Larry nodded again.

"I seen more people studyin' that piece of paper—like it gave 'em some respectable reason to go in," said Cyrus. Then he looked hard at Larry. "Except that Detzer ain't come up with a respectable way to get 'em back out again. Nope. The way I see it, a man's gotta give up some of that respect to ever get out of there for good. I figure ol' Todd Blakemore ain't got too much respect left. And what little he has, he sure don't wanna lose now..." He paused, aiming a reflective look at the floor. "It's gonna be hard on that young'un—awful hard," Cyrus said, shaking his head sadly. He swept up a little pile of dirt, then leaned his broom against the counter as he went to fetch the dustpan. He paused, and looked again at Larry. "Of course, I can't say for sure."

"So where do you fit in?" asked Larry. "I mean, why do people come talk to you about it? Are there more like Todd?"

"Lord 'a' mercy, yes! A fair lot more!" exclaimed Cyrus.

"And?"

"I try to give 'em back some o' their respect."

Larry waited before asking his next question. The old man had swept the dust into the dustpan and was ambling toward the dented, army-green trash can between the end of the counter and the wall beside the swinging doors.

"Have you ever been, Cyrus?" Larry finally asked.

The baker stood stock-still, his eyes glittering at Larry. Larry looked at the old man, who stood facing him on the other side of the counter. Cyrus looked neither up nor down as most people do when they are recalling a memory or a fact. Rather, he returned the stare. As if the memory lived and breathed before his eyes, he said, "I been there once, Pastor."

"What was the occasion?" asked Larry.

"I'll tell you, if you don't mind me leavin' out a piece or two."

"I don't mind," said Larry.

"Well," said Cyrus, "I had occasion to follow a young man through those doors one hot July night. He was a good man when he went in...better than most folks thought. But he was never the same when he come out. And..." The baker scratched his nose, leaving a white trail of flour dust behind, "I can't say everything went well for me neither, after that night."

"When was that?" Larry asked.

"Must have been about five years ago," Cyrus replied. "Pretty soon after the place opened."

"What became of the man?" asked Larry.

Cyrus took off his long apron, folded it, and walked across the room where he placed it on the corner of the display case. He peered carefully at Larry.

"Hadn't you better be gettin' on home, Larry?" Cyrus asked. "It's pretty late—or early by now, I guess. Won't your missus be worried?"

"I guess you're probably right," admitted Larry, following Cyrus toward the door.

But he found himself oddly fascinated by the old man's reluctance to answer his last question. While Cyrus was turning the doorknob, he tried again.

"So, anyway... What became of the man?"

"I don't know exactly—not yet," answered Cyrus. "But if I knew for sure, I'm afraid the answer might break both our hearts."

Larry looked perplexed, but Cyrus said only, "Well... Good night."

Larry stepped out. Behind him, Cyrus pulled the door firmly closed.

THE NEXT STEP

"FOR YOU know what the Scriptures say: 'As a man thinketh in his heart, so is he.' That's all, Mavis—Thank you."

Larry laid his notes aside and clicked off the dictaphone. He ejected the cassette from the machine and laid it in his "out" box, where Mavis would retrieve it and type it into outline form for Sunday morning. He set the microphone aside and looked out the window. It was a bitter Tuesday in a month that seemed to have lost the knack for warmth. There were six more days until the taping of the television show, which was to air a few weeks later, just before Christmas. Larry wondered if there was any significance to the timing of the broadcast.

In the middle of his office floor were piled the components of the church's ancient manger scene. The time-worn plastic figures had been around the church since long before Larry began his tenure, and were somewhat the worse for wear. Although the baby Jesus remained intact, and Joseph and Mary still made a decent-looking—if slightly faded—couple, summer storage and winter weather had gotten the best of the remainder of the cast. The Christ Child slept peacefully under the watchful eye of a one-winged angel. And an electrical short inside one of the wise men gave him the tendency to blink on and off. Because of this, Nigel had dragged the whole assembly out, to attempt to track down the source of the mage's inconsistency, as well as make such refurbishment as might be possible with the other figures.

Something happened to Larry as he stared at the pile of plastic statuettes. Had the thoughts come one at a time, he might have been able to fend them off. But they attacked in droves. A blinking mage, insecure children, a lost friend, a receding marriage . . . a forgotten rose. They rushed at Larry, thrusting, parrying, driving him into an emotional corner. He chewed his lower lip and turned his wedding ring.

Across the parking lot Larry could see the parsonage. He looked at his watch: five thirty-two. Dinner would be on the table soon, he thought, wistfully. If only he had an appetite.

"You need to face up to your greatest fears . . ." he quoted to himself. Wasn't that what Nigel had told him in their counseling session? In a way, wasn't he about to do just that? Nigel couldn't be *that* wrong, could he? He picked up the phone and dialed his home number.

"Hello?"

"Hi, honey," he said, forcing a cheery tone that he didn't feel. "Listen . . . I've got to go see a fella who lives a ways out in the country. I may not be home for dinner—"

"Oh, Larry!" she moaned. "What excuse do I give the kids *this* time?" He winced at the tone of her voice, as she continued. "Why can't this person meet you at your office, *after* you eat dinner with your family, for the first time in I-don't-know-when? He *does* realize that pastors eat, doesn't he?"

Larry rolled his eyes and shook his head. She wasn't about to let him off the hook. Clenching his jaw tighter, he said, "Rose, believe me, I tried that. I asked him if we couldn't meet here. But his—his problem is such that he doesn't want to be seen coming into my office. I've got to meet him where he is, Rose. Try to understand." Larry hardly noticed the lie rolling off his tongue.

There was silence on the other end, then the soft sound of sobbing. "Oh, come on, Rose, honey," he pleaded. "Don't! I won't be that late, honest!"

"You're already late," she said in a tear-laden voice, "and getting later all the time. I don't know you anymore, Larry... and it frightens me."

She hung up the phone. Larry's chest began heaving with the unfairness of it all. Why did everything become so complicated, just when he was trying to accomplish something he felt so strongly about—something God had called him to, in fact? He licked his emotional wounds for a few moments, indulging himself in the salty taste of self-pity. Then he stood, put on his jacket, switched off the office light, and headed for the door.

GUNNER half-stumbled out of the Sunset Grille into the waning light of the evening. Glancing about quickly, he ducked his head and made off down the street, as if he had been walking for some time now.

He noticed the sign above the donut shop across the street, its glow pale against the falling dusk. He slowed, then stopped, then turned to cross the street to Cyrus's place.

Gunner opened the door, went in, and slid into a chair by the window without bothering to remove his coat. He stared blankly at the backs of his hands, resting on the tabletop. He glanced up only when Cyrus tapped him on the shoulder. "Oh, hi, Cyrus," he said, dropping his gaze back toward the tabletop. "I didn't hear you coming..."

"What can I getcha, Mayor?" Cyrus asked.

A long silence. "Just a cup of coffee, I guess," Gunner answered listlessly, looking across the street. Cyrus's eyes followed the line of Gunner's vision. He looked back at Gunner, then turned to fetch the coffee.

In a moment he returned with two mugs and a pot of freshly brewed coffee. He poured one for himself, another for Gunner, and sat down, uninvited, across from the distracted mayor.

"What's on your mind?" the old man asked, leaning forward over the table.

Gunner started. "Who, me? Oh..." Again the vacant stare. "Nothing... much..."

"Seems I been hearin' that a lot these last couple of days," observed the baker. "So far, ain't nobody said it that convinced me." His eyes honed in on Gunner's until the mayor was forced to acknowledge the burden that lay, unwrapped but not unseen, on the table between them.

He gave a pathetic little smile. "I guess you're right, Cyrus," he admitted, taking a careful sip of the steaming coffee. "I do have a few things on my mind. Didn't know it showed that much."

"Sure does," returned Cyrus. A moment more he studied Gunner's face and posture, then pointed, with his chin, at the building across the street. "Have anything to do with that place, reckon?"

Gunner's nostrils flared, but he made no answer, other than a tiny nod of the head. Cyrus nodded too, saying, "Thought so." He got up and walked across the shop, coming back with a glazed donut, still warm from the frying vat. "Have one of these. They're pretty fresh."

Gunner's eyes thanked Cyrus, and he picked up the donut between a thumb and forefinger, biting off perhaps a third of its circumference. "Good," he said around his chewing. "Like always."

Cyrus nodded. "Glad you like it. Like I always say, ain't too many holes in a man that a good donut can't fill."

Gunner's chewing slowed, then resumed, his eyes locking reluctantly with the baker's intent, searching look. When he swallowed and had another sip of coffee, Gunner cleared his throat and said, "I guess you heard what happened down at the church."

"Maybe, maybe not," Cyrus replied. "How about you tellin' me your side?"

"Well..." A long pause, punctuated by several dry swallows. "They 'churched' me," Gunner said bitterly. "Told me to stay away until I had 'rectified the matter' —that was the phrase they used. But they kicked me out, Cyrus! That's the long and the short of it!" His look pleaded for commiseration, for understanding—for anything other than judgment.

Now Cyrus studied the tabletop, and took a slow sip of coffee. He looked up slowly, opened his mouth several times, then finally asked, "Did they have a reason, Gunner? I never heard of 'em chuckin' somebody out just for the fun of it."

Gunner's breathing came faster, his nostrils flaring with suppressed emotion. He was silent for so long that he thought perhaps Cyrus would give up and go away, but the old man just sat there, waiting. At last, Gunner managed to mumble, "They said I was...in there." He shrugged in the direction of the window.

"And were you?" pressed Cyrus, in a gentler voice than he had yet used. "Were you in there?"

In the stillness, the rattling of the wall clock seemed almost loud. The two men sat quietly, the one hunched over the tabletop, the other in an attitude of attention, waiting for his answer. "Yeah," moaned Gunner at last, "I was. And . . . it wasn't the first time, either."

Cyrus reached across the table and gripped Gunner firmly on one shoulder. There were no more words to be said, just now.

Minutes later, Cyrus glanced out the window at the right moment to see Larry Ravelle driving by, his face tightly drawn.

LARRY drove west on the main highway for ten miles, before reaching the narrow, two-lane blacktop road that meandered south across the shoulders of the rolling farmland.

He was usually struck, on the rare occasions when he came this way, by how little the scenery had changed since the days of his childhood, when this drive was a daily ritual seen through the windows of a school bus or Dad's pickup. True, a few of the old two-story white frame dwellings had been torn down, replaced here and there by modern brick-and-skylight houses erected by the more prosperous farmers; and some of the fencerows were missing a few of the trees they once sported; but the essence, the primary identity of the farms and ranchland, remained the same as in his memories of youth. He found this of slight comfort tonight, though, for his mind was on other matters.

He reached the graveled turnoff to his home of many years before. As a precaution he switched off his head-lights, navigating the long driveway by the residual glow in the western sky. Nearing the house, he could see that no lights were on. Since it was too early to be in bed, even for his antisocial brother, Larry concluded that, true to Billy Bobb's assessment, John was in town, being entertained at the Grille.

Larry pulled around back and stopped his car. He

walked to the pump house, perhaps twenty paces from the back door of the dwelling, ignoring the yapping of a blustery-but-harmless terrier. He opened the door to the small shed, feeling in the dark for the spare house key that had hung, since his and John's youth, on a rusty nail beside the light switch.

He went to the back door and let himself inside. He was standing on the porch, awash in the smell of tractor grease and sweaty work clothes. He pulled a small flashlight out of his pocket and shone it on the tangled assortment of coveralls, implement- and seed-company caps, boots, and denim jackets that hung on pegs and lay piled on the floor beside the kitchen door.

He found a pair of coveralls buried beneath a layer of coats and old sweaters, and selected a well-soiled cap from the available inventory. Then he went back outside, locking the door behind him. He tossed the clothing in the back seat of the station wagon, replaced the key in the pump house, got in his car, and drove back toward Ellenbach.

"SO ANYWAY," Gunner was saying, "now people from the church cross the street to avoid having to speak to me. It's just awful, Cyrus. I feel like dirt!"

Cyrus sat quietly, his eyes encouraging Gunner to continue.

"The way I figure it," Gunner said, "I can at least go in there and sit and be around some other people, and not feel like I'm getting darts thrown at my back." He raised his face, a hint of truculence in his eye. "They don't look down on me over there, Cyrus. I *can* say that for them."

Cyrus looked down, then up again. "Well, Gunner," he said softly, "I don't believe you can say I been lookin' down on you, can you?"

Gunner dropped his eyes. "No...of course not, Cyrus," he murmured.

"And, if you'll pardon me gettin' on my soapbox," the baker continued, "when you think about other folks, stop and consider this: It'd be pretty hard for two hogs lyin' in the same mudhole to look down on one another, now wouldn't it?"

Gunner had no reply.

"And I'll say one other thing," Cyrus went on. "I'd lay you odds that the main reason you're over there ain't the fellowship—is it? Ain't it more the chance to be nobody for a while...maybe do some things you wouldn't especially want your name attached to?"

Gunner hung his head in silence. Cyrus got up, brought the coffeepot over, and freshened the mayor's cup. Gunner took a long sip of coffee and drew an unsteady breath. "Well, Cyrus," he said reluctantly, "I got to admit there's some truth in what you say. It's for sure that place hasn't done me much good."

Cyrus nodded in agreement, his eyes never leaving the top of Gunner's head—which was all he could see at the moment. "Everybody I've ever talked to about it says the same thing, sooner or later. And I'll tell you what, Gunner," he said softly, looking across the street, "it's going to do more harm before it all comes to a head."

III.

THE BATTLE

IT WAS Friday and it was sundown, and there was a noise in the parking lot beside Larry's station wagon. It was Pitch and Stool shouting for us to come out. Gravel-throated Stool's voice rose above that of his partner.

"Truck it out here, boys. We don't got all night!"

Dias and I accompanied Larry down the steps to the parking lot, and saw the two standing there. Stool had shouted at Larry too, but Larry, of course, hadn't heard him. That's one of the most iniquitous things about the way demons work: They order you about from a distance, and when you do their bidding, they make you think it was all your idea in the first place.

Making sure Rose and the kids were occupied at the back of the house, Larry stepped into the garage, found his brother's work clothes where he had hidden them, and put them on. In the short time it took to walk to the car and open the driver's-side door, he already was feeling the weight of his decision. The "how-could-I's" had begun. I could feel the anguish in his soul as the tiny part of him still attuned to my influence fought against the onslaught of Pitch's ministrations. *This is no way to accomplish God's will,* the tiny remnant was saying, *by sneaking about and letting people think you're someone else.*

But what'll they say when they figure out it's my shoe? the rest of him countered. *Found at the slaughterhouse . . . with the magazine!*

Pitch sneered in my face as he got into the backseat. I hurried to join him. It appeared hopeless, but I couldn't abandon my mission.

Stool hopped on the hood and bade Dias to follow.

Dias jumped quietly aboard only after Larry began backing out onto the street. If he thought Larry was lost, he didn't let his voice or demeanor show it. I admired his bravery.

Larry inched along the street, then pulled around behind the church building and stopped, staring blankly through the windshield.

"Your friend is very preoccupied tonight," said Pitch as he watched Larry lean over and probe about for something in the glove compartment. "That can be dangerous for a man with so many responsibilities, don't you think?" He smirked at me a moment, then turned his eyes back toward Larry.

The pastor finally felt what he was searching for, pulling out a stack of dusty index cards, bound with a rubber band. Larry unwrapped the cards and shuffled through them.

"My, my! What has the pastor drug out now?" said Pitch lightly, leaning over Larry's shoulder.

They were relics from seminary—Bible verses long ago committed to memory and then, ultimately, to that wasteland of maps, expired auto club cards, and eraserless pencils. The verses were in his own cursive handwriting.

Pitch stiffened when Larry selected one and read it aloud:

"No temptation has overtaken you but such as is common to man . . ."

Pitch scooted away from Larry like a cockroach scurrying from the middle of a suddenly lit floor. I leaned forward and prayed with my lips close to Larry's head.

"Stop it!" Pitch cried, his hands over his ears. Larry continued.

"And God is faithful . . ."

"Drive, you idiot!" Pitch screamed at Larry. "Get this crate rolling—we've got a lot to do tonight!"

". . . who will not allow you to be tempted beyond what you are able . . ."

Pitch, in desperation, pulled on the handle, but the door didn't budge. Larry had locked it from his control panel after starting the engine, and his finger remained on the button.

Pitch started through the door, but then jerked his arm back with a yelp of pain—the passenger side of the car was close to an evergreen hedge. In Pitch's distracted state, he couldn't summon the substantiality to withstand the tiny lances of the bush's needles. He looked in alarm at his damaged wrist, cradling it in his lap and moaning in panic and hurt. He began cursing at the top of his lungs to drown those hated words. But they kept coming.

". . . but with the temptation [God] will provide the way of escape . . ."

There was a loud thud on the roof of the car. An ugly, contorted face flattened against the windshield. There were blotches of grease where skin met glass.

"Stop reading!" cried Pitch.

". . . that you may be able to endure it."

With Larry's pronunciation of those final words, Pitch shrieked and turned his tirade upon his battered partner.

"Get up, Stool, you weakling! Get up or I'll . . . I'll . . . I'll report you!"

Stool's eyes bugged out further at the mention of this. He wriggled in Dias's mighty grasp. Dias was now standing on the hood of the car, forcing the demon's face against the glass. He was expressionless as he executed his job. Stool's nose flattened to one side until it appeared it might snap . . . then with a little popping noise, it did snap. The demon clawed at the windshield wipers. His legs flailed about behind him. I could see the rotted teeth at the back of his jaws, the coal-black hole where his tongue disappeared into his gullet.

Larry placed the cards on the seat beside him and began to back the car out of the church lot. I opened my eyes and looked through the glass at Dias. There was a confused look on his face, and Stool was breaking free of his grasp.

"Yes!" croaked Pitch. "That's it. There's plenty of time . . . plenty of time to consider those verses later."

Stool pushed hard against the windshield, and was able to turn his head from side to side.

"Excellent! I knew he could do it," panted Pitch. "I knew it all the time . . . Now," he continued, gaining strength with each passing moment, "there's no immediate use for these cards." Pitch reached over the seat and scattered them on the floor as Larry rounded a corner.

Stool clambered to his feet. He faced Dias with renewed hatred in his eyes. Around the hood they sparred, each waiting for an opening to dart in and grab hold.

On the way down Washington Avenue, Larry suddenly thought of turning at the light on Terrence Street. There were several older church members in this neighborhood who were ailing. *I'll just make one or two calls on these folks, and . . .*

"Green, fool! It's green!" shouted Pitch in Larry's ear.

Dias shot in for a leg-hold on Stool just as Larry pressed the accelerator and drove through the intersection. *Someone else in the church needs a chance to minister,* Larry told himself. *I've got to focus for now on the Grille . . .*

Stool brought his weight down hard on Dias, then clamped his fingers around my partner's throat. Through the windshield I could see him choking Dias, shaking him like a rug. The station wagon drove north.

With every street sign we passed, the demons grew stronger, and Larry weaker. He attempted one last time to take the Way of Escape. Cyrus's words went around in his brain until he spoke them to himself: *They ain't countin' on the devil workin' on the forty-first day . . . the forty-first day . . . the forty-first day . . .*

Larry drove past the Sunset Grille and turned left into an alleyway behind Paradise Donuts. The heater knob was turned to its highest setting. A sweat droplet ran from Larry's temple to his jawbone.

"Why are we stopping here?" Pitch demanded, looking over his shoulder toward the Grille. "Over there!"

Larry put his head down on the wheel, closing his eyes as the engine idled softly. He thought of Rose . . .

The car shook as Dias flung Stool from him, getting slowly to his feet.

Larry held an image in his mind: Rose at home . . . in bed. He saw her gentle face, her hand patting the pillow beside her, bidding him to join her. He saw the form of her body beneath the sheets, which covered but did not hide her beauty.

Dias grappled with Stool, then tripped the demon, flinging him onto his back atop the upthrust hood ornament. The demon's back arched high in agony. His lips cocked open, and he spluttered and frothed horrible curses. Dias shook him back and forth, plunging the ornament further into his enemy's back. Stool hissed and jolted about spasmodically.

Inside the car, Pitch was frantic again. He climbed into

the front seat and put his face right up under the wheel where Larry leaned his head. Pitch looked in his eyes. He spoke into them as if to reach the brain and the meddling image.

"Get on with it! Back this heap out of here and do what you came for," he hissed. "Besides—there's so little excitement in a woman you can have any time you want!"

Rose faded from Larry's mind. He felt the engine's heat blast up at him from the vents, felt the sweat trickling down his armpits, beneath his brother's denim coveralls. *There's nothing exciting at home,* he thought . . .

He raised his head, and just as he put his hand to the gearshift, he paused, studying the steamed-up windows of the donut shop. Cyrus waited inside, no doubt, with warm donuts and good advice. He reached to turn off the ignition.

Stool, who had almost wriggled loose from the hood ornament, screamed and arched even higher, as Dias shoved a forearm against his throat.

"Wait!" shouted Pitch. "Your shoe! Your reputation! Have you forgotten that?" The hint of a smile came over his lips as he watched Larry remove his hand from the key and put the car in reverse.

"Yes! Now go! Just go! Do it!" Pitch babbled eagerly.

Larry backed out of the alley, then crossed Washington Avenue. He pulled around the corner a block or so past the Grille, lest a parishioner recognize the pastor's car in front of the place. Looking all about to ensure there were no witnesses, he opened the door and stepped quickly away from the station wagon, flinging the door shut behind him.

With a thump, the door closed, wiping out any wispy remains of Rose's image. Larry paced down the dark sidewalk, down the side of the red brick building, around its corner and through the door of the Sunset Grille.

Pitch followed close behind, cackling and rubbing his hands with glee.

Standing on the sidewalk, I looked back toward the front of the car. A black dog stood on the hood, hunched over Dias, whose chest was pinned beneath the foul beast's front paws. The Stool-dog's mouth was covered with foam, and there was a shining opening on my partner's neck. Dias's body was limp. The dog sniffed at the wound. He licked it and rolled his head backward, letting the warm life-essence drip down onto his chest. I could watch no longer. I rushed at the car, and was halfway there when I remembered I was unarmed—not to mention forbidden to fight. But I had to do something to help my partner! I shouted and waved my arms.

"Go on! *Git!*" I screamed.

The dog let his black eyes roll back, unmoved by my performance. I froze when he jumped down from the car and crept toward me, growling. I heard his thoughts.

Little angel, if I had more time I'd destroy you too . . . I could smell his rancid breath as he grinned at me through his fangs. He trotted past me disdainfully, headed toward the Grille. He stopped, and turned to face me once again.

Someday, when I have the time, I'll finish the job . . . He bounded across the street, and followed a patron through the door of the Sunset Grille.

I raced to Dias, who lay draped across the car. His clothing had staunched the flow of his wounds. But it stuck to the skin around the edges, and looked as if it would be quite painful to pull loose. I bent down and touched him. He lay still as a rock.

I held his head in my hands, and looked into his face. After a while, his eyes fluttered open.

"Didn't . . . do so well . . . this time," he panted weakly.

"No, I'm afraid not," I said. "We've got to get you somewhere . . . get these gashes patched up."

"Just a while longer," he wheezed. "Getting—stronger ... but not yet, all right?"

"Of course, Dias," I said, wincing in sympathetic suffering for my wounded, brave partner. I was worried about the pain he must be experiencing. Just because we aren't mortal doesn't mean we can't be hurt. In fact, our nature is such that we experience pain on more levels than humans can imagine—and the Supreme One on levels far beyond ours.

As the stars wheeled above Ellenbach, and Larry prowled the inside of the Grille on his benighted errand, I held Dias's head, and wondered how on earth or in Heaven we would ever complete this mission in time to catch the pipe.

THE SHOE

LARRY slipped inside the Grille, and moved toward a booth near the back of the eating area, remembering to limp in imitation of his brother's damaged leg. He could just barely make out the shadowed entrance into Billy Bob's office. His brother's clothes felt loose on him. Without them, though, he would not be here tonight. A waitress startled Larry.

"Hello, John. What can I get for you tonight?"

It was the first time since high school—the years when the twins grew rapidly and irretrievably apart—that Larry had been mistaken for his brother. Even though this was the precise goal of his foray into the Grille tonight, it took a moment for him to recover from the scare, and another to hide the signs of being surprised. Given all this, Larry did a fair job of covering when he responded flatly—as the detached, reticent John would have—"The usual, please." He wondered if he should have omitted the "please."

When the woman returned with "the usual," she had a puzzled look on her face. "John," she said as she placed the drink—straight whiskey—in front of him, "It's Fri-day night. This isn't your normal—"

"Extra time on my hands," Larry interrupted, looking down at his knuckles. "I'd like to spend it here—if I may," he finished gruffly, imitating John's brusqueness as accu-rately as memory would permit.

"Well...sure, John," answered the waitress nervously. "I didn't mean to make you mad—" Flushing, she wheeled and retreated to the bar.

The door to the office remained closed during the en-tire time Larry sat there, trying to look nonchalant while toying with a drink he had no intention of consuming. An hour passed that seemed to take three, and he decided to investigate. Casually, with a motion that he hoped appeared practiced, he tossed a five-dollar bill on the table beside the untouched whiskey. Then he sauntered toward the short, dark hallway leading to the manager's office.

There was a sign on the door which, from his seat, Larry had been unable to read. As he approached the door, the message became clear. In red block letters it read: "MAIN OFFICE MOVED DOWNSTAIRS."

Larry felt his breathing suddenly stop. When it re-sumed, his breaths were shallow...just like in the slaugh-terhouse. The allure of risk and the scream of danger beckoned him. The doorway to the floors below was just a short stroll away. As he stood there, he played the same mental games which he had been playing for decades. He prayed...but he didn't really mean it. His mind was made up. He was going through those green doors.

He had been walking slowly toward them during all these attempts at self-justification, and his hand was on the knob when he heard his brother's name again.

"John! What a surprise to see you here on a Friday!"

Larry knew the voice immediately. Its owner put a

warm grip on his shoulder and spun him around good-naturedly.

"What's the occasion?" said a smiling Billy Bobb.

"Poker game canceled," answered Larry. If he had thought about it, he would have been amazed at how easy deception was becoming for him—but, of course, he didn't.

"Too bad, Johnny boy. Well, we're glad to have you with us any time. Say...you been losing weight lately?" Billy Bobb gave him a wrinkle-browed, appraising look.

Larry thought quickly.

"Far too busy to eat."

"Then you better order up. In fact, it's on me tonight!"

"Thanks, but no," said Larry. "I've had dinner, actually."

"Suit yourself," said the manager, smiling, as he turned to make his rounds among the customers on the first floor.

Larry, emboldened by the success of his camouflage, tossed caution to the winds. "Before you go," he said, and Billy Bobb turned back toward him, "I noticed the sign." He pointed to the office door.

"Oh, that. Yes...well, we decided to move downstairs for managerial purposes. Kinda funny, ain't it?"

"How's that?"

"You know...Seems like most people are wantin' to climb *up* the ladder of success, and here I am, wantin' to go the other way," chuckled Billy Bobb. Then, he added, "That seem odd to you, John?"

"I jus—" too wordy for his brother; try again—"Perhaps."

"Anyway, I'm downstairs now, Johnny boy," the manager said, turning away again. "Good luck to you." And Billy Bobb was off to glad-hand and mingle with his clientele.

Larry looked around him one more time, then pushed through the doors and stepped down the stairs.

There was obviously no office on the floor with the booths, so Larry continued on down to the third level. He arrived in a small, dimly lit room, in front of a door attended by a muscular-looking man with a scar on his cheek and a nose so flat it had to be devoid of cartilage. He looked at Larry, taking in the questioning look on the familiar face.

"Evenin', John," he said in a flat voice. "You wanna take in the show tonight?" he asked, laying a hand on the door handle.

Larry was in a quandary. There was no unobtrusive way he could ask this man, who obviously knew his brother, about the location of the office. Why would John want to know such a thing? And if the shoe's absence was noticed, all it would take would be a phone call to his brother to implicate the town's pastor in this bizarre burglary. Larry's mind whirled. All he could think of was to go inside and perhaps ask someone in there about the office.

"Maybe so," he replied casually. "How much, again?" he asked, reaching for his wallet. He had noticed the cash box on the table beside the attendant.

"Same as always, John," the fellow laughed. "Five bucks. You gettin' forgetful in your old age?"

Larry laughed easily at the jibe, then wished he hadn't. His gruff brother probably would have ignored the joke, or given a sour rejoinder. He laid his five on the table, and the man swung the door open. "Enjoy the show, John." Larry nodded tersely and went inside.

So—this is the live entertainment, he thought.

The room was dark, except for a bank of red, blue, yellow, and green lights flooding a small stage at the front. On the stage, a woman was dancing. Her eyes were never still; with them she seemed to give each member of her audience a special invitation, an intimation that she would like to spend a more personal time with him and him alone. Wearing no clothing and no constraint, she was entering into their souls, and possessing them—some for the first time, some for the thousandth.

The music accompanying her dance was loud, its tune inconsequential, for it was the rhythm that really counted. It was the age-old rhythm that had thrummed inside the temples of Astarte on the Chaldean plain, the rhythm known by the priestesses of Artemis and the devotees of fertility cults from the Baltic Sea to the forests of ancient Britain. It was the rhythm of a human heart pounding with passion, fueled by the powerful elixirs of untrammeled, undisciplined, rampant desire. The men heard it, felt it, unwittingly entered into it, were carried along on its intoxicating currents. The woman heard it, and smiled. She had summoned it, and she knew.

If Larry had moved among the oddly quiet men in the room, and asked for the identity of the dancer on the stage, he would have received strange looks, shrugs, shakes of the head. Very few in the room could have described her face to him with any degree of accuracy, not so much because they didn't look at it—they did—but because, if they had paused to think about it, they would realize that each time the woman danced, her face was slightly changed from the last time. No one knew her name. It had never occurred to anyone to ask. She was the dance—and that was all.

Larry watched her. Since the slaughterhouse he had sworn to himself he would never lay eyes on such stuff as this again. But here he was, taking it in, wanting to walk away, but without the willpower to move his feet. Only the image of his shoe saved Larry from melting completely into the dance, in parallel orbit with the other entranced watchers. He literally had to think about the motions of turning away... first his head and feet together, followed by his torso, until all of him had turned toward the back of the room.

Larry looked about at the back for anything that might indicate an office. There was a recessed area bounded by a small counter with the word "Bar" in red neon above it, and an area furnished with unoccupied pool tables ... but no office.

Larry eased up next to one of the men seated at a table close to the exit at the rear of the room. Though his back was turned, he fancied he could feel the liquid, electric gaze of the dancer on the back of his neck. His hands shook, his breathing was fast and shallow. And though his eyes were focused on the face of the man he was about to address, Larry knew he could turn around at any moment and fantasy would embrace him in her arms. He steeled his mind: He would not, could not go back to that. *You're here for another reason,* he shouted at himself.

The face of the man he approached was slack with fascination. His tongue rested lightly on his lower lip, his mouth partially rounded. He caressed the arm of the chair in which he sat, and Larry well knew what the man was touching with his mind.

"Pardon me," growled Larry, raising his voice above the pounding of the soundtrack.

The man jumped, his eyes snapping around to Larry in a startled jerk. Larry didn't know the man, and breathed an inward sigh of relief.

"Sorry," he said. "I didn't mean to scare you. Tell me ... is there an office on this floor?"

The man was very polite, once he got over being surprised. He affected an air of nonchalance, as if nothing could be more normal than for him to be sitting in a dark room with at least thirty other men, bewitched by the seemingly tireless moves of a female body.

"What can I do for you?" said the man, cocking an ear toward Larry, while keeping one eye on the stage.

"Where can I find the main office?" Larry repeated, a little louder.

"The main office . . . the main office. Seems to me it's on the top floor."

"No," said Larry. "Not any more."

"Oh. Then have you tried the next floor down?"

"I . . . No, I haven't."

"Well, then . . ." The man gave the appearance of pondering as his voice trailed into silence and his eyes followed every movement of the dancer's limbs and torso. In a moment, with difficulty, he brought his attention back to Larry.

". . . Then it must be on the bottom floor, because I've never seen it here." Again the wandering, vacant look, the slack jaw.

"You've been there?" asked Larry, curiously.

"The bottom floor?" the man smirked, as if Larry had suggested something off-color. "No, I've never been. That's the hard-core stuff down there! I just like to take a little look now and then, you know." He gave Larry a conspiratorial wink. "Just a change of scenery once in a while, right?"

Larry nodded, smiling and moving toward the door.

"No harm in that, right?" the man grinned, jerking a thumb toward the stage.

Larry glanced up—and she was looking at him with those inviting eyes.

His heart choking him, he wheeled toward the door, knowing he couldn't stay a moment longer.

DIAS grimaced as I helped him pull off his mail shirt. Stool's fangs had gashed him deep, but the wounds were

213

well on their way toward healing—for nothing of Hell can permanently alter or scar that which had its abode in Heaven. Great, closed welts were what remained of the jagged tears of the Stool-dog's teeth—that, and the fatigue of battle which still sapped the strength of my partner as he leaned against the wall of the attic room above the donut shop.

We had limped up the stairs only a few moments ago, with me straining to support Dias's greater weight and bulk as he limped along, one arm draped over my less-than-broad shoulders. Cyrus had been working in the kitchen when we came in, and for just the briefest moment I could have sworn he saw me—but of course that was impossible. I looked again, and he was turned away from me, carefully placing glazed donuts on a rack in the display case, humming to himself in a monotone. Then Dias staggered against me, and I had to return my attention to the task at hand.

"What are we going to do about Larry—in that place?" Dias asked, wincing as he slowly rotated his sword arm above his head.

"I don't know," I answered, shaking my head as I applied salve to the few remaining open wounds on my partner's left shoulder. "Whatever we do, we haven't got much time. We're to be taken up in the pipe in less than seven days." I felt despair making thrusts at my resolve. "Maybe we've allowed Pitch too much too soon," I speculated aloud. "Maybe I should have shielded Larry more—"

"No. You had your orders," Dias stated firmly. Then he looked at me. "You did what you had to do. Larry's got to do his part."

Somehow, those words didn't bring much comfort just then.

Dias looked at me, a thoughtful expression on his face.

"What about Rose?" he asked. "Isn't there something we could do for her?"

LARRY pushed open the door at the bottom of the stairs, and stepped cautiously inside a room on the other side.

A dim red glow pulsed faintly from the corner where the walls met the ceiling. In the center of the room, taking up most of the available floor space, was a round structure with wooden walls, ten feet high. There were doors all around the thing, through which several men came and went while Larry was watching. Each time a door opened he tried to catch a glimpse inside, but always it would shut before he saw anything. Above the structure hung white track lights, beaming down upon whatever it was that was inside. Out of the center came music, and laughter, and other sounds which would, under different circumstances, have been proper, joyful—but here were sinister, seamy—and utterly seductive.

Larry circled the structure warily, averting his eyes from anyone that passed him. The round thing was absolutely the only furnishing on the bottom floor. No furniture, no wallpaper, no signs; nothing had been allowed which might detract from the focal point of the room.

He heard it beckoning him, sighing its promises of satisfaction and ultimate release. *It's here, Larry. Everything you've ever imagined it could be is just inside. Come and see. Come and taste*...The voice inside the round thing whispered to him, throbbed within him with an insistency that was...his own. He dared not go inside—and he could not refuse.

Along the walls, men stood talking. At first he assumed they were employees of some sort, but a second glance revealed they were less than comfortable in this setting. They looked at the round structure, then away;

looked at each other, then away. They smoked their cigarettes and made stumblefooted talk, trying to appear at ease—perhaps, thought Larry, trying to forget. Families. Wives. Honor.

Behind the round thing, in the wall farthest from the stairwell, was a door. Seeing it, Larry felt hopeful. Perhaps he could find the object of his search and quit this place of dark enticement. He walked quickly to the door and knocked on it. He repeated this several times, but there was no answer. Larry touched the knob and turned it just a fraction ... it moved! Then fear set in. *What if Billy Bobb is in there after all ... there at his desk, tricking me with silence? What if he went down the stairs while I was on the other floors ... waiting in here to hold up the shoe and gloat over me?*

Larry's hand moistened the doorknob. The heat of this bottom floor was subtly making itself felt. It twined its way up from somewhere, and did not rise to higher levels as expected. Instead, it lingered in this room ... enveloping his middle. He felt the witching voice reaching toward him from the round thing. *It's here, Larry ... It's all here ...*

As he wavered in front of the door, Larry noticed the lettering on the wall to his left. It read, "FURNACE ROOM." It was painted in red, making it barely discernible in the room's lighting.

There was no office after all, he thought with chagrin, and he could descend no further. But this was Larry's last chance. There were no other floors to search. He turned the knob and peered through the crack in the door.

Inside, the room was dimly lit by a small night-light, plugged into the wall behind the desk. Larry stepped in and closed the door behind him. His eyes slowly adjusted to the near-darkness. As they did, Larry was surprised to see furniture instead of the old mops and ductwork one

216

would expect. To his left was a ratty loveseat, spilling its stuffing onto the cement floor. To his right, an old vinyl-covered chair. And directly in front of him was the desk. Behind it, the wall was covered with half-assembled metal shelves. Why anyone would be more comfortable down here than on the main floor, Larry couldn't imagine.

As Larry stood here, his nerves wound to the snapping point, his imagination began to play the same sort of tricks it had that evening at the slaughterhouse. The coat rack in the corner became a gallows. And Larry had to force himself to gaze for several seconds at a beanbag chair to be convinced it was not a black dog glowering at him from the corner. He laughed nervously, the sound coming out tinny and hollow. *Nothing is really what it seems here,* he told himself.

Where is that dratted shoe? On the shelves, maybe? He had to step around the chair to the far right corner of the desk. Then he sidled along the narrow space between the desk and the wall. Moving gingerly behind the desk, he bent and peered through the dim shadows cast by the night-light. He looked carefully in all the empty spaces between the jumbled books—nothing.

Maybe in one of the desk drawers? He turned in the small space, lifting his hand slowly to touch the smooth wood, to run it along the desktop, and, if by chance the shoe remained, to save his reputation. No shoe. He opened the lap drawer, his heart pounding with the fear of discovery. No shoe. The top left drawer. Nothing.

He looked in every drawer of the desk, his anxiety mounting with each unsuccessful attempt. Where had Billy Bobb put that shoe? He had to find it! Getting on his hands and knees, he searched about beneath the desk. Perhaps the shoe had been tossed on the floor . . . But no.

He sat back in the manager's chair, a sigh of desperation puffing between his lips. It was all over. In his panic-ridden mind there was only one explanation for the absence of his loafer: Billy Bobb had somehow divined its owner, and surmised the connection between the shoe and the magazine on the killing-floor of the slaughter-house. He closed his eyes, feeling a wave of self-loathing wash over him. How could he have been so careless...

And then, it called him again. Through the closed door of the heated office, it called him. *No hurry now, Larry. You're already down here—might as well have a little fun. Come on in. You won't be disappointed...*

Moving as if in a trance, he walked around the desk and out to the office door. He opened it, and it was waiting—there, in the center of the room. Slowly, Larry paced toward the nearest door of the round thing.

THE ARREST

Rose Ravelle tossed on her bed. Though she was weary, rest eluded her tonight, as it had now for so many nights.

It was all because of the Sunset Grille, she told herself. She realized with the sad wisdom of retrospection that from the day two months before when Larry had told her of his decision to confront Ellenbach about its den of iniquity, her husband had been moving away from her. And in these last weeks the estrangement had widened at a frightening pace, pushing her further into the gauzy numbness of depression, dragging leadenly at her will.

The children were becoming more difficult to handle. They couldn't help noticing the unspoken coldness between their parents. She knew that the darkness tugging at her heels was worming its way into their young spirits, as well. Yet she was so emotionally exhausted, so dreadfully drained by the constant struggle against apathy, that she herself had few resources to offer them. Always before when she or Larry had been a bit down, the other mate was there to take on more of the burden, to offer respite and solace. It had always been a partnership. But now she felt like the sole crew member in a leaky lifeboat. Her children were quietly screaming for rescue, and she couldn't bail fast enough to keep them all afloat.

As for their relationship as husband and wife, the alienation she was feeling toward him lately made the thought of physical union almost repugnant. For weeks now he had not been a husband emotionally or spiritually—why should she feel any biological desire?

And yet . . . she couldn't forget the way things had once been, before this strange darkness had come over their marriage. Despite the way she felt now, she knew deep in her heart that life with Larry had once been better. Before she had been happy to be the mate of Dr. Ravelle, had been filled with quiet pride at the way the community doted on her husband—for she knew that his public persona was closely matched by his private demeanor. He was fun; he played with the children; he did little things for her to show he still cared for and valued her. Oh, of course there had always been minor frictions: forgotten school pickups, church meetings which ran an hour longer than he anticipated, curtness when a sermon idea wasn't coming together as he hoped. Like any minister's wife she sometimes chafed at the glass house they were forced to occupy, the ideals which, like it or not, the community expected them to exemplify.

But all those, she realized, were mere irritations, nothing more than inconveniences compared to the wailing emptiness she now felt in the deep places of her heart. Larry was putting so much of his self-worth on the line with this Sunset Grille thing, he had absolutely nothing left to give any of the rest of them. When he began this crusade she never dreamed he would become so distant, so detached from the wishes and needs of the other human beings whose lives were so inextricably bound to his. He might save Ellenbach from the scourge represented by the Grille; but, she wondered, would that scourge claim his family in the process?

HE OPENED the door, and was greeted with a loud blast of sound from mounted speakers encircling the top of the round structure. There was a platform just inside the door which ran the entire circumference of the enclosure. Like a carousel, the structure turned slowly clockwise. On the platform was a near-solid ring of men leaning on a waist-high railing and peering into the center.

In the middle was something like a large turntable, spinning sedately in the opposite direction of the surrounding platform. The turntable was furnished with brightly upholstered couches painted with garishly tinted clown's faces. On the couches were women—and men.

As Larry stood there, the whole room appeared in motion; there was no still, steady anchor to which the senses might cling. The eyes, the mind, the imagination were sucked in, forced to kneel in homage to the wanton carnality below. In only a few moments—while he looked on in shock and revulsion, seeing the women who beckoned, invited, pulled the watchers' wills toward them with a steamy, hot force, and seeing a couple of the spectators quickly overcome by the dizzy, obscene wooing and stepping down to pay their money and join the figures on the couches—in those short moments, Larry realized the reason for the uneasy mannerisms of the men standing outside. They had been in here, had seen and felt the raw power of this altar of the flesh. They were trying to leave, but could not quite rid themselves of the desire for a last look. They might leave tonight, but they would come back, again and again—and eventually they would give in. And once a man ever surrendered to that insistent pull on his desire, he would leave behind him on the platform the last shreds of his self-respect, the last ragged scraps of his own notions of decency. That was the price demanded of the worshipers in this sanctuary: their souls.

A SUDDEN panic flared within Rose. With a vivid, heartsick clarity that she had, until now, shoved far back in her mind, she could visualize the dissolution of her marriage—perhaps her life. Lying on her back, staring wide-eyed at the ceiling of her bedroom, she cried out in a half-moan, "Please, God! Help my husband! Help me!" She turned over and sobbed into her pillow, *"Please, dear Lord, have mercy on us!"*

AN ABRUPT, cloying claustrophobia descended on Larry like a net-snare dropped from above. Panting, his teeth gritting with the severity of the effort, he shoved himself away from the railing of the platform. No more—he could withstand no more. His will, his restraint were stretched to the very breaking point, and there was no time for anything other than full retreat. He had to get out, had to get away from the horrible, decency-mocking magnetism of this place. Neither his career, nor his dignity, nor even his cause against the Grille had any place in his frenzied mind at this moment. His was the unreasoning flight of self-preservation—for to stay here an instant longer was to die.

He slammed open the nearest door, half-running toward the stairs. One or two of the men leaning against the walls stared at him in curiosity as he left; he neither saw nor cared.

Legs pumping violently, he pounded up one flight of stairs, then the next. The third flight brought him to ground level, and to the double green doors through which he had begun this pilgrimage into depravity. Striding toward them, heedless of the artifice of his disguise, he had just placed his hand to the knob, when he felt it turning—as if of its own will—in his hand. The door was pulled open from the other side, and two men jumped back, startled, as the opening portal brought them face-to-face with him. One of the men was Billy Bobb, who now spoke.

"John! I was just—" He glanced at the other man beside him. "That is, we were just coming to . . . to look for you."

The other man was Red Sweeney—the sheriff. Involuntarily, Larry stiffened.

"I see you've been downstairs again," Billy Bobb continued, uneasily.

"Yep," responded Larry, not yet dropping his disguise.

"You and the sheriff know each other, don't you?" asked the manager, shoving his hand into his hip pockets and looking everywhere but at Larry's face.

"Sure," said Larry. He reached to shake hands with the sheriff. When he did, a ringlet of silver flashed in the other man's hand, clamping tightly around his wrist. Red Sweeney's voice clicked on like a taped monologue.

"John Ravelle . . . You're under arrest for the rape and murder of Emily Hansen. You have the right to remain silent. You have the right to an attorney present at all questioning. If you choose to waive the right to an attorney . . ."

THE
CONFESSION

THE GOSSIP ran throughout Ellenbach with the disorganized efficiency which is the hallmark of small towns. There was no question which piece of news was the juiciest morsel of the two. That John Ravelle was capable of such a despicable act was no great surprise to a town which had learned, from his boyhood, to distrust him; but that Red Sweeney should have first arrested, not John, but *Larry*, and that the pastor had been disguised as his brother, and had just come from the basement of the Sunset Grille—it was almost too much for the town to accept.

Almost, but not quite. For no news is received with such secret, half-ashamed glee as that of the fall of one who has had long tenure atop the public pedestal. *Well!* they thought as they heard it, *I never expected such a thing from* him! *Makes you wonder what is down there.*

IT WAS Sunday morning, and the worship service had begun at the Ellenbach Community Church. But Dr. Larry Ravelle was at home, sitting in a chair in the living room, holding his head in his hands and contemplating a world in ruins.

Of course, there was no way he could stand in front of the congregation and deliver the sermon he had prepared. It would have been like bathing in acid, mouthing pious platitudes while looking into that knowing sea of faces. Impossible. So, he had called the seminarian who had served as his ministry intern the previous semester. The young man had agreed to come—thankfully, without asking too many questions—and Larry had retreated in humiliation to this room, where he had sat, eaten, and slept for the past thirty-odd hours, weaving around himself a cocoon of shame.

Rose was in the back of the house, which was a bitter relief. He couldn't withstand the reproachful looks she would surely heap on him—and deservedly so. He had disgraced her, disgraced their marriage, disgraced everything he had so loudly proclaimed he stood for. She avoided him, and he didn't need to wonder why.

The children had gone on to church, Rose having told them that Daddy and Mommy were sick this morning. Apparently, she had decided that they would be spared, at least for a while, the whispering accusation and veiled disparagement which their father had so richly earned. It was only a matter of time, though, Larry reasoned. One of their friends would say something on the playground.

My daddy says your daddy is a hypocrite!

Oh, yeah? What's that, smart-face?

That's somebody who lies about how good they are.

You're a liar!

Oh, yeah? Well, a hypocrite's the same as a liar...

The cocoon closed tightly about him; the darkness wove a close-knit web of despair before his vision.

"VISITOR to see the prisoner," the deputy announced.

Red Sweeney looked up from the paperwork he was

filling out. "Why, hello, Cyrus. What brings you around?"

"Just like the man said," replied Cyrus, nodding toward the deputy. "I'm here to see John Ravelle."

The sheriff slowly put down the pen he had been using, peering carefully at the wrinkled, grizzled face of the old man. "Who's minding the donut shop, Cyrus?"

"Closed 'er down this mornin'," Cyrus answered. "Been thinkin' about closin' on Sundays, anyway. Now— you gonna let me in to see John, or not?"

Red Sweeney shrugged. "I guess so, Cyrus," he said, rubbing the side of his nose as he leaned back in the squeaky oak swivel-chair. "No harm, I don't reckon... Sure," he finished, motioning toward the deputy. "Let him in, Doyle. Give him... oh, say... fifteen minutes."

"Thanks, Red," said Cyrus. "I appreciate this."

Again the noncommittal shrug. "Sure, Cyrus. I don't guess it'll make any difference anyhow."

Cyrus halted and aimed a mystifying look at the sheriff. "Well, now, Red," he said quietly, "I just believe it might make all the difference in the world." Then he turned and followed the deputy toward the lockup.

"Crazy old coot," mumbled Red Sweeney, returning to his paperwork.

THE CELL door clanged shut behind him, and Cyrus stood, looking down at the wretched heap crumpled onto the jailhouse cot.

John Ravelle turned his head, peering with a single eye to see who had been stupid enough to come visit him. When he recognized the baker, he dropped his chin back on the cot. "I don't recall ordering any maple bars."

"Or iron ones neither," answered Cyrus. "John, I'm here 'cause I thought you might need to talk to me."

John gave a sour laugh, turning his face toward the

wall. "Of all the things I need, chit-chat with you isn't one."

"Well, now, that just shows you how wrong people can be sometimes," Cyrus remarked cheerily, plopping down at the foot of the cot. "I think you need to talk, and I'm here to listen."

John pulled his feet in, half-rising from the cot in angry surprise. "What's wrong with your ears, Cyrus?" he asked. "I'm not interested in talking. Will you leave, or should I have Doyle haul you out?"

Cyrus smiled, shaking his head as if at a favorite, mischievous nephew. "Now you know you don't mean that, John," he said in a calming tone. "Besides . . . if I leave, who's gonna protect you from the bony men?"

John's eyes went round and white, and it was several seconds before he could draw another breath. "Who told you that?" he whispered finally in a strangled voice.

"Never you mind, son," said Cyrus softly. "It's enough that I know—and I understand. Just like I understand the devils that are chasin' each other through your head right this minute."

John sat bolt upright, his back jammed against the wall at the head of his cot, his eyes riveted on Cyrus's kindly old face.

"You need to talk, son," Cyrus insisted. "How else you gonna purge that poison from your soul? You ain't got a whole lot of time on your side, John," he urged calmly. "I think we both know that, don't we?"

John stared at him for three or four breaths—then nodded.

"Well, all right," the old man continued. "That's settled, then." He reached out and patted John companionably on the shin, like the father John's father had never been. "Come on, now, boy," he soothed, "let it all come out. You been needin' this for a long time . . ."

∗ ∗ ∗

CYRUS walked into Red Sweeney's office, smiling. "Thanks again, Red," he said. "I'll be on my way now."

"Okay, Cyrus," responded Red in a perplexed tone. "Be seein' you."

Cyrus turned toward the door to the outer office, then stopped. "Oh, by the way, Red," he said, snapping his fingers at a sudden recollection, "John told me to tell you he was ready to make that one phone call you said he was allowed."

Sheriff Sweeney looked down the hall toward the lockup, then back at Cyrus. "I . . . I'll bring him right out," he said, clearly mystified.

"You do that. Well . . . take 'er easy, Red," the baker said, again turning to leave.

The sheriff sent a clench-browed look at Cyrus's vanishing back. "What's that old geezer up to, anyway?" he asked himself.

THE PHONE beside the bed rang, then rang again. On the third ring Larry reached over and brought the receiver to his ear, with a slightly annoyed expression on his face. As if he didn't have enough problems . . . "Hello?" he said.

There was a long silence. Was this a prank call? Had it started already? "If there's somebody there—"

"Larry?" The voice sounded tight, constricted—and familiar.

"Yes," he said, "this is Larry Ravelle. To whom am I—"

"It's John. Your brother."

Now it was Larry's turn to be silent. He wondered, not for the first time, if John knew about the mixup and where it had occurred—then finally decided there was no way he couldn't know.

"Larry, I . . . I'm sorry to call you like this, but—"

John? Apologizing?

228

"—but I . . . I really need to talk to you, Larry."

"Ah . . . sure," he stumbled, trying to get his lips and brain synchronized. "Sure . . . Go ahead. I'm here."

"Not like this," John said. "Could you come down here? To the jail?"

Another long silence.

"What I have to say is best said in person," John insisted. "I . . . I need you to come down, Larry."

John? Pleading?

"Well . . . well, okay. I'll be there in just a few minutes."

He hung up the phone, his brain fogged with circling questions. Slowly he turned to Rose, who was gazing up at him with a bleached-out look.

"Rose . . . I just got a call."

She didn't move.

"From the jail—it was John."

Her eyes flickered toward him; her head moved the slightest fraction.

"He wants to talk to me. He was pretty insistent."

A furrow appeared above the bridge of her nose. "He *wants* you to come see him?" she asked. Apparently, John's unfamiliar behavior had even cracked the frozen crust of Rose's lethargy.

Larry nodded. "Yeah." He looked up at her. "I think I'd better go to him, Rose." Something like a sense of purpose began kindling in his chest. His brother needed him. How long had it been . . . ?

Now Rose nodded slowly. "All right. Yes . . . I suppose you'd better go." Her head fell back onto the pillow, and her eyes returned to their disinterested contemplation of the space between the curtains.

LARRY walked into the sheriff's office, passing next door the city hall where he had, a few weeks and an eternity ago, stood before the people of Ellenbach and railed against the place where he had been arrested by mistake. But, for the first time since the slaughterhouse episode, his mind wasn't on the Grille, or on himself, or on the guilty secret he carried within him which was now the stuff of street gossip. At this moment, for however brief a time, his thoughts were of his brother, locked in a cell in this building. John had called him. His twin brother needed him, and he was answering the call.

Red Sweeney looked up as Larry entered the office. "Oh, hello, Reverend Ravelle," he said in obvious discomfort, his eyes guiltily avoiding the pastor's.

"Hello, Sheriff." A long pause.

"Say, I sure am sorry about the mixup the other night," Red began.

"It wasn't your fault, Red," Larry said quickly. "You were just doing your job." *And I was in the wrong place at the right time,* he finished to himself.

"Well...I appreciate your taking a tolerant view, Reverend," Red said, uneasily shuffling papers on his desk. "Never in a million years would I have wanted a mistake like that to happen."

"I know that," Larry said. "And, please—could you call me Larry? 'Reverend' doesn't seem to fit, somehow."

Another moment passed before Larry cleared his throat and said, "Red, I'm here to see John."

Sweeney nodded, grabbing a silver ring strung with keys from a desk drawer. "This way," he said, striding down the hall toward the lockup. Larry followed.

When the two brothers were alone in the cell, they stared at each other for perhaps two full minutes, neither speaking a word. Then John cleared his throat, tore his eyes away, and said, half-gesturing toward the bunk beside him, "Sorry I can't offer you a chair—I'll scoot over."

"No, that's all right, John," returned Larry, squatting on the floor at the foot of the bunk. "I'll just sit over here."

John shrugged. "Suit yourself." He looked again at the floor, while Larry peered at the air above his brother's head. Neither of them knew how to begin.

"I'm glad you—" Larry started, just as John spoke.

"Thanks for—"

They both stopped, looking at each other. "You go ahead," Larry said.

John ran his fingers through his hair, then looked his brother directly in the eye. "I'm going to plead guilty, Larry," he said, his jaw barely quivering. "I'm not going to fight them. I deserve whatever I get for . . . for what I did . . ." His voice faded into a rough whisper. He clenched his jaw as a single tear spilled from his right eye and traced a wobbly track through the gristle of his two-day-old beard.

Larry's eyes dilated. His throat was frozen with the enormity of what he was hearing.

"It was like a sickness in me, Larry," John continued, jabbing his thumbs into his damp eyes. "Something I always had to fight, ever since—" he looked at Larry— "since we were kids."

Larry nodded, trying vainly to swallow with a throat suddenly as dry as silica.

"That's why Karen left me, you know," John continued, the tears dripping in a steady stream by now. "I could never have normal feelings toward her. I was always wanting . . . things she couldn't provide—things I now realize no woman should have to provide."

Larry's mind churned. *The darkness . . . The pictures . . . The bony men . . .*

"She finally had all she could take, and ran out. And I can't blame her—not really."

Larry closed his eyes. *The craving . . . Nothing exciting at home . . . Just a look; it won't hurt . . .*

"You know, Larry, it got to where . . . all I could think

about was women: how much I wanted them...how much I hated them. And then—I went down into the Sunset Grille."

Larry's breath was coming in ragged grasps by now. It was all he could do to keep from running to the cell door, screaming for Red Sweeney to let him out. John looked at him. "Larry? You all right?"

The slaughterhouse...The dancer...The turntable...The eyes—the beckoning, seducing, cajoling eyes...

"No, I'm not all right...not by a long shot," Larry said softly. "I think I needed your call about as badly as you needed to make it."

John's face slackened. "It's got you, too, doesn't it?"

Larry's eyes, captured by his twin's intent, knowing look, blinked once, twice. Then he nodded.

"I guess," said Larry haltingly, "I guess the same trouble got into me..." He held his face in his hands. "And now—I know it's nothing compared to what you're facing—but now...everything I worked for, everything I believed in...all gone...gone..." He began to sob softly.

Larry felt his brother's rough hand on his shoulder, then along his back. Instinctively he leaned into John's embrace.

The two brothers sat that way for a long, long while.

THE REUNION

"NO FAIR!" screamed Pitch, twisting his body, flailing his arms, pounding his feet. "His wife wasn't part of the deal, and you knew it, you deceivers!"

In John Ravelle's jail cell, while John and Larry gave silent comfort to each other's hurt, Dias and I watched Pitch fume. Stool was crouched silently beside him, ready for another bout with Dias. I was fearful of the outcome—only Dias and I knew how weak he still was from the battle on the hood of Larry's car.

"In the first place, Pitch," I retorted, brandishing my finger in his face, "we didn't *use* his wife; we tried to comfort her. In her distress, she called upon the Name— and you know as well as I what happens when a human does that."

"Maybe so—but she was just grasping at straws," pouted Pitch. "And what about that blasted phone call? What about John? He's been ours for a long time. That was blatant cheating!" he accused.

"Rose grasped the *right* straw," Dias growled from

where he leaned in the corner, "and she called upon the Name with a sincere heart. You're a sore loser, Pitch."

"I haven't lost yet, you overgrown fledgling," threatened Pitch, brandishing a fist. "Stool should have finished you outside the Grille."

Dias rolled his eyes and looked away.

"In the second place," I continued firmly, "Rose Ravelle was, is, and always will be part of the deal. She's Larry's wife, and her life is forever bound to his in the Supreme One's view. When she uttered the prayer of faith, however inarticulate, she was heard. You know the Supreme One doesn't require eloquence on the part of those who beseech Him. Your boss, not ours, is the one who delights in technicalities. You ought to understand that by now."

Pitch only snorted.

"And as for John," I said, "I don't know what you're talking about. We had no contact with him. You'll have to blame someone else for that. Maybe you should complain to the Supreme One," I finished pertly, starting to feel a bit cocky.

Pitch was fairly seething by now, his mouth gashed in a hate-filled snarl, flecks of spittle standing in the corners of his mouth. "Don't lecture me, twerp," he panted, his fingers curling into claws. "This isn't over yet..."

I met his livid stare, willing my face to remain calm. I couldn't suppress the shudder which ran down my back, however. Such rage, such absolute, distilled malevolence...

Looking into the contorted visage of the demon, a sudden memory rushed upon me from an unguarded spot in my mind...

His face dipped below the edge and withered into a hideous mask...I looked through the hole in Creation, and a demon's face stared back at me from where, moments ago, my brother's face had been... "Don't let go! Don't drop me!" *he wailed.*

"Lukas!" *I screamed, as he slipped into the yawning darkness below.*

He tore my bracelet from my wrist as he fell...

My vision jolted back to the present: to the jail cell, to the two weeping brothers, and the panting, glowering Stool, and...to the bracelet on the wrist of that embodiment of utter darkness which my brother had become. Slowly my gaze traveled up his arm, across his chest, to his neck, his chin...

His eyes. "*Lukas?*" I whispered.

The demon's breath stopped when I said the name. His orbs gaped from his head. A slow, evil smile began spreading over his features.

"Well, well, well," he smirked, stepping a pace or two closer to me.

Dias stirred from his corner, but I halted him with a gesture. "No, Dias...it's...it's all right."

"You hurt him," Dias growled at Pitch, "and I'll—"

"Don't worry," chuckled Pitch, his nose almost touching mine by now, "I wouldn't dream of it! After all," he finished, breathing the stench of Hell into my nostrils, "we're family, aren't we, Skandalon? Why would we possibly want to hurt one another?"

"Be careful, Skandalon!" warned Dias, from somewhere in the dim recesses of the periphery. "He's trying to work on you! He's trying to cause you to doubt."

"Doubt?" murmured Pitch, his brow wrinkled in an expression of concern. "Oh, no, my musclebound friend. Skandalon and I needn't trouble about doubt—or hope. We know where we stand, don't we, *brother?*" The last word sounded like a curse on his lips.

I couldn't move, couldn't breathe—could do nothing

but look into those seething eyes and remember, and try to understand.

"We work the same way, don't we, little Skandalon?" Pitch went on. "We test, we obstruct, we—" The next phrase bloomed in his mind, bringing a fresh sneer to his lips. "We *try* them, don't we, Skandalon? After all," he whispered, reaching out to slowly take my throat in his clawed hands, "we're *twins!*"

With a war cry, Dias charged. But by now, Stool had regained enough strength to meet him halfway across the cell. The two crashed together in a mingled bellow of rage and pain. This time Pitch joined in. I tried to shove past him to come to my partner's aid, but my twin shoved me hard against the bars of the cell, then struck me a blow in the face. Everything faded to black.

"Well," said Larry, sniffing, "I guess I'd better get on back."

"Yeah," said John, giving his brother a final pat on the shoulder before rising and seating himself on the bunk. "I guess so."

Larry nodded, raising himself to his feet. "This was good for both of us, John," he said, looking into his brother's eyes. "Better than we may ever know." A long, quiet gaze passed between them.

Larry turned to call Red Sweeney. "Larry," John said, "whatever you do, don't let go of what you have. Do whatever it takes . . . okay?"

Larry turned this over in his mind for a long time. "Okay," he whispered at last. He reached out, and the brothers squeezed hands a last time. "I'll come back—after the TV show, okay?" Larry said.

"Great," John nodded. "I'd like that a lot."

Stool groaned, and rolled off the still form of Dias. Pitch struggled to his feet, gazing about him in disgust at the prone figures of the two enemy representatives, and the milksop humans who, despite his vastly superior intellect and skill, were for the moment beyond his reach.

"Come on, Stool," he cursed, kicking the damaged but victorious ogre, "let's go. There's nothing more we can do here..."

The demons limped out with great difficulty. As he departed, Pitch cast a final glance back at Larry, who awaited the coming of the jail attendant. "You're mine," he vowed, his lip curling in contempt.

LARRY pulled into the driveway of the parsonage just as the worship assembly was being dismissed across the street. He sat in his car a moment, looking through the windows at the church members making their way to their automobiles, some with children in tow. A few glanced in the direction of the parsonage, then away.

It occurred to him that he ought to go among them, begging their forgiveness for the embarrassment and reproach he had caused in his self-righteous hypocrisy. He owed them that—and so much more.

But he tore his gaze away, focusing on the front door of his house. There was another matter to be tended before anything else, one that was long overdue. He would see to it first.

He got out of the car and went inside quickly, with the real or imagined stares of the homeward-bound congregation prickling at his back. Shutting the front door behind him, he leaned against it, eyes closed. He was summoning strength for the short walk back to his bedroom—the longest walk of his life.

Rose was still lying on the bed. When she heard the door creak, she turned to look at him, her eyes limpid pools of vulnerability and despondence. He went to the bedside, knelt, and took one of her hands in both of his.

He could not yet look at her face. So he bowed, almost in an attitude of prayer, and spoke his discourse into the muffling folds of the Dutch Doll quilt atop the bed.

"Rose, I . . . there's something I have to say. More like a million things, really . . . I haven't been honest with you, Rose. I've kept something from you all these years, because I was ashamed to admit it to you—and I guess because I was ashamed to admit it to myself," he murmured.

At the tone of his voice, her brow wrinkled. Hesitantly she turned to look at him. This was something different—something real. She sensed a meekness, a humility that had been lacking in him since—when? The words now stumbling from his lips had none of the easy fluency he used in his sermons, none of the high-handed manner he had lately adopted in justifying his long, unexplained absences. This was a new sound . . . the sound of unrehearsed contrition, of abject defenselessness. Almost against her will, she began to listen carefully.

"I guess the roots of the problem go back a long way," Larry was saying, "to when John and I were kids. Talking to him at the jail just now, it hit me—the thing I've been hiding from you; from everybody. But it's finally caught up with me, and I can't hide any longer.

"Rose," he said, his voice breaking on the soft contours of her name, "I . . . I'm an addict." For a moment he could say no more, sobbing softly into the quilt.

Slowly her hand came unclasped from his—and reached, with a few starts and stops, to his shoulder, where it began to rub in small, comforting circles.

"It's not a drug—not really," he was saying in a soggy voice, "but it entraps and enslaves just as surely as heroin or cocaine ever did. And when I think of the vain, conceited way I stood up there on Sundays," he added, softly pounding a fist against the mattress, "and spouted spiritual clichés at the church, as if I didn't need to be kneeling in shame on the floor..." His voice broke again.

When he could continue, he said, "Rose, I always thought I could overcome this on my own. I thought there'd be no need to tell you any of this. But talking to John, I realized I've been ignoring all this time the advice I gave others. Like, *'Confess your faults one to another, and pray for one another, that ye may be healed...'*"

Rose was blinking rapidly as tears spilled from her brimming eyes. Both her hands now rested on his shoulders. He looked up at her, and her fingers traced the line of his jaw. Again he spoke.

"Rose, I'm addicted, obsessed, plagued—whatever you want to call it—with pornography. I have been ever since Mom died and Dad...went wrong." His eyes begged her for understanding, his fists clenched the quilt as if it were a lifeline, a tether to her compassion.

"The only times in my life I've been able to forget my cravings, just for a few minutes, have been the times when I've been totally focused on you," he said, his voice trembling. "Please, Rose...forgive me, if you can. Don't give up on me. With God's help, and yours, I'll get past this...this filthy fixation." His head fell into her lap, and great, raw sobs racked his frame.

Her hands stroked his hair, the back of his neck, his arms. As she comforted her husband, she hummed in her mind, over and over, a one-line hymn of thanksgiving for the answered prayer she had scarcely been aware of uttering: *Thank You, Lord. Thank You for bringing him back. Thank You...Thank You...*

The front door opened, then closed. The sound of small footsteps was heard in the hall. "Mom? Dad?" called Peter doubtfully, as Annie trailed her big brother through the empty house.

"In here, kids!" called Rose in a shaky voice. The door opened. The children saw their parents, and then the four of them were tangled in a great, laughing, crying heap.

THE TAPING

IT WAS Monday afternoon, and downtown Ellenbach was abuzz with excitement. A large van, emblazoned with the logo and call letters of the television station in Laird, had arrived at midmorning in the street in front of the Sunset Grille, and crew members had been scurrying to and fro all morning, carrying booms, microphones, cameras, lights, and sundry other nameless equipment into the red-brick building on Washington Avenue. This was the most excitement the town had seen since anyone could remember.

The taping was scheduled to begin at five o'clock. Kurt Stedley's research team had done its work. They had contacted a number of Ellenbachians on both sides of the Sunset Grille issue, assuring the presence of a large and vocal number from both constituencies. Kurt's interest in the program had skyrocketed after he heard about the arrest mixup and the discovery of Reverend Ravelle inside the Grille. Kurt's show thrived on controversy and spectacle—and this program appeared to have plenty of both.

Kurt himself arrived on the set at four o'clock in a station-owned van. It had begun to snow. The van pulled up curbside in front of a crowd of oglers and autograph-seekers who stood about chatting in the white, wintry dusk.

As the van's door opened, Kurt was taking a final drag at a cigarette. He thumped it into the street and was immediately all smiles, stepping—as quickly as decorum and ratings would allow—through the crowd swirling about the door of the Sunset Grille. When the door had closed behind him, the smile evaporated like alcohol on the back of the hand. He stared about the cable-strung room cluttered with microphone booms, light stands, and camera dollies.

"Where's the preacher?" he bellowed at the top of his voice to no one in particular. Charlie, the director for the show, hurried up to Kurt, a dutiful look on his face. He began speaking in a rush.

"Kurt, I asked Pam before we left the station this morning if all the principals were lined up, and she said yes. I asked her if we told everyone to be on the set by three-thirty and she said yes. When I got here a while ago, I asked the makeup crew if the pastor showed up for his call and they said no." The director shrugged help-lessly.

"Get on the phone, Charlie!" Kurt shouted, a blood vessel standing out prominently on his forehead.

Charlie winced—the blood vessel was always a bad sign.

"Get that guy down here!" Stedley continued. "You *know* I want my guests on the set an hour and a half before taping starts! Now do it!"

Charlie scurried away, desperately searching for a telephone.

Kurt watched him go, satisfied he had made his point.

He blew out his cheeks, looking around at the preparations for the show. He felt the familiar butterflies in the pit of his stomach—which was good. It told him he hadn't lost the edge, the adrenaline-induced state of alertness he would need to bob and weave around the emotions and reactions he intended to induce in his audience. His personal motto was, 'If they're not mad at you when you've finished, you didn't do your job.' He doubted this show would present any problems in the reaction department.

Billy Bobb Detzer walked up, smiling and sticking out his hand. Kurt took the offered greeting. "Hello there, Mr. Det—rather, Billy Bobb."

"That's more like it, Kurt!" said Billy Bobb jovially. He looked around at the foreign tangle of cords, cables, and broadcasting hardware scattered around his establishment. "I hope your folks have everything they need in here. I don't think we have room for anything else except a few people."

"The setup looks okay," Kurt assured him. Taking the manager by the elbow, he guided him to a nearby barstool. "Now let me tell you what I plan to do, Billy Bobb. First off, we want to give the viewers a hook—a zinger, something to make them want to stick with the show once they've started watching. So I plan to lead in by telling exactly what you've got to offer here: good food, good drinks—and beautiful girls. You with me so far?"

Billy Bob nodded thoughtfully.

"Now, then," the reporter continued, "the next thing we've got to do is get them solidly on your side. I figure the best way to do that is playing up the economics issue—poor farmers losing their farms, lousy grain markets, all that kinda stuff. Right?"

Billy Bobb nodded again, pursing his lips.

"Then—I just thought of this while driving over—it would be a great touch if we could get one or two of the girls—from downstairs, I mean—on camera. Let them really sell, you know? Talk about how much they enjoy their work, and—What's wrong, Billy Bobb?"

Billy Bobb was shaking his head firmly. "Can't do that, son," he said in a tight-lipped voice. "I won't allow it."

"What do you mean?" Kurt asked incredulously.

"The girls downstairs ain't gonna be on camera; that's what I mean."

Kurt stared at him, blinking. "Why?"

"The girls downstairs don't mingle on the ground floor," the manager said, his jaw adopting a truculent set. "It's . . . it's bad for business—and that's all I'm gonna say about it."

An exasperated look came over Kurt. "Come on, Billy Bobb!" he pleaded. "You've got some real lookers down there, I know you do! Why in the world wouldn't you want them on camera for everyone to see? You said yourself you were after publicity on this thing! Why not let our viewing area have a peek at what you're—"

Kurt's voice halted, stopped in its tracks by the expression on Billy Bobb's face. Kurt had the same eerie, goosebumpy sensation he'd had the first time he met the white-haired man, a feeling as if some nameless threat lurked just below the surface of Billy Bobb's eyes. Kurt knew, with a certainty beyond understanding, that he didn't want to arouse that threat.

"Okay, okay," he said placatingly, "if it's got to be that way. . ."

"It does," the manager grunted.

"Then we'll just do without the sex appeal, I guess," Kurt sighed. He glanced toward the door at the tallish, attractive, clean-cut man who had just entered. He turned toward Billy Bobb. "Is that—?"

"Yep," nodded Billy Bobb. "That's him."

Kurt walked toward the newcomer, holding out a hand and giving off his most polished smile. "Hi! I'm Kurt Stedley, and you must be—"

"Larry Ravelle," said the other man softly. The pastor looked past Kurt as they shook hands, nodding gravely at Billy Bobb. Kurt glanced over his shoulder in time to see Billy Bobb return the greeting.

Like two knights before a joust, Kurt thought. "Well, Reverend Ravelle—"

"Please," the other man cut in, "call me Larry."

"Well, then, Larry," Kurt amended without missing a beat, "we'd better get you over to the makeup girls. The cameras start rolling in less than an hour, you know..." He walked off, his arm around Larry's shoulders, chatting companionably as if they were old college roommates.

I WOKE up, lifted my head, and saw John Ravelle lying on his cot, staring upward into the corridor beyond the cell. I turned my head, moaning with pain, and followed his gaze to a high, barred window. Through it I could see only the night darkness.

I turned my head again—and saw Dias. His chest had been torn open by the demons' claws and fangs. He lay in the middle of the floor, and wasn't moving—at all.

He must have put up a titanic struggle. Small patches of demon tissue decorated the bars of the cell with a grisly memento of the valiant defiance of my poor, defeated friend.

Grimacing with pain, I crawled to him and knelt beside him. He wasn't dead, of course—that's impossible for us—but clearly there was nothing I could do for him now. He slept in that place where Heaven's warriors are comforted while their bodies heal. I couldn't lift him, even had I been in full strength instead of badly hampered by pain.

I had to get out—to find out what had become of our adversaries, and Larry. Also, I knew the time was drawing near—tomorrow night, wasn't it?—when the pipe would open for our return journey. Again I looked at Dias's face. Would my partner be well enough to get to the pipe when it was time? I didn't see how. His wounds were too great; it would be a long while before he recovered enough to lift himself.

I unbuckled his sword—the weapon he had been unable to use in this last fight—and hung it, like a bandoleer, across my chest. Without Dias's strength to protect me, I might have to make such use of the weapon as I could. The notion gave me little cause for comfort. I didn't at all relish the thought of continuing an already shaky assignment without his strength and bulk to provide reinforcement. So far I hadn't done too well against my designated opponent, Pitch. I wasn't eager to undertake a solo confrontation with him and Stool combined.

"Sleep well, my brave companion," I whispered, leaning above his motionless face. "If I can, I'll come and get you." With a final, pained glance at his horrible wounds, I rose to my feet, and tottered from the cell.

Red Sweeney was reading a newspaper in the outer office. I looked over his shoulder, and gasped. Today was Monday! I had lain dormant in the cell for an entire earthday! The clock on the wall told me the rest: It was nearly time for Larry's television interview. And tonight at midnight the pipe would open for my homeward journey. What would Pitch do at this critical juncture, if left unhindered?

I had to get down to the Grille—and fast.

THE CROWD gathered inside the Sunset Grille was quiet and attentive. Kurt Stedley had just finished explaining the procedures and formats to follow while the show was taping. As usual, he had done an excellent job of building rapport with the audience, making them feel at ease while turning on all the charm he possessed in order to win their loyalty. He stood in front of one of the cameras. They were almost ready to begin.

Seated to Kurt's right in a canvas folding chair was Billy Bobb Detzer, looking calm and relaxed beneath the bright lights and swaying microphone booms. To Kurt's left was Larry, seated in a similar chair and appearing somewhat more agitated and ill at ease than his white-haired counterpart.

"Everybody ready, folks?" beamed Kurt, taking in the audience with his practiced grin. "All right, Charlie—count us down, and let's get started."

The director spoke softly into the headset connecting him with the people in the sound van outside who were running the board and the videotape machine. He then looked up at Kurt, raising an index finger: "Three . . . two . . . one . . ." He pointed at Kurt just as the red light atop the camera winked on. From the monitor speakers came the familiar theme for the Kurt Stedley Show, and the taping was under way.

"Take a rural setting," said a toothy Stedley, "in a country where constitutional rights and freedom of speech are still respected. Add to it a progressive form of entertainment and one man's outraged sense of morality. Shake well. Heat. And you've got our topic for the day. On this edition of the Kurt Stedley Show, we'll take a look at the controversy that's rattling the small town of Ellenbach, a battle raging over a place called the Sunset Grille. Some say it's just a great place to eat, some say it's a den of iniquity. Stay with us, and see what you think! We'll be right back after this . . ."

The music broke in and the red light went off. In this spot would be inserted a commercial by the major sponsor for the Kurt Stedley Show. After Kurt had consulted his notes for the next segment, Charlie gave another countdown, and the taping resumed.

"Welcome back to the Kurt Stedley Show, folks!" he grinned, then allowed his face to assume a more serious, purposeful cast as he continued. "Today we're in Ellenbach, a small community being ravaged by a struggle that is polarizing its citizens along moral, religious, economic, and social lines. We're coming to you from inside the Sunset Grille, that controversial business establishment which, depending on whom you listen to, is either the salvation or the damnation of this town in our nation's heartland. The first order of business today will be getting to know the principal players in this real-life drama."

Kurt turned to Billy Bobb with a cordial smile. "Mr. Detzer, you're the manager of the Sunset Grille here, I believe?"

"That's right," said Detzer. "And, Kurt," he continued in an easy, familiar manner, "I told you to call me Billy Bobb."

"So you did, Billy Bobb, so you did," chuckled Kurt delightedly. "Tell me, Billy Bobb," he asked, his brow furrowing in photogenic puzzlement, "what made you want to operate a place like the Sunset Grille—here in a small town like Ellenbach?"

"Well, now, Kurt, I'm glad you asked that," said the manager, turning to look meaningfully into the camera, as if he'd been doing it all his life.

In his chair, Larry felt his apprehension deepening. It seemed apparent that Stedley and Billy Bobb were getting along famously—at least on camera. How would the reporter, well known for his badgering interview style, treat him when his turn came?

"When representatives of the organization came to

me," Billy Bobb was saying in an earnest, forthright voice, "they told me they wanted to open a first-class place here in Ellenbach, a place where folks could come and enjoy a fine meal, if that's what they wanted, or have a nice, quiet drink if that was what they were after. And . . . if they wanted to, they could even see a live floor show—"

In the front row of the audience, Fig Pemberley huffed audibly. Billy Bobb glanced at her, and went on.

"Now, Kurt, I don't want our viewers getting the wrong impression. Not everything that goes on here at the Sunset Grille is intended for general viewing—"

"The 'floor shows' you just referred to—is that what you mean?" Kurt asked helpfully.

"Right," nodded Billy Bobb. "There's no way in the world I would ever allow youngsters, for example, to see things that might be inappropriate for them. And that's why we keep all that kind of thing on the bottom floors, where the attendants can keep a real close eye on everybody that goes in and out."

"So—you're pretty careful about who you let in to see the floor shows—is that it?"

"You bet," Billy Bobb affirmed. "After all, Kurt, this great nation of ours was founded on the principle of freedom of speech and expression, right? And, as long as what a man does in his free time doesn't hurt anybody else, why shouldn't he be free to enjoy himself however he wants?"

"What about Emily Hansen?" shouted someone from the back of the audience.

Kurt grimaced, then pasted on his patient, good-humored grin. "Now, just a minute there, folks," he chuckled, facing the audience. "There'll be plenty of time later in the show for audience participation. As my viewers know, I believe in letting everybody have their say.

But, please," he begged, "wait until we've had a chance to hear both sides of the issue. Then, I promise, you can ask all the tough questions you want. Fair enough?" he asked, the very picture of wide-eyed impartiality.

"Kurt," interjected Billy Bobb, "can I say something?"

Kurt turned back to the white-haired man. "Go right ahead, Billy Bobb."

Again the manager peered into the camera's lens with a soulful, sincere gaze. "I don't guess there's anybody in Ellenbach that feels any worse than I do over what happened to that poor young girl. Like everybody else, I was just sick when I heard about it—that's all, just sick." He paused to blink and swallow. "And, yes, it's true; the man who was arrested for the crime had been in here once or twice—"

Larry felt himself bridling. He clenched his fists in his lap.

"But folks, I ask you: How can you blame my girls for what happened to that young victim? Did they tell that man to commit such a vile act? I just don't see the relationship between a man spending a little time in my place and the perpetration of such a horrible crime." By now, Billy Bobb's eyes had the drooping, melancholy look of a basset hound. It would be difficult for anyone, seeing this man's face for the first time, to equate such a sincere, compassionate plea with sponsorship of a violent crime against a woman.

Larry didn't know which was more abominable: Billy Bobb's facile misrepresentation about John's patronage of the Grille, or his slick disassociation of himself from the activities downstairs. How could he sit there and put on such a hypocritical act? He fumed in his seat, eagerly waiting for his chance at the microphone. *I'll make him sick for sure,* he promised himself.

"Well...thank you, Billy Bobb," Kurt intoned in a

serious voice, nodding thoughtfully, as if to himself. "And now, let's meet the other figure in this morality play," he said, pacing evenly to his left, toward Larry. As the overhead mike followed him toward the pastor's seat, he said, "Your name, sir, is Dr. Larry Ravelle, and you're the pastor of the Ellenbach Community Church—is that right?"

"It is," Larry said.

"And, of course, Dr. Ravelle, you are familiar with the Sunset Grille—would that be a fair statement?"

Larry nodded tersely. "Correct," he said.

"And you, Dr. Ravelle, you take an opposing view to that just expressed by Mr. Detzer—would that be a fair statement?"

"Absolutely," said Larry decisively. "Mr. Detzer has cleverly skirted the true crux of the matter here, and I want to say—"

"Let me get something straight for our viewers, Dr. Ravelle," cut in Stedley smoothly. "The Sunset Grille operates within the codes and statutes of the city of Ellenbach, does it not?"

Larry paused doubtfully. "I suppose so—"

"And you have mounted a drive to get the codes changed so that the Sunset Grille could no longer do so—is that right?" Gone was the affable, smiling interviewer. In his place was the efficient, no-nonsense investigator, aiming his questions in a rapid-fire manner at the object of his interrogation.

"Ah, yes," stuttered Larry, flustered by the sudden change in the tenor of the questioning. "There was an initiative to restrict businesses serving alcoholic beverages from providing the sort of—live entertainment offered by Mr. Detzer's establishment . . ."

I limped into the Grille, and saw that the taping was under way. I looked around the crowded, floodlit room and spotted Larry, a camera zooming in for a closeup of his face as the interviewer fired questions at him from point-blank range.

Larry was sweating profusely, and his words were coming out in a disorganized tangle. But that wasn't what bothered me.

At his shoulder stood Pitch, shouting in his ear. "You'll show them all," he was telling Larry in a rough, commanding voice. "If you just get the chance, you'll show them what hypocrites and liars these media people are—not to mention that scumbag Detzer over there!"

But Larry wasn't getting a chance to show anybody anything. Though delaying for now any mention of Larry's visit to the Grille—"a hot one for the close," Kurt had decided—the interviewer kept up a barrage of leading questions, slanted steeply toward the Grille's side of the argument. And Pitch was maintaining such an unceasing level of noise and harassment that Larry had no chance to gather himself, to begin to say what he had really intended.

"Where is the cutoff point, Dr. Ravelle, for the church's involvement in community business?" Stedley asked.

"That would be," said Larry, "when there is no longer any need for its involvement."

Kurt paused in thought. "And who is to be the judge of that?"

The cameras zoomed in on the pastor's glistening face.

"When the sheep have gone astray," Larry said, "then that's the duty of the shepherd."

"Which would be you. Is that correct?"

"In some cases, yes. That's correct."

At that, loud hoots sounded from a number of farmers in the audience. Significantly, Stedley did nothing about this interruption.

Fig shifted nervously in her seat. Kurt Stedley stroked his chin and paced back and forth with all the savvy of a prosecutor.

"Are any of your sheep here today?" Kurt asked in a mocking tone.

"Of course . . . yes."

"Now seriously, Dr. Ravelle! 'The shepherd,' 'the sheep'—for the benefit of those of our viewers less familiar with such terminology, how about some plain answers? What drove you, for example, to try to inhibit free enterprise through tampering with the existing liquor laws? What's your real motive here? Is it just a chance to demonstrate your clout, your control over this community? Is this your chance to polish your image? And maybe get a bigger pastorate in the process?"

"Sir, I'm afraid you've lost me," said Larry through clenched teeth.

Kurt couldn't resist that opening.

"Imagine that! A shepherd—lost!"

Several in the audience snickered, but Billy Bobb wisely maintained an air of pained detachment. When the laughter died down, Larry tried to explain himself.

"I was referring to your statement about my motive, sir. I have only one, if you are really concerned with it. Would you like to hear it?"

"Be my guest," said Kurt.

"My motive is to expose darkness wherever it exists," said Larry through tight lips. "Surely a man, such as yourself, would describe what goes on below us as 'darkness.' Wouldn't you?"

Kurt was mildly annoyed by the question. The ratings demanded that his audience believe the worst—or best, depending on the point of view—about the Sunset Grille. But how could he prove this without showing some of the female entertainers? Until now, he had done nothing to include the farmers. Turning toward the camera, Kurt made the switch like a pro.

"With us tonight are several spokesmen for the grain and cattle growers of this fine community. Perhaps it is these men and their families who feel Dr. Ravelle's pressure the most. These are decent people who have found it more and more difficult to hang on to farms and ranches that have been in their families, in some cases, for decades. They're not the type you or I would describe as 'dirty old men.' We'll talk to them—right after this..." The theme music faded in.

THE CARD

I RUSHED to Larry's side when the red light blinked off. Pitch was so absorbed in his caustic monologue of denunciation that he didn't notice my approach in the crowd.

"Larry! You've got to tell them!" I shouted at him. "Remember the promise you made to Rose! You can't win by using the same weapons they use—they won't ever fit your hand! Remember! Look in your pocket!"

A troubled look came over Larry, and his hand strayed to the inside pocket of his jacket. He withdrew something from it, then looked down: It was one of the index cards from his seminary studies, inscribed with this message:

To keep me from becoming conceited because of these surpassingly great revelations, there was given me a thorn in my flesh, a messenger of Satan, to torment me. Three times I pleaded with the Lord to take it away from me. But he said to me, "My grace is sufficient for you, for my power is made perfect in weakness." Therefore I will boast all the more gladly about my weaknesses, so that Christ's power may rest on me. That is why, for Christ's sake, I delight in weaknesses, in insults, in hardships, in persecutions, in difficulties. For when I am weak, then I am strong . . .

When Pitch saw the card, he screamed with pain and revulsion. Leaping back, he glared at me as I stood at Larry's side.

"You miserable meddler!" he raged.

"I'm not meddling. I'm assigned to this man—remember?" I made my voice as hard and determined as I could muster, meeting his maddened gaze calmly—I hoped.

"I thought I finished you back in the cell," he growled. "Blast that big friend of yours—he kicked up such a fuss I must have gotten careless . . ."

"Must have," I observed laconically. "Anyway—here I am. And this time you're going to lose, Pitch."

"Oh, is that right?" he sneered nastily. "We'll see how your tepid pastor reacts when he realizes what your plan will do to his career, and to his precious, ragged reputation—"

"He knows, Pitch," I responded. "We don't conceal any clauses in our agreements—unlike yours. He's accepted the consequences as an inevitable result of his actions—for which he's been forgiven."

"Forgiven, eh?" snarled Pitch. "He won't feel so forgiven when they drum him out of that pathetic little pulpit down the street—"

I shrugged. "Feelings have little to do with it, Pitch. Feelings don't change the facts. And the facts are—you've lost this man. And he's won. You tried to make him forget that, but I've just reminded him."

Pitch uttered an inarticulate scream of rage, followed by a string of sordid curses. "You won't get him!" he screeched at me, shaking his fist in my face. "I'll have him—and *you*—in Hell before this is all over!" He flung his words at me. "Do you hear me? Do you hear, *brother?*"

I saw the director frown, then jiggle his headset. Music came over the loudspeakers. It was time for the show to continue.

After a smooth lead-in and summary of the show thus far, Kurt turned toward a group of farmers and ranchers seated on the front row of the audience.

"What do you gentlemen think of the proposed ordinance?" He held his microphone out to capture their responses.

"It'd take food from my children's mouths," said one man.

"Billy Bobb's place helped me pay my bills when there was no other way to get it done," said another man. "He's a saint, if you ask me."

"Well, can't the Grille continue?" asked Stedley earnestly. "I mean . . . without the floor shows?"

"Don't think so," opined one of the men. "Another restaurant—Frank's Place, I believe it was called—tried that a while back. Didn't work out. People wanted more reason to drive all the way out here."

"Yeah. If there can't be a show where there's booze," said a third, "then there ain't gonna be people where there's no show. And then the Grille would have to close, and we'd all be hard put to find as good a market for our stuff."

"Hardly sounds right, does it?" asked Kurt sympathetically—"taking away a legal establishment that enables you folks to earn your living." The men nodded their heads in agreement.

Kurt, with the sure, confident manner of a lawyer who

knows his case to be watertight, approached the place where the forlorn pastor sat. *You poor sap,* he thought, *never sell vice short. Everybody knows that.*

"Well, Dr. Ravelle, you've just heard from some of the people who would be most directly impacted by the closing of the Sunset Grille. What do you have to say to them?" He waited, not allowing the smirk he felt to show on his face.

"Now!" I yelled at Larry. "This is the time! Do what you decided to do!"

"To Hell with all of them!" Pitch was shouting in his ear. "These clods aren't worthy of you! They'll never understand any of this! You spill your guts to them, and all they'll do is laugh in your face and humiliate your wife and kids! You owe them nothing! *Nothing!*"

Larry's hand twitched, then moved to the outside of his jacket—the place where the index card lay concealed in his pocket... *For when I am weak, then I am strong...*

He looked up, first at Kurt Stedley, then at the people in the audience silently awaiting his reply. His eyes never flickered toward the camera. Instead, he gazed steadily toward the people of Ellenbach as he spoke.

"Before we go any further, I... I have something to say that's... that's just about the hardest thing I ever had to say in my entire life." Larry halted, swallowing hard several times.

The audience grew very still, each person shifting in his seat, the better to view the pastor's face. Even Stedley's face betrayed an expression of honest bewilderment. *What is this Bible-thumping nut going to do now?*

On his chair, Billy Bobb shifted uncomfortably. Things had been going so well. He scented a change in the wind, and not, he suspected, for the better.

"I was born and raised right here in Ellenbach," Larry

was saying. "A lot of you people in this room knew me when...when my brother and I were kids."

Members of the audience glanced uncomfortably at one another at the reference to John Ravelle.

"You were with us when my mother died, and you saw the way my father suffered." Several more swallows. "Our dad was an unhappy man—I guess that's no secret. He had to raise John and me the best he could, without Mom around to help out.

"But there was something you didn't know," Larry said, his voice beginning to tremble, his eyes glazing with tears of shame. "My brother and I shared an awful secret for most of our lives, a secret I had tried in vain to escape, up until yesterday, when I was talking with John in his cell at the county jail..."

Larry rubbed his eyes with the heel of his hands, then looked directly at Kurt. "You see, Mr. Stedley, and anyone in your audience who doesn't already know it, the man Billy Bobb was talking about earlier—the one who raped and killed Emily Hansen—that man is my twin brother—John Ravelle."

Kurt almost gasped to hear Reverend Ravelle bring up this spicy bit of information on his own.

Larry continued: "You go and ask him, Mr. Stedley, if what he saw and heard in the basement of the Sunset Grille had any influence on what he did that night. Go and ask him if you want, but I can tell you the answer he'll give you. I can tell you, because I've felt the same hideous influence working inside me that my brother John felt that night—just after he left the Sunset Grille.

"Ever since John and I were kids," Larry said, his voice cracking repeatedly, "we've both been addicted—"

Kurt's mouth came open again.

"—addicted to...lust."

Behind the cameras, the crewmen kept their lenses

trained unwaveringly on Larry Ravelle's tear-streaked face—though they were unaware of doing so. Like everyone else in the room, they were completely captivated by the spectacle of a well-respected, influential pastor baring such untidy secrets not only to his hometown, but to an entire television viewing audience.

"Maybe it had something to do with Mom's death—or Dad's reaction to it," Larry was saying. "Or maybe John and I were just more susceptible somehow. I don't know exactly why it got started. But I do know this." His eyes went back to the people of his community. "I knew then, and I know now, just as surely as my brother John knew on the night he committed that crime, that it was wrong, and that I ought to stop—immediately." His eyes roved among them, challenged them to dispute the truth he had just asserted.

"We both knew it was wrong, but, for whatever reason, we didn't have the strength to stop. We went on and on—never satisfied, never admitting to ourselves that we were allowing something to sink its claws into us that would never leave of its own accord.

"It affected us in different ways, John and me," he continued. "John wasn't quite as able as I was to keep it under wraps. So," he said, his chest heaving with the effort of controlling his voice, "John's lust cost him his marriage; and it infected him with a jaded, pathological view of sexuality that tainted the image of every woman he ever saw. That was what brought him here," Larry said, looking angrily at the manager, "night after night after night. He saw women who paraded the sick view he already had—who seemed to justify any base desire his imagination could conceive. Night after night, he had his sickness confirmed, fueled, encouraged. And one night it just got to be too much for him to handle. The opportunity presented itself, and . . ."

It was some moments before Larry could go on. It was time for another break in the taping, but neither Charlie, nor Kurt, nor any of the crew in or outside the Sunset Grille took any thought of halting the tape.

"The things I'm telling you aren't supposition or conjecture," Larry explained when his voice had returned. "My brother told me all this yesterday in his cell. He knows how hideous his actions were, and he's prepared to suffer the consequences. In a way, he's almost relieved."

Soft sobs were heard among the audience by now. Even the farmers on the front row had a guilty, saddened look on their faces. John Ravelle had been one of them, even if he wasn't the most popular man in the county.

"But what about me?" Larry asked. "What about the pastor, Dr. Ravelle—the golden boy," he scoffed, "the darling of Ellenbach? Surely Larry Ravelle didn't ever have the same sort of feelings that culminated in the rape and murder of Emily Hansen!" Again his eyes glittered a challenge. "Wrong. I was just as guilty as John ever was, folks. I just didn't get caught.

"No, I didn't ever actually lay violent hands on a woman," he said. "But that doesn't excuse the things I thought about sometimes. Maybe I didn't go down to the basement of this place as often as my brother did— but I was here millions of times in my mind.

"I've walked past the newsstands, and seen the covers of the magazines," he went on, "and sworn I wasn't going to look, wasn't going to give in, wasn't going to let the desire overtake me...and found myself walking back, pulling out my wallet to buy my dollar's worth of filthy fantasy. I've gone on trips to other towns, stayed alone in hotels where no one knew who Larry Ravelle was—and watched the X-rated movies on the TV, wondering if even I knew who Larry Ravelle was."

Many of the men in the audience were hanging their heads as they listened to Larry confess the secrets of their hearts.

"In God's name, listen to what I'm saying! No one is immune, people!" he cried. "No one! This stuff can creep into your hearts, and curl around your soul, and choke your honor to death—and all the while telling you it isn't going to hurt you or anyone else! It can poison your relationships with those dearest to you..." He swallowed and blinked, then went on. "It will kill you slowly, and tell you you're enjoying it. I know," he finished in a whisper, "because I've seen what happens on the bottom floor of the Sunset Grille—and it almost killed *me!*"

Pitch howled in rage and torment, and his scream was taken up by all the demons inside the Grille. I could see their grotesque figures whirling in the air about me, writhing in agony as Larry pronounced the true name of the Grille's product: death.

One of the demons—a snakelike apparition with the jaws and teeth of a dragon, twined about one of the main power cables, snapping and biting in frenzy at everything within its reach. As I watched, I saw its teeth clench the cable, biting down harder and harder.

ONE of the technicians in the sound van jerked his headset away from his ears and threw it on the floor, looking at it as if it were a live serpent. "Did you hear that?" he asked, his eyes wide with alarm.

"Hear what?" asked another.

"Oh, man!" intoned a third, pointing her finger at one of the monitor screens. "We've got real trouble in there!"

The others looked. One of the cameras had turned away from its full-frame closeup of Larry Ravelle, and was trained on the corner of the room where the power cords were located. A huge tongue of flame had bloomed from amidst the tangle of cables, and even as the technicians watched in horror, it licked eagerly up the back wall of the Sunset Grille.

INSIDE, the acrid ozone-smell of electricity filled the air, along with the smoke that quickly billowed outward from the burning wall. People in the audience, coughing and crying aloud in panic, had scrambled from their seats and were climbing over one another, trying to escape the conflagration which ran toward them on eager, glowing feet. In the face of the fire's terrifying threat, questions of morality, ethics, economics—even identity—succumbed to the onrushing flood of hysteria that roared from the other side of the room.

The fire ripped up the back wall behind the bar. The heat caused the massive mirror hanging there to burst, spraying slivers of glass like shrapnel.

In the main room at ground level, smoke was so thick that even the people farthest from the place where the fire had started were about to be overcome. Desperately, they belly-crawled over furniture, sound equipment, and each other toward their one hope of freedom: the front door.

Those who first reached the door grasped the handle, frantically trying it. But it was a cold, wet evening in Ellenbach, and the latch was jammed. "It's stuck!" coughed one of the farmers, jerking maniacally on the stubborn latch.

Then the door crashed open, pulled from the outside. As a surge of people fell outside onto the sidewalk, Cyrus stepped up and peered intently into the smoke-strangled room. "Where's Larry?" he shouted in vain to the choking, coughing refugees from the inferno. "Has anybody seen Dr. Ravelle?" The heated handle of the door had burned the skin of Cyrus's palm when he gripped it to pull the door open, but he scarcely heeded this in his anxiety. "Is Larry Ravelle still in there?" he shouted. No one answered him.

And then Larry stumbled through the doorway, just ahead of a pile of blazing timbers which crashed down from the burning ceiling. The pastor was half-carrying a semiconscious Kurt Stedley. The two men fell through the blazing doorway into the arms of the just-arrived firefighters and medical team. Oxygen masks were clapped over their faces, and they were whisked away on wheeled stretchers, amid the wail of sirens and the hacking of emergency vehicle radios.

When Cyrus saw Larry, he climbed through the tangled mass of coughing victims, pacing quickly beside the stretcher as the medics wheeled it toward the waiting ambulance. "Larry! Can you hear me? It's Cyrus!"

The pastor coughed into his mask, wincing at the pain in his chest. His eyes opened, recognizing the old man. He nodded weakly.

"You done real good in there, son," said Cyrus, gripping Larry's hand tightly. "Real good."

Larry struggled to lift his mask. "I think we were the last two inside—" he began.

"No, I mean before that," interrupted Cyrus. "What you said. Real good."

Larry's hand squeezed Cyrus's. "Thanks," he husked. And then he was inside the ambulance, the doors shut. Cyrus stood still and watched as the vehicle pulled away toward the hospital.

"Real good," he said once more, then turned back toward the chaotic crowd outside the Sunset Grille.

* * *

INSIDE, the oaken bar was now engulfed in the center of the flames, becoming a glowing, twisted metal skeleton. And all around it, fiery timbers crashed through the burning floor to quickly spread the blaze through the lower levels.

THE PIPE

I STEPPED from the burning Grille just as Larry and the interviewer stumbled through the doorway, then watched the ambulance take them away.

The hour for my return was almost at hand; I had to reach the pipe in the attic of the Paradise Donut Shop. But in front of me I saw a crowd of frenzied demons who had fled the burning Grille, and now clotted the street and sidewalk between me and the donut shop. And behind me I heard Pitch emerge from the flames, cursing and thrashing, then screaming out to his cohorts: "After the Trial! Get him!"

The great pack of demons came for me. I spun and raced toward the outskirts of town. I'd have to lead them away, then try to double back somehow. Once I'd reached the attic above the donut shop and taken the pipe, this rabble could rage and threaten all they liked—they wouldn't be able to touch me.

As I ran, the blade of Dias's sword slapped at my legs. I was beginning to regret my decision to bring it, since I had more skill at using my heels than a blade. But there wasn't time to discard it now; the hell-horde was rallying to Pitch's crazed admonition, rising to the chase like a pack of hounds.

I could look back and see the reddish glow of the Sunset Grille burning behind me. I also saw black shapes rushing over the rooftops, gaining steadily. Great bat-shaped devils beat their wings furiously. I could hear their threatening growls as I ran.

I ducked into an alley, followed it, and at once turned back toward the blaze and the confusion surrounding it. Soon I dashed past the chief of Ellenbach's volunteer fire brigade. He was in a panic as he watched the flames leap from the roof of the Grille to adjacent buildings. He ran from one hose to another, screaming at his men. All of Ellenbach, it seemed, stood gaping nearby, their shadows scattered across Washington Avenue in the cold December night. As I dodged among them, I heard snatches of conversation.

"Did they all get out?"

"Don't know. There was a bunch of 'em in there for the TV show..."

"Anybody downstairs?"

"Don't know..."

"Anybody seen Billy Bobb yet?"

"Nope—not over here..."

A loud sound roared low over my head. Looking up, I was shot through with terror. By the light of the fire I saw three huge demons landing on the roof of the donut shop with their feet apart and their leathery wings drawn back. One of them pointed toward me, and the three again took wing, joining the pursuit.

I fled the fire scene again. At my back, the Grille rumbled and hissed its death-groans. I dashed down another alley behind a downtown store, vaulted a fence, and set off among the houses of Ellenbach. My pursuers moved with the cautiousness of those who have freshly arrived from the weightless underworld. They dipped and dodged, and did their best to stay out of contact with the cruel, unwelcoming earth.

A band of them were closing quickly on me, from several angles—I could hear their eager panting, just at my back. If I so much as stumbled, they would be upon me. I dodged sideways across a lawn, and they were whipped senseless as they tried to follow me through the winter-stripped branches of a weeping willow. I turned sharply right and hid in the lee of a concrete-floored shed while they disentangled themselves. Like macabre marionettes with their heads thrown back and their yellow-fanged mouths howling at the sky, they danced on strings that cut them viciously. Finally, they broke away from the limbs and flew toward my hiding place with death in their eyes.

I crouched in the shadows behind a bag of fertilizer, watching and calculating as they bore down on me. When they were barely five paces away, I shoved as hard as I could, spilling the small, round fertilizer pellets from the opened sack. The demons' feet contacted the pellets, which to them must have felt like rolling coals of fire. They screeched and tumbled in a vain attempt to halt their forward momentum, colliding with one another and the ground.

Before they could regain their feet, I raced from the shed. The moon shone through the bare trees, casting long, fingerlike shadows on the dead grass of the lawns over which I raced. I glanced over my shoulder to see two gargoyle figures flapping madly after me. They flew barely above the ground. Their talons touched the snow, and they winced with pain, as a human might whose knuckles have been scraped across a heavy grade of sandpaper. The thought crossed my mind that these might have been among my playmates—before the war.

Across the next lawn was a rusty sprinkler, still attached to a hose. *Here is something to pray for,* I thought. *Let it not be filled with ice...* My legs pumped up and down. The gargoyles flapped close behind, shouting the awful things they would do when they caught me. I reached the spigot and cranked it all the way on. The two alighted on the grass on either side of me, just as the hose lurched and the sprinkler spit watery buckshot in all directions. I crouched in a doorway and watched them writhe in the crossfire. Suddenly a man came to the door, muttering under his breath. "Durn kids," he said, throwing open the screen and starting down the steps. With a turn of the spigot, he halted my salvo.

Off I went again with my enemy following behind, slower by now, but considerably more infuriated as well. I quickened my pace.

Stretching before me in the shadows of the next yard were icicles hanging from the low eaves of a garage. A narrow sidewalk, flanked on the right by a privet hedge, ran the length of the building. I slowed down, calculating my chance of success with the stratagem I planned. My pulse pounded within me. Labored breathing, interspersed with curses and threats, closed in behind me. Taloned footsteps rounded the corner.

"Here he is!" said the leader, a big demon with the head of an alligator and the body of a gorilla. I willed myself to be still, to wait. Just as a claw touched the back of my neck, I bolted. Straight through the row of icicles I ran, not disturbing a one. The demons followed blindly, not noticing the swords of winter. In an instant they were slivered by frozen sabers into fragments from which they would require quite some time to remake themselves.

I stopped at the end of the sidewalk and turned around. The icicles were intact. In the morning the sun would be out, and the delicate points would be melted to the hilt long before noon. "Sheath yourselves, my friends," I said aloud. "Sleep well, for tomorrow you'll be gone." I felt Dias's sword against my side, and turned my thoughts toward gaining access to the pipe. Apparently I had confounded most of my pursuers. I decided to try stealing back again toward the donut shop.

I crept through the door of Paradise Donuts at ten till midnight, earth-time. Cyrus was still across the street, assisting victims who needed help, and running errands for the firemen or the police. I had been able to avoid detection or renewed pursuit on my way back, for which I was thankful. But there was no time to waste.

At the top of the stairs I went through the door and found myself standing again in the little room where my mission had begun. I left the door ajar and looked around. Nothing had changed. The warmth from the room below radiated up the staircase. Boxes of flour and sugar were stacked against the west wall. And above me was the opening to the pipe, hanging in midair like the welcoming beacon of a sailor's home port.

There had been little time to think of Dias since the battle in the jail cell. Now, as I reached inside my shirt and felt the leather pouch around my neck, I remembered. There was sadness in returning without my partner. "I'll miss you, Dias," I whispered aloud.

"Oh, the poor little angel," came an ugly voice from the corner. "Whatever will he do without his friend?"

I whirled around to see the scar-chested Stool step from the shadows. My hand went to my sword.

"Use it, if you can," he laughed. "You've seen what I can do to a trained fighter. Guess what I'm going to do to you?" he leered, crouching for a spring.

I leaped for the pipe and caught hold of the lip with both hands. My fingers trembled against the smooth material of the opening. Half my body was within it when I felt Stool's grip on my ankles. He yanked hard, and my grip was torn loose. I fell out onto the floor. I twisted and kicked, but his knees pinned me down. He raised his sword above his head when another voice halted him.

"Not yet, Stool. Not that easily. Let him think about it a while..."

Pitch stepped forward into the light coming up the staircase from below. He knelt beside me, a gruesome smile exposing his fangs as he leaned near my face. "Well, brother of mine," he snarled, "you may have saved your weak-kneed pastor this time, but there will be others. And with you unable to take the pipe," he chuckled, "you won't be able to help much, will you? Pity, that. I'd almost hoped we might square off again sometime.

"Just imagine," he went on, clearly relishing my helplessness. "You'll be trapped here from now on, little Skandalon. No way to get back up there." He motioned with his head toward the pipe. "Abandoned. Marooned. Stuck like a human on this little ball of mud."

"Not forever, Pitch," I panted. "One day, the final pipe will be opened—"

"Ah, yes...the famous legend of the final pipe," sneered Pitch, as Stool chuckled above him. "Do you still believe that tripe, Skandalon? All that business about your boss's return, and that vulgar courtroom stuff?" Pitch giggled, shaking his head in mock wonder. "How gullible he's made you all! How trusting, how naive you all must be..."

I heard the door downstairs open, then close, "People will be wanting some donuts," I heard Cyrus mumble. "Best get some mixed up—Uh-oh. No mix. Oh, well..."

Pitch stood then, dusting his hands. "Very well, Master Stool," he said, grinning nastily down at me. "You may finish your work. But slowly, Stool—and carefully."

Now the baker's feet clomped on the stairway, as he came to the attic for a bag of ingredients. If only he were Dias, I thought to myself. But what could one old human do to help me?

Stool's lips parted in a snarl. His sinews tensed as he raised his blade above his head.

Just then, Cyrus topped the stairway. His toe caught on the last step. "Whoops!" he said, as the armful of pans he had been carrying flew from his grasp. He flailed his arms about, trying to regain his balance.

The pans flew straight at Stool, slicing him like so many saw blades. He looked down at me, a surprised, pain-filled expression filling his features, just before he evaporated into the fabric of nothingness which hangs between earth and the infernal realm.

I jumped to my feet, drawing Dias's sword and forcing Pitch to the wall with its point.

"Go ahead, brother," he scowled, as he saw me hesitate. "Do it! I don't think you've got the guts to, but go ahead—if you think you can!"

Cyrus had been clumsily and hurriedly picking up pans. As he reached over for another one, he stumbled into me, jarring my elbow and driving the sword point home—through Pitch and into the wall behind. Just as he vanished, following Stool empty-handed back to Hell, Pitch looked at me with a snarl of hatred I could never have imagined. For a moment, he hung before my vision, the very embodiment of malice and spite. Then he was gone.

With a start, I realized that Cyrus's touch had been tactile—tangible! I whirled about, and the old man was smiling at me, his eyes studying me intently.

"Well, young'un," he said at last, his gaze flickering toward the pipe, "hadn't you better get a move on?"

I felt my jaw dropping in surprise. "You ... *you can see me?*"

"What's the matter, boy," he chirped merrily, "don't you know what happens when an angel misses a pipe? If I could, I'd shinny up there and be Home. But," he said with a trace of sadness, "that pipe isn't mine. I missed mine . . . so I'll have to wait for the final pipe, like all the rest of us that missed theirs. . . ." His eyes gazed past me, reaching outward from this world lodged in time, longing for the greater, final, complete world floating unfettered in destiny.

"But *you* don't have to wait!" he said, returning to the present. "Go on, now, git! I'll tidy up down here, don't you worry none about that. Besides," he said, "there's lots of work in this town before it's all said and done. Now, up with you!"

I caught the lip of the pipe, crawled inside, and felt the welcome pull that drew me toward Home.

THE ROSE

LARRY carefully folded the newspaper, laying it aside with a thoughtful look on his face.

He had just finished reading the report of the fire at the Sunset Grille. By all counts, no one had been lost to the flames which had so suddenly erupted inside the building during the taping of the television show.

No one, that is, except Billy Bobb Detzer. Unaccountably, the manager of the Sunset Grille had not made for the door with the rest of the people who were trapped inside. Instead, his charred remains had been found among the debris on the lowermost level of the Grille. And there had been another grisly detail: Usually the heat from a fire caused a victim's muscles to contract, forcing the corpse into a fetal position—a fact known to anyone, the fire chief said, who was ever associated with the grim details attendant to fires and their aftermaths.

But it had not been so with Detzer. When the workers had found his remains, the skeleton was in a fully extended position; the arms were flung out wide—almost as if the victim had been embracing the flames which consumed him. As Larry considered this he shuddered.

No other remains were found on the bottom floors— or anywhere else in the Grille, for that matter. Only Detzer. No trace of any female victims, or any paraphernalia on the bottom floors—nothing. All consumed, or otherwise vanished. Almost as if none of it had ever been . . .

The door slammed open as Peter and Annie bounded into the hospital room, closely followed by a smiling Rose. The children hopped onto the side of their father's bed while their mother leaned over and gave Larry a long, lingering kiss.

"Daddy, we came to take you home," announced Annie matter-of-factly. "Mommy says you can't stay here anymore."

"Amen to that," agreed Larry, pulling Annie close. "I don't suppose you cleared any of this with the nurses outside?"

"Sure," said Peter. "It's all set. All you have to do is get some clothes on."

"Here," said Rose, handing her husband a pile of folded clothing. "I brought these from home, since your others were ruined."

Having been cleared for release by the charge nurse, Larry walked down the hall toward the front door of the hospital, one arm around his wife and the other around both his children. "Hey, guys, I know what," he said as they started down the front steps. "Why don't we stop by the donut shop for one of Cyrus Daye's specialties before we go home?"

"Yeah!" chorused the children.

The Ravelles walked into the donut shop and were greeted cordially by an unfamiliar young man of rather impressive size. "Hi, folks!" he called as they entered. "Come on in!"

Cyrus came out from the back, wiping flour from his hands onto the apron he wore around his middle. "Well, if it ain't the Ravelle family—and the sick one with them," he winked, smiling at Larry. "Say," he said, gesturing toward the man who had greeted them, "did you meet my new help?"

"I don't believe we were introduced," said Larry.

"This here is Chris Dias," said Cyrus, as the friendly young man nodded at them. "I took him on as a . . . whatchamacallit—apprentice, that's it," the old man said. "I figured it was about time for me to teach someone else the ins and outs of the donut business. I can't work all the time, you know."

"Absolutely the right thing to do," commented Rose.

Chris wiped his hands, grinning. "Cyrus says there's plenty to do here—and I believe him," he said.

"Well, Dr. Ravelle," observed Cyrus, cocking an eye at Larry, "I guess you'll be back in the pulpit by next Sunday, by the looks of you."

A thoughtful look crossed Larry's face. "Well, Cyrus," he said, "I'm not so sure. First I've got some tough owning up to do with lots of those folks—especially with Gunner McGuffy. After that, I'll let the church leaders decide how best to proceed. But as far as filling the pulpit goes, I wonder if the Ellenbach Community Church needs to hear another voice for a while."

"But if you don't preach," Cyrus asked, "what'll you do? A man's got to do something, you know."

"I don't know for sure," Larry said. "Maybe take over the farm, now that . . . now that it's vacant." *I'll start by tearing down the barn,* he told himself.

"Yeah, maybe so," agreed Cyrus, his look taking on a

trace of sadness. "You know, Larry: Your brother—I just kinda believe he's had a change of heart, after..."

John's hearing date was next week. It was common knowledge by now that he planned to plead guilty to all charges.

"I think you're right, Cyrus," mused Larry. Then he looked up at the old man. "And somehow, I think you may be the only person in Ellenbach who's not surprised about that."

Cyrus shrugged, smiling. "Well...let's just say that I been keepin' my eye on him for quite a long time...." An indefinable glance passed between the old man and his new apprentice.

"And I've had my eye on these donuts for a long time," announced Peter impatiently. Everyone laughed.

Later, with donuts and milk cartons in hand, they drove toward home in the station wagon, with Rose in the driver's seat. As they passed a certain corner, Larry sang out, "Stop, honey! Right here!"

The station wagon squawked to a halt. As the others glanced at each other in mystification, Larry opened the door and sprinted into a nearby shop. When he emerged he was carrying a single red rose in a bud vase. Grinning from ear to ear, he walked around to the driver's door, as Rose rolled down her window.

He leaned through the window, handing his wife the flower.

"Rise, Rose! A new sun has risen," he announced.

For a long moment, they gazed into each other's eyes. "It certainly has," she said.